Tempting Boundaries - Special Edition

A Montgomery Ink Romance

Carrie Ann Ryan

Tempting Boundaries
A Montgomery Ink Novel

By
Carrie Ann Ryan

Tempting Boundaries
A Montgomery Ink
By: Carrie Ann Ryan
© 2014 Carrie Ann Ryan
ISBN: 978-1-63695-248-2

Dedication

To Kennedy. Love you darling. Just watch out for the squirrels!

Acknowledgments

I just love a best friend's little sister book! Thank you to my book soulmates for loving these tropes as much as I do. You know who you are.

Thank you to my writing group for pushing me through this novel. I wake up every morning, work out, then drink coffee with you so we can start sprinting. You're the reason I wrote this book when I did. So Shayla, Lexi, Carly, Angel, Kennedy, Stacey and others, thank you!

Again, thank you to my editors Devin, Saya, and Debbie for helping me clean up my work and find the characters that might have been buried.

Charity, darling, thank you for being my brain when I needed it. Dr. Hubby, thank you for being so understanding since I wrote this book during a cross country move and while we were living in a hotel waiting to close on the house. Seriously, this couldn't have been fun!

As always, thank you readers for loving my books. Every buy, review, link share, and casual mention over a cup of coffee means the world to me. Y'all have loved this series so far and its exceeded far beyond my expectations. Thank you for reading. You guys are amazing.

Tempting Boundaries

NYT Bestselling Carrie Ann Ryan continues her Montgomery Ink series with a forbidden romance worth the risk.

Decker Kendrick has kept away from her for years, but now his best friend's little sister is stepping up the game. No matter how hard he's tried to stay away from Miranda, once she sets her sights on him, there's no backing down.

Miranda Montgomery has loved her brother's best friend for as long as she can remember and won't walk away until he knows how she feels and what they could have together.

Only once they give in to their temptations, not all is at it seems. Decker's father is out of jail, and someone from Miranda's past refuses to stay away. And if he isn't careful, Decker will lose her before they even have a chance.

Chapter One

There was just something about the scent of a grill, the feel of a cold beer in his hand, and the company of a family that truly loved him that made Decker Kendrick want to relax after a long day's work. If he added in the fact that he could go home and have the woman at his side under him, over him, and all around him, it would be a pretty fantastic way to end the day.

Colleen, his date to the Montgomery family barbeque and engagement party, leaned into him and batted her false eyelashes. He had no idea why she wore them. He thought she looked decent without them. But whatever—it was her body to fake up any way she wanted to. He'd been seeing Colleen off and on for a few months, more often in the past month since he'd called her up, hoping to get his mind off a certain long-legged brunette he shouldn't be thinking about in the first place.

The woman in question hadn't shown up to the party yet, and Decker was grateful. Hard to ignore her and keep her off his mind if she kept popping up everywhere he went. Though that wasn't really fair considering she was part of his family.

More like *he* was part of hers.

He was an honorary Montgomery, and she was the little sister.

Totally not for him.

"Decker? Baby?"

He blinked and looked down at Colleen. Not the woman who haunted his dreams and kept him up late at night. Jesus, he was a bad man. A very, very bad man. Sure, he was keeping it casual with Colleen—something she'd put on the table to begin with—but he shouldn't be thinking about a woman with long legs he couldn't have when he was here with someone else.

That wasn't the kind of guy he wanted to be.

"Colleen?" he answered back, keeping his voice low. He didn't normally bring dates to the Montgomery family gatherings, and as such, he didn't want everyone to hear everything he said. They were all nosy in the we-are-family-and-we-can-be-nosy-if-want-to sort of way, and he'd learned to deal with it. He hadn't planned on bringing her at all, but when she'd called to ask him to dinner, he'd mentioned he had plans, and she'd sort of invited herself along. It hadn't bothered him too much then, but now he felt kind of like an awkward ass about it. Since this was the first time he'd brought Colleen to any type of function with the Montgomerys, he'd been prepared to have the family question the two of them until they pecked them to death.

So far, that hadn't happened, and frankly, that was more telling about what the others in his life thought of the relationship. Their politeness and lack of prodding meant they didn't see a future. Considering Colleen hadn't wanted a future to begin with when it came to her and Decker, that was just fine with him. He didn't see himself marrying the woman anyway. They were friends. Sort of.

"You're thinking too hard." She rubbed the little spot between his eyebrows, and he frowned. She wasn't usually so touchy-feely or attentive. Weird.

He pulled back, uncomfortable with the display of affection—or whatever it was—in front of the family that had taken him in so long ago.

"Just tired. Hauling a total of a half-ton of porcelain up and down stairs all day makes for a long workday. We also punched out our other project the day before. So I'm ready for a nap. Or another beer."

She wrinkled her nose, probably at the mention of his work. Another reason he'd never get too serious with her. She hated the fact he was a blue-collar worker and not some suit-wearing businessman who could keep her in diamonds and silks. She worked her butt off at her job and wore the expensive clothes that came with her world. That wasn't something he wanted in the long run. He worked for Montgomery Inc., the construction arm of the family businesses. He was the project manager right under Wes and Storm, the Montgomery twins who had taken over the family business when their parents, Harry and Marie, retired.

Wes was the OCD planner of the company and got his hands dirty daily with the bump and grind that came with being one of the top privately owned construction companies in Denver. Storm was the lead architect and a genius when it came to finding the right flow for a refurbished building or how to start from scratch with a piece of land that could be used carefully.

Decker had started out as a teenager working under Harry doing every kind of grunt work he could get his hands on. He'd gone to college only because the Montgomery twins had, as had his best friend, Griffin—another Montgomery—and because the state had helped him out. He wouldn't have been able to afford it otherwise. He'd gone to the local university, busted his ass for his degree, then went right back to working for the family that had raised him when his own blood family had failed.

He ground his teeth.

Best not think about the others right then. Not if he wanted to stay civil—he looked down at the beer in his hand—and sober.

"Must you talk about those matters with me?" Colleen asked, breaking through his thoughts.

He shrugged. He honestly didn't know why he'd

brought her that evening other than because he was in a rut, and he hadn't thought to say no. They liked each other well enough, but they weren't in love. He hadn't slept with her in months either. Despite the fact that his balls were so blue from lack of sex—his right hand could only do so much—he hadn't wanted to sleep with one woman when his mind was on the other. Sure, he'd been trying to date to get those thoughts out of his head, but he wasn't about to use another woman fully like that.

"I work with everything that goes in a house or building," Decker said, his voice low. He had a deep, growly voice according to the-woman-who-shall-not-be-named, and when he got annoyed or emotional, his voice just got deeper.

Colleen didn't care for it.

"Yes, dear, but you don't have to talk about it." She raised her chin and looked out at the yard. He'd helped with the initial landscaping years ago when he was trying to find his place within the business. He'd been better at digging the holes and lifting bags of mulch, rather than doing the actual planning. Marie was the brains behind that. She'd told them what to do, and he and her boys had hopped to it.

In the end, the place looked great with tons of vegetation that looked as though it was natural, rather than lines and perfectly square things that made no sense.

"Did you hear me, Decker? What is going on with

you? I said don't talk about things like that, not to stop talking at all."

He barely resisted the urge to roll his eyes. "Sorry to bother you," he mumbled, not sorry in the least. "Why don't you go talk to, uh, the girls over there while I get another drink?" He couldn't remember the two girls who worked with Sierra, the newly engaged woman and star of the party, but they seemed to get along with anyone. Hopefully, they'd make friends with Colleen so this evening wouldn't be a total waste.

She raised a brow and looked pointedly at his hand. Seriously? Jesus Christ. He shouldn't have brought her here. Or rather, he shouldn't have let her invite herself in the first place. She didn't belong, and he didn't know why he was kidding himself by trying to make it work when neither of them truly wanted it.

"I've had one beer, and I'll have one more since we have a couple hours left. I won't drink more than that." He wouldn't have had to explain himself to the Montgomerys. They knew enough about where he'd come from that him getting behind the wheel, even slightly buzzed, wasn't an option.

"If you say so," she clipped then strutted off to the girls on the other side of the backyard.

His shoulders relaxed marginally, and he cursed himself for it. He *liked* Colleen. He really did. She wasn't a bad person. She just didn't understand him.

Whose fault is that?

It wasn't like he'd told her all that much about himself, and he'd never once mentioned his past.

"Shit, bro, you look like you ate something rotten," Wes said as he walked toward him. He had the Montgomery blue eyes and chestnut hair, only his was neatly clipped and worked with his OCD persona.

Storm, Wes's twin, walked beside him. While Wes was a bit lanky, Storm had more of a build on him. He was also a bit more rugged with his shaggy hair, light beard, and flannel shirt over another light shirt, while Wes had his button-up shirt over nice jeans. It never made any sense to Decker that the twin who worked with his hands more often than not as the other general contractor preferred dressier clothes on his day off while the twin who sat behind his desk drawing when he wasn't in the field wore more rugged clothes. Well, considering each of them worked side by side with Decker and sweated their asses off regularly, it didn't matter what they wore now, as long as they worked hard during the day.

Which they did.

"Bro?" Decker asked, a smile on his face. "You working with the kids at Austin's shop now?" Austin was the oldest Montgomery and owned half of Montgomery Ink, the tattoo shop side of the family business, with their sister, Maya. It was also Austin and Sierra's engagement party and the reason they were all at the barbecue that evening.

Storm snorted. "We say bro sometimes. Doesn't make us some college kids who want bad ink."

"I don't do bad ink, asshole," Maya snapped as she came up to them. She wrapped her arm around Decker's middle, and he hugged her back. Why couldn't he be this comfortable around *all* the Montgomery women?

She pulled back before he could squeeze her tighter. Maya liked her space, and Decker liked her all the more for it. Her dark brown bangs were severe across her forehead, and she'd done a weird eyeliner thing that made her look like some fifties rocker pin-up. The red lipstick just made her look like she'd smile at you—then kick you in the ass.

"I meant that he wants bad ink because he doesn't know what good ink is," Storm said, backtracking. Wes and Storm might be the second oldest in the family, but no one messed with Maya and walked away without a limp. "Not that you give bad ink."

Wes laughed then shut up as Maya glared.

Decker, being the smart one of the group, kept his face neutral.

Maya narrowed her eyes at the three of them then nodded. "Okay, so tell me what's going on. Jake couldn't make it today, and I'm bored."

"When are you just going to admit that Jake is your boyfriend?" Wes asked.

Decker closed his eyes. It was like the twins *wanted* to die by her hand tonight.

"He's not my fucking boyfriend," Maya growled then lifted her chin, speaking softer this time. "He's my friend. I don't know why a guy and a girl can't just be friends without the rest of the world wondering if they're fucking."

Decker raised a brow then looked at the space between them.

Maya waved him off. "You're a brother, not a friend. So the world wouldn't ever think you'd be fucking a Montgomery girl. That'd be all kinds of wrong."

He swallowed hard and tried to keep the frown off his face. Shit. She was right. No one would think he'd ever be with a Montgomery girl. Maya was like his sister, as was Meghan, the eldest girl. Meghan was even married to an asshole, but married just the same.

Miranda though...Miranda was his best friend's little sister and had welcomed him into her family to boot.

There was no way he could ever think of her as more.

Or rather, he should *stop* thinking about her as possibly more.

"Anyway," Wes continued, "we came over here to ask what's up with Decker. He looked like he stepped in shit or something."

Decker rolled his eyes. Wes really liked making things sound worse than they were. "I'm fine. Just a long day." He rolled his shoulders, and the twins did the same. They'd hauled right by his side, and he knew they ached just as much.

"Tell me about it," Storm grumbled. "I never want to look at another toilet again."

"Charming," Maya said dryly.

"So, have you found a new receptionist yet?" Decker asked Maya, changing the subject from toilets to the running joke of the family. The shop had been through four or five receptionists this year alone. They had fantastic artists and had even just promoted their apprentice, Callie, to full time. However, they couldn't keep a receptionist to save their lives. The college kids always left for greener pastures, and the other ones thought it was fun to come in high around pointy needles. It might be legal to smoke, but that didn't mean they wanted their staff lit up while working.

"You can't have Tabby," Wes put it. "She's ours." Tabby was the Montgomery Inc. receptionist and a goddess with organization. She and Wes were a team in OCD heaven.

Maya cursed under her breath. "I don't want Tabby. She'd color code my ink in a weird way, and then I wouldn't want to move anything around. And no, we haven't found a receptionist. I don't know what it is. This latest guy just wanted free ink. Free. I pay for my own tattoos, you know. I won't let Austin do it for free because his work is *worth* my money. Wanting it free in our place just shows disrespect."

Decker snorted. "At least you get the family discount." Maya looked over her shoulder and discreetly flipped him off.

Decker frowned since she tried to hide it then smiled

as Meghan's kids, Cliff and Sasha, ran into the backyard, barreling toward their uncles on the other side of the yard. They'd be over here soon for sure to see the rest of them. He loved those damn kids.

"You get the discount too, brother mine," Maya said. "But the discount isn't all that much in the scheme of things. This idiot wanted it all for free. So he huffed away and found another shop most likely." She shrugged. "Not as good a shop as ours, but whatever."

"There's no shop as good as yours." He rubbed between his shoulder blades. "Speaking of, I need to make an appointment for the ink on my back." Maya's eyes brightened, and he cursed. "With Austin, hon. It's his turn." All of the Montgomerys took turns with the other siblings when it came to their ink. Both of them were talented, and picking one over the other was nearly impossible.

Besides, they both had nasty tempers if they didn't get to be part of the siblings' and parents' art.

"Fine. I see how it is. You like him better." She sniffed and wiped a non-existent tear at the edge of her eye. Not that she actually touched her makeup in the process, but the move worked for her.

Decker rolled his eyes then punched her softly in the shoulder. "Shut up. You *just* did work on my arm, and you get my leg next. It's Austin's turn now."

She smiled, and he wasn't sure if it was a good one or a *you'll be sorry* one, but he rolled with it.

He looked over his shoulder to see Colleen in a conversation with one of Sierra's girls so he let her be then looked at the empty beer bottle in his hand. "I'm going to get a refill. Any of you want something?"

They shook their heads, and he said his goodbyes before walking over to the cooler. Alex, another Montgomery—seriously, there were eight siblings and countless cousins so he was always walking over a Montgomery or two—stood by the cooler, a tumbler of amber liquid in his hand.

Decker looked over his shoulder at the crowd and frowned. "Where's Jessica?" Jessica was Alex's high school sweetheart and wife. When they'd first gotten married a few years ago, she'd always come to the family events, though she never exactly fit in. It wasn't like she tried, either. The Montgomerys had tried on their part to welcome her into their midst, but for some reason, it never really took. Now, come to think of it, Decker hadn't seen her at one of these events in awhile.

Alex snorted then took another drink. From the glassy look in his eyes, this wasn't his first drink.

Well fuck. This wasn't good.

"Like she'd come to one of these," Alex drawled. He didn't sound drunk, but Decker could never tell with Alex. The fact that he knew something was off at all was because of experience. He'd dealt with enough drunks and near-drunks to last a lifetime. "She's off with her girls at the spa or something. She didn't feel like celebrating Sierra and Austin's engagement since she's never actually met Sierra."

Decker's eyebrows lifted toward his hairline. "She hasn't met Sierra yet? How is that possible?" Jessica was already a Montgomery, and it wasn't like Sierra was new to the family. She already lived with Austin and was helping raise his son.

"It's possible when you're Jessica." Alex took another drink and looked the other way.

Okay then. Conversation over.

Decker shifted from foot to foot. Alex had always been the one to joke and make people laugh. That wasn't what Decker saw now, and it scared him a bit. The man in front of him looked angry...and drunk. Decker knew drunks. He'd lived with one off and on until he'd finally been able to break free.

He didn't want to see it again.

"You want a water, Alex?" he asked calmly. Tiptoeing around it wouldn't help, but coming right out and asking if the man he called his brother was an alcoholic wouldn't either.

Alex gave him a small smile instead of getting angry, which surprised Decker. "I'm good." The man didn't leave to refill his drink, but that didn't mean he wouldn't do it once Decker was out of sight. He didn't know what to do, but as long as Alex knew he was there, maybe that could help.

"Okay. Just...you know I'm here, right?" he asked softly.

Alex's face closed up, and he lifted his chin. Damn. "I'm good," he repeated.

Decker searched his face and couldn't find a way past the barriers. He'd keep an eye on him though. This man was his brother, blood or no.

He got a soda instead of a beer, his stomach not quite ready for booze after that, and walked over to his best friend, Griffin. The man held the same look as the rest of the Montgomerys, dark hair and blue eyes, but with the same slender build as Wes, rather than the brick-house look of Austin or even Storm. Griffin was the easiest going of the family, the writer who spent most of his time in his own head, rather than in the real world. His mess of a house reflected that, but Decker loved him anyway. They were the same age, so they'd grown up like twins after a while. Decker might have more in common with Austin on some levels and work closely with Wes and Storm, but Griffin was the one he knew best.

"Glad to see you finally found your way over to me," Griffin joked. He sat in one of the outdoor chairs and waved at the empty one. "Take a seat. I'm people watching."

Decker laughed then did as he was told. "First, you could have come over to me. It wasn't like I was blocking you. Second, this is your family. Why are you watching them?"

Griffin took a sip of his beer then shook his head. "You were with Colleen, and as I can't stand that giggle of hers, I didn't want to join in."

"Giggle?" Decker asked, a little annoyed that Grif would judge his date. It wasn't like he and Colleen were married, but still. Pointing out something like that didn't seem right.

"Giggle," Griffin repeated. "You know it. Whenever she giggles, your shoulders tense, and you get that little twitch at the corner of your mouth."

Huh, now that he mentioned it... Nope, not going to think about it. He still had the rest of the night and probably more nights with the woman. It wouldn't do to nitpick and then zoom in on those quirks for too long. He wouldn't be able to get over it.

"You noticed all that?" he asked, draining some of his soda.

"Yep. I told you. I people watch. In fact, I'm watching that asshole and my sister right now. I really want to beat the shit out of him, but I'm not sure she'd appreciate that. She doesn't like when the rest of us threaten to maim or murder her husband."

Decker frowned then looked over at Meghan and her husband, Richard. Meghan was three years older than him and had always struck him as warm, friendly, and not to be messed with. She was like the mother hen of the clan and stood up for herself.

But not now.

Now she had her shoulders slouched and her head down. Richard was snapping about something, and each time he spoke, Meghan turned in on herself just that much more. Nope. This wasn't going to do.

Decker stood up, set his soda down, and then rolled his shoulders. "You ready?" he growled at Griffin, who had stood with him. Like there was any other way to react when he saw someone he cared about being beaten down emotionally.

"Yep. Let's not beat the shit out of him since their kids are here, and it's Austin and Sierra's time, but yeah, I'm ready."

They stalked toward the couple, and Richard puffed out his chest as he noticed them. The man had once had a decent build and hair on his head. Now it looked like he was balding a bit, but he brushed it in just the right way that you couldn't tell unless you'd seen him before. He also had a little bit of a gut that came with lack of activity. Though he wore suits that shouted their worth, the effect was lost at the straining button on his stomach.

"What?" the bastard snapped.

Decker smiled, but it wasn't a nice one. He put his arm around Meghan, who stiffened. He let that pass and kept his arm on her. The more people who cared about her, the better.

"Just wanted to say hi to my sister, that's all," he said smoothly.

Richard scoffed. "She's not your sister. You're just the trash. Get your hands off my wife."

He didn't even wince at the word trash. He'd heard worse and usually from people who should have meant more to him than this sack of shit.

"Richard," Meghan admonished, her voice gaining strength. *Atta girl.* "Decker is family."

Decker squeezed her shoulders, but she didn't relax. Damn.

"She's right about that," Griffin said easily.

"Well then, wife, you're not a Montgomery anymore," Richard said, baring his teeth. "You'd do best to remember that. Go get the brats. We're leaving. We said our hellos to the happy couple—they won't be happy for long knowing the way that brute is—so it's time to go."

Why the fuck was Meghan still with this man? He treated her like shit and beat down on her emotionally. Decker didn't think Richard touched her with his fists, but one could never tell. Decker should know.

Flashes of meaty fists and breath tainted with cheap booze filled his mind, and he shook it off.

"Once a Montgomery, always a Montgomery," Griffin said from his side.

"Pretty much," Decker said smoothly. "If you're in a hurry, you can head out and we'll get Meghan and the kids home when they're ready to leave."

"She's *my* wife. Not yours."

"Decker. Griffin. Let it go," she whispered.

Decker shook his head. "Sorry, hon, Austin and Sierra's party just started, and we haven't done the toasts yet. You should stay. If Richard needs to go, he can go." He looked into her eyes and prayed she understood he meant more than for that one night.

"Fine. Keep the brats here."

"I need the boosters," Meghan whispered.

"Then you should come with me," Richard snapped.

Meghan glared. Good. There was still some fire in her. "I'm not risking my children's lives because you want to leave early."

"Our children, Meghan. You best remember that." He smiled coolly, and Decker froze.

So that's why she stayed. For the kids. That motherfucker.

"We got boosters in the house," Griffin said. "Mom and Dad keep them in case they have the kids." He didn't mention that Decker had bought them when Richard had left Meghan alone with the kids and taken her car one time.

She didn't need to remember that. On second thought, maybe she did.

"Fine." Richard didn't even say goodbye to Cliff and Sasha before stomping away. Meghan visibly relaxed when the man left.

"Meghan..." Decker started, but she held up a hand.

"No. Not here. I need to take care of my children."

He nodded, knowing she was stronger than his own

mother. At least he hoped. "I'm here if you need me."

"Me too," Griffin added. "We all are."

She cupped both their cheeks and smiled sadly. "I know. I love you both. Now go and talk to Austin or Sierra or something. I need a moment."

Decker nodded before leaving her alone with Griffin. His friend would take care of her until she pushed him away because she thought she was too strong to lean on someone. He wouldn't let her situation grow to be what his past had been, but he also knew there was only so much a person could do without physically pulling them away.

That wouldn't help anyone.

"That prick gone?" Austin growled when Decker reached him. Sierra punched her fiancé in the stomach, and he winced before wrapping his arm around her.

"Watch your mouth," she whispered and looked over his shoulder.

Austin and Decker looked as well. Austin's son, Leif, stood near, his attention on whatever Storm was saying and not on Austin's words thankfully. Leif had come to the family after his mother had passed and Austin had found out he was a daddy. Strange as hell to think of it all, but Decker loved the boy like he'd been raised with them from birth. He fit right in.

"Yep. That prick is gone. I'm worried about her. Alex too." He might as well let it all out. Austin was his big brother, and Sierra was going to be a new sister. They were family.

Sierra shook her head. "We all are. They know we're here, and if there's anything we can do, we'll figure it out."

Decker pulled her from Austin's arms and gave her a tight hug before pressing his lips to hers in a hard kiss.

"Hey, get your mouth off my woman."

Decker pulled back and smiled at a flushed Sierra. "But she's such a pretty woman." He tucked her into his side. "See? She fits just right."

Austin growled then pulled a laughing Sierra to him. "No, she fits against my side. You're an ass."

Decker grinned. "A hot ass. And you know it."

"You two are idiots, but I love you." Sierra laughed at her words, but Austin growled. "I mean I love Decker in a brotherly sort of way. I love you in a sexy, sweaty way. Okay?"

Decker raised his hands in mock surrender. "I so do not need to think about that. I'm going to go see how Harry's doing. Let me know when you want help with your toast or something."

Austin nodded, but his eyes were all for Sierra.

Fuck, what would it be like to have a love like that? A person who was by your side no matter what.

Decker didn't think he'd ever have that. Not with the way his mind and body wanted the one person he couldn't have. In his experience, love didn't last, and marriages were only shackles he knew some people could never be rid of.

Of course, that wasn't quite true since the couple he'd

just left seemed to be on the right path, but he wasn't sure yet. Then of course, the couple he was in front of had been together for over four decades and still looked like they were more in love every day.

But love hurt when one person was sick.

Harry Montgomery had always been larger than life. He was a big man with an even bigger heart. Yet the man in the chair in front of him didn't look like that now. The extracorporeal radiation therapy—Decker had been reading up—that targeted Harry's prostate cancer had taken a toll. The man looked so much smaller, weaker, and paler than Decker had ever seen.

The doctors told him they'd caught the cancer early and things were looking good, but the treatment looked like it hurt worse than the cancer. And now, in Decker's eyes, Marie was forced by love, duty and circumstance to stand by her husband's side as he grew weaker and weaker. How was that reward for love? How could that be worth it? The pain and loss that could come with growing close to someone didn't make sense to him, and he wasn't sure he deserved it in the first place.

"Come here, boy," Harry growled out, a sparkle in his eye.

Thank God.

Decker crouched near him, his hands shaking. He didn't know what to do. Did he hug him? It looked like, with just one hug, Decker would break the man he thought of as his father.

"How you feeling?" he asked. And damn if his voice hadn't choked up.

Harry patted his arm as Marie came to Decker's side, kneeling so she could hug him. He put his arm around her, inhaling that sweet Mom scent that had worked so well to calm him as a kid.

"I'm doing better," Harry said softly. "It doesn't look like it, but I'm not dying. Not yet."

Decker felt like he'd been stabbed in the heart with those words. Jesus. He couldn't lose Harry. He couldn't.

"Hey, don't look at me like that," Harry said. "I told you all I'd be honest with you about my recovery. We caught it early. The radiation hurts like a bitch, but we're pushing through. Now I wanted you to come over here because, one, you're my son and I wanted to see you, and two, because you helped with that prick of a husband my daughter chose. I couldn't get up to fix it, so thank you." The slight helplessness in Harry's eyes was too much.

Decker swallowed hard and willed his eyes not to fill with tears. Fuck.

"I'd have kicked his ass..." He shot a look at Marie. "I mean his butt, but the kids were there."

"You can say ass when it comes to Richard," Marie put in. "He *is* an ass."

Decker threw his head back and laughed. "I love you both. I just wanted to make sure you knew that."

Marie's eyes filled with tears. "Oh, that's the sweetest thing. The sweetest thing. We love you too, baby."

Harry nodded, and Decker leaned into the strong woman's arms.

The hairs on the back of his neck rose, and he stood up slowly. He turned to see Miranda walking into the back-yard, her long legs bare under her sundress.

Holy fuck, she looked amazing.

He willed his cock not to fill, considering he was standing between her parents. Griffin came up to his side, and Decker knew there was a special place in hell for a man who lusted after his best friend's little sister.

Harry and Marie gave him a knowing look, and he held back a groan. Yep. He was going to hell. He was going to burn, and he'd deserve every moment of it.

Miranda turned to them and smiled brightly, her eyes twinkling.

He fought to keep his gaze on her face and not on her breasts or her legs that never quit.

He could do this.

This was Miranda Montgomery. The woman who was a girl no longer, and she was not for him.

He wouldn't drool over her. He wouldn't make an ass out of himself.

Griffin gave him a weird look, and Decker groaned inwardly.

Yep.

Going to hell.

Chapter Two

Miranda Montgomery was in love. In fact, she'd been in love since she was six and he was twelve. Her love had grown, faded, come back in full force, and evolved into what it was now.

Unrequited and painful as hell.

She smoothed her hands down her dress and put on a bright smile. She was late to Austin and Sierra's engagement party because she'd been doing last-minute brush-ups on her lesson plans for the next day, and now she wished she'd been able to make less of an entrance.

Of the seven siblings, their spouses, their dates, kids, neighbors, and friends, the first person she'd seen had been the one person she dreaded to see at all.

Colleen.

She shouldn't be pissed that Decker had brought a date to a family event. If Miranda had been dating seriously, she would probably have brought him with her. She'd had that one date last month with one of the most boring men on Earth but that was it. Maybe she needed to start looking past the man she was in love with and find her own life.

Maybe.

Miranda didn't like Colleen. Although Colleen had the man Miranda wanted, her dislike wasn't just because of that.

Colleen didn't like Decker's job. At all. If a person had to get their hands dirty to earn a living, they were beneath Colleen's notice. Miranda's brothers and sisters were tattoo artists, construction workers, a writer, and a photographer. There were no slick suits in this family. And Colleen was all about status and prestige. Other than Colleen's looks, Miranda couldn't see the connection between her and Decker.

In addition to the job issue, Colleen couldn't seem to understand why the Montgomerys considered Decker family.

Decker had come to the house with Griffin one day when Miranda was a baby, and except for the rare occasions when he was forced to return to his birth parents, he had never left. Her parents had taken him in because his parents had failed to do the one thing they were supposed to do—raise their own child. The law didn't allow the Montgomerys to adopt Decker, but her brothers thought of Decker as one of them nevertheless.

Miranda, on the other hand, never thought of him as a brother—she'd been too in love with him for that—but to her, he had always been more than family.

She was nearly certain that Colleen didn't know any of Decker's history. Anyone could see that she was clearly confused about Decker's place within the family. Decker's past was his story to tell. The fact that he hadn't confided in Colleen meant that she wasn't solidly ingrained into Decker's life yet.

Miranda had overheard Decker talking with Griffin about how the relationship with Colleen was casual and nothing serious on either end, but that didn't give her the right to jump in and try to make Decker hers.

She wasn't petty, and she wasn't a bitch, but she was thinking like one, and she didn't like herself at the moment.

It wasn't like she could ever have Decker anyway.

Or could she?

"Aunt Miranda! Why are you sad?" Cliff, Meghan's son, asked. God, why had Meghan allowed her husband to name the poor child Cliff? He was teased over his name, but he lived through it with his head high.

Miranda smiled then knelt down in front of him. She hadn't heard him come up, but her little buddy was the perfect medicine for a hurting heart.

"Hey, Cliff. I'm not sad. Just lost in my own world. Can I have a hug?" She held out her arms, and he jumped on her. She let out an oof and hugged him hard. "You smell like chocolate. Did Grandma or Grandpa sneak you something?" She tickled him when he shook his head until he fell on the ground laughing.

"Mercy. Mercy!"

"Tell me!" Miranda laughed and kept tickling.

"Chocolate is yummy," he whispered through his giggles.

"I know. Now I want some," Miranda whispered and kissed him on the forehead. She let out another oof as Sasha, Meghan's daughter, jumped on her back. At three years old, she was a tiny little ball of energy compared to her six-year-old brother's tornado of even more energy.

God, she loved these two kids. She couldn't wait for Austin and Sierra to start making babies so she'd have more nieces and nephews to spoil. She'd fallen for Austin's son, Leif, at first sight and wanted the boy to have siblings soon. She had a feeling with the way Austin and Sierra were talking, that might not be too much of a wait. She'd once thought she'd have Alex and Jessica's children to romp around with, but after all these years, she wasn't sure that was happening. Jessica wasn't one of the nicest people around, and as much as Alex would be a great father, Miranda was worried about the woman as a mother.

Damn. When did she become so judgmental? Time to put a stop to that.

She shifted Sasha off her back and tickled her, too. The children laughed under her attacks, and she smiled at the two. They could make anyone's day brighter, and she was glad for it.

"I see the minions have found you," Meghan said from above. Miranda looked up and got a foot to the chin in the process. "Cliff! Watch your feet, honey. Are you okay, Miranda?"

Miranda rubbed her jaw, her eyes stinging. "Yep. He didn't hit hard." Thank God, since she wasn't sure she had time to get her teeth replaced. Or the money for that matter. "I just got distracted." She put her hands on her waist as she sat up. "Okay, crew. I think you've learned your lesson."

"Lesson?" Sasha asked and batted her eyes at her. Oh yeah, this girl was going to be a heartbreaker. Adorable.

"I'm your favorite aunt. Remember that."

"I heard that!" Maya called from her side but didn't come over.

The kids giggled and smiled at her.

Meghan grinned. "See? Favorite. No matter what Maya says." Cliff and Sasha got up, kissed her on the cheek, and then ran off to play with Leif. The next generation of Montgomerys was out in full force, screaming and playing like they had all the time in the world.

"There's my M&Ms," her dad said from her side. She looked over and smiled at her dad, trying to ignore the fact that Decker was standing right next to him.

Her parents had named each of the boys in the family without thinking of cute nicknames. Though Alex and

Austin started with the same letter, none of the others did. They'd named the three girls though, Meghan, Maya, and Miranda Montgomery. M&Ms. In light of everything that had happened in the past months, Miranda wouldn't change that for anything. She liked having that special connection to not only her sisters but her parents as well. It made her feel oddly special in a sea of Montgomerys.

Miranda stood up quickly and hugged her father, holding back tears. Damn it. She was stronger than this, and breaking down at the sight of her father so weak wouldn't help. Decker loomed by her father's side, his face a mask. She didn't know what he was thinking, but she damn well knew she had to be made of stronger stuff than this.

"Hey, Daddy," she whispered then hugged him softly. He didn't hug back as hard as he used to, and she bit her lip.

Decker pulled her to his side like he'd always done, his arm around her shoulders. She sucked in a breath and forced herself to relax. He'd always been good at reading her moods and making sure she was taken care of, but that meant only that he cared for her like a brother...not anything else. Nothing had changed, and if she remained as she was, nothing would ever change.

That, though, was something she'd have to think harder on later. Right now, she needed to focus on the present, not a future of what-ifs.

Meghan hugged Harry then started talking about Cliff

and Sasha. Miranda listened with half an ear, her attention on Decker. He'd left her standing there to get a chair for Dad but carried two in his other hand.

She would *not* look at his sexy forearms as he held those chairs.

Would. Not.

Maybe just a peek.

No, get a hold of yourself, Miranda.

Miranda sat in one of the chairs. Meghan waved off the other one then went off to be with her kids. Decker sat on the other side of Dad in the empty chair. It should have been awkward, sitting so near the man she loved and couldn't have, but it wasn't, not really.

These people were her family, and always would be, no matter what.

"Decker? I need to head home. I have an early day."

Miranda smiled at Colleen. See? She could be the bigger person.

Oh, she *wanted* to push the other woman away and throw herself at Decker, but that didn't mean she *would* do that.

Decker took out his phone and checked the time, frowning. "Okay. Let's say goodbye to Austin and Sierra, and then we can head out."

Colleen sighed, but Decker didn't seem to notice. It was getting harder and harder to pretend to like this woman, although it wasn't as if Miranda was doing a good job of it anyway.

"We're going to head out." The announcement wasn't really necessary. He turned to Harry, "Be sure to let me know how you're doing and if you need me to help out around the house."

"You know I will," he answered as he held out a hand. Decker gave him a man hug instead and stood up again.

Miranda stood awkwardly for a moment then held out her arms. She *always* hugged Decker. Today wouldn't be any different. Decker gave really good hugs, too. He didn't just gently pat you on the back and call it a day. He really gave his all to those in his circle. With anyone else, he kept his distance.

Colleen took one of his arms in hers, smiling sweetly up at him. Seriously? Decker blinked, looking between them. Well, shit. There was no good way to get out of this and not look like an idiot, or at least as petty as Colleen. Miranda let one arm drop then patted his free shoulder. Had he always been this well-built?

Yes. Yes, he had.

"Good to see you. Bye now." See? Bigger. Person.

"Okay then, pipsqueak."

Gah. How she hated that name.

She was an adult, damn it.

Not that he saw that.

Not that anyone saw that. She was the Montgomery little sister. The baby. There was no changing her birth order, but it would be nice if others treated her like the adult she was. Sitting here pouting about it, on the other hand, wasn't the most mature behavior.

Instead, she smiled at the couple. "It's Miranda, not pipsqueak. I haven't been pip in years. Night, all."

Her father's hand slid into hers, and she relaxed some. "You're my little girl, hon. You don't get to change that."

Miranda turned away from Decker and Colleen and looked down at her father. "You can call me that if you'd like. You've earned the privilege." She saw the light in his eyes brighten at her words, and she knew she meant what she said with all her heart. She'd be her daddy's girl—as long as she had a dad.

Cancer sucked.

She felt more than saw Decker and Colleen leave, and she finally relaxed all the way. Every time Decker was near, her body went into overdrive, calling out to him like some siren. A siren couldn't lure a man apparently, but whatever. Of course, when she was near Colleen, she tended to turn into some uptight bitch, and she needed to stop that. It wasn't the other woman's fault Decker had chosen her—even if Decker said it was casual.

She visited with her brothers and sisters for another hour or so, and then knew she had to head home. She had an early day the next morning, and she couldn't look like she'd spent the whole night partying. It might only be a little after seven, but it was still a school night.

She grinned. A school night. Her whole life had been about school one way or another it seemed. Now that she was a high school math teacher, it would remain that way until her old age. She loved everything about it, especially the challenge of students who didn't want to be there. If she could find just the right catalyst, she knew she could change their minds. She might not reach them all, but if she reached just one, that was what mattered.

On her way out of her parents' backyard, she said her goodbyes, hugged her father again, and then headed home. She lived only ten minutes or so away from their house, but it was far enough that she felt like she was on her own. That was the point. She loved Golden, Colorado. Like Arvada and Westminster, where some of her family lived, it was a western suburb. It pressed right up against the mountains rather than the plains in the east. There were breweries and quarries all around her, and her apartment had a small forested park surrounding it.

It helped that Decker lived in a house a mile away.

Not that she chose the suburb because of him. She'd chosen Golden because that's where the job opening at the school was. It was hard as hell for people in the state to find jobs to begin with. It was a lucky coincidence that Decker lived so close.

And now she felt like a stalker.

Enough of that.

She pulled into her parking lot and made her way into her apartment. She loved her place. Even though it was a small one-bedroom—all she could afford on her meager salary—it was *hers*. She'd decorated it with comfy furniture, bright colors, and since the kitchen had a breakfast bar, instead of a small dining table, she had her desk where she could work. She didn't need much more.

She was perfectly fine as she was. She had her small apartment, a job she actually liked, friends and family who loved her, and students who liked her. At least most of them did.

What she was missing was a man in her life. She didn't need one to live—she wasn't that far gone—but she was romantic enough to know she needed...companionship.

She snorted.

And sex. Sex helped. She *liked* sex. She just hadn't had it in so long it was getting annoying. Yes, she should go to bed, use her trusty nightstand friend so she could relax, and dream about a bearded, tattooed man she couldn't have.

At least not yet.

"ENJOYING YOUR SECOND WEEK OF SCHOOL?" JACK, her co-worker, stood beside her in the teacher's lounge.

Miranda turned, coffee in hand, and nodded. "Actually, yes, I am. It's only the second week of my first year on my own, but I'm not disillusioned yet."

"The epiphany comes for everyone, honey," Mrs. Perkins, their sixty-something-year old English teacher said from her spot at the table. Jack and Miranda stood by the counter, fixing their coffees, while other teachers milled about, getting ready for the first period.

Miranda just shook her head and smiled. "I'll take the happiness for now, if that's all right."

Mrs. Perkins looked over her glasses, her pointed chin and mouth scrunching. "If that's what gets you through, keep at it. When you crash and burn, you know where to come."

Pessimist much? Miranda so did not want to turn into Mrs. Perkins when she got older. The woman wasn't a mean old crone or anything—not like some of Miranda's past teachers—but she wasn't too happy either.

"Don't listen to her," Jack whispered in her ear. His breath warmed her neck, and she took a step to the right. He didn't make her uncomfortable per se, but she was at work and didn't need any rumors about the new girl and the—according to the older students and some of the staff —sexy history teacher.

Miranda turned, increasing the space between them. "I won't," she said softly back.

Jack smiled, and she saw what others did. He had a great smile. His blue eyes seriously sparkled under the right light. He had that angelic look with his tousled blond hair and tanned skin. It seriously wasn't fair that he was so good looking...and a history teacher. He was also the closest to her age at the school from what she could tell. He had to be around thirty to her twenty-three. Not that it meant anything anyway. She had to get over a certain somebody before she even looked at another person. Looking at a co-worker that way wouldn't be the smartest thing to do right out of the gate.

She drained the last of her coffee and looked at her watch. "I better get to it. These kids aren't going to teach algebra to themselves."

"It'd be easier if they did," Mrs. Perkins put in. "With all the testing the state wants us to do, they'd be better off that way anyway." The older woman stood up, dusted off her matronly outfit, and left the lounge.

Miranda looked down at her cute flats, linen pants, and silk top. She might not look like what others thought of as a teacher, but she liked clothes. Sue her. She had a feeling that, as she grew older, what she wore now would look dated. She'd grow into her own high school teacher persona as time went on.

"Have fun today," Jack said before leading the way to the hallway. He grinned at her, and she smiled back. She didn't feel that flutter she experienced whenever Decker smiled in her direction, but Jack was a nice man to look at nonetheless.

She made her way to her classroom and got the camera table ready. The school had just updated to a projection system that didn't require erasing on plastic and dim lights. She could put the textbook right under the camera and show what she was talking about, as well as write out words in real time. She also used the white boards when she was lecturing since she had space on either side of the projection screen, though she mostly used that for getting students out of their seats to show their work. And if she noticed too many droopy-eyed kids, she could move around to wake herself up as well.

Mrs. Perkins had been right about the state testing and all the bureaucracy that came with a public school, but Miranda took it in stride. It wasn't as if the low pay, long hours, no budget, overworked teacher trope was a new thing. She'd known that going in. Now she just had to work with it. Well, she'd see how she did by the end of the school year. Teacher burn-out wasn't a thing of the past, after all.

The first bell rang, and students started trickling in. First up was ninth grade algebra, though she had a few tenth graders blended in. Many of the students in her school had taken it in eighth grade and had now moved on to geometry—the next period's class—but she had a good grouping anyway.

The second bell rang, and the last students ran in, looking harried and, if Miranda was right, a bit mussed. The boy gave her that cocky grin while the girl on his arm blushed. She ran to her seat while he strolled.

It seemed the tradition of making out in the hall hadn't ended with her generation.

Kids today.

She grinned, noting down their names in her head just in case. "Good morning. After the announcements, we'll be starting on our friend, *x*, so open your books to chapter two please."

There were the normal groans and whispers, but she took it all in. This was her life now. She was going to live it and enjoy it.

No matter what.

BY THE END OF THE DAY, HER LOWER BACK HAD started to hurt, and she knew she needed to increase her core yoga sessions. Getting aches and pains from standing all day wouldn't end any time soon if she didn't try to battle against it. She'd made it to her car, the previous day's homework papers stuffed in her shoulder bag, when Jack came up to her.

She blinked, surprised to see he'd parked right next to her. She hadn't noticed that when she'd come in. Of course, her mind had been on her schedule for the day, not the cars in the parking lot.

"Enjoy your day?" Jack asked, sliding her bag off her shoulder. She gripped it, not wanting to let her students' papers out of her hands. Privacy was important, and she didn't want to look like the little woman who needed help.

She was a Montgomery. She could handle things on her own.

"I've got it," she said nicely. He let go of the bag, and she brought it closer. "But thank you. And yes. I did. It might be Monday, but it's still the end of August, so we have energy. Right?"

He nodded then leaned against her car. "I'm glad you started working here, Miranda. You're bringing fresh air to the place."

She hoped so, though she needed to go home and start grading, get ready for the next day, and then call her dad to make sure his treatment went well. Okay, she was getting a bit tired just thinking about all of that.

Perk up, Montgomery.

"Thanks for saying that, Jack."

"So, how about I take you to dinner this weekend to celebrate your new position?"

She blinked, a bit stunned. He was asking her out? She didn't think he thought of her that way. He was a nice guy, and she hadn't heard he was a player or anything so that was something. Yeah, they worked together, but a few teachers had dated each other within the school, and the world hadn't ended. It wasn't in their contracts that they weren't allowed to fraternize.

But still.

She wasn't quite ready.

She needed to get over Decker...or something.

"Oh, um. I'm really busy." Not a lie. She did have tons of work to do. She also wanted to check in with her dad about his treatments and then Sierra on the wedding arrangements. She hated hurting people's feelings. Why couldn't she just say no? "Maybe some other time." Why on earth did she say that?

Jack gave her a quick grin. "No problem. I'll be sure to take you up on that. Drive safe, Miranda, and I'll see you in the morning."

She nodded then got in her car. Jack got into his and drove off. Her body relaxed, and she started on her way home. The man was a nice guy and really good looking. She probably should have said yes so she actually had a social life beyond her brothers and sisters, but as she'd told herself before, she wasn't ready to date someone while she was in love with another person.

She pulled into her parking lot, grabbed her things, and made her way inside her apartment.

She screamed when she saw Maya on her couch and her sister's friend, Jake, looking in the fridge.

Maya screamed back, and Jake cursed.

"Damn it. I hit my head on the freezer," he mumbled. The man was seriously hot, and Miranda didn't know how Maya kept her hands off him—or if she even did—but that didn't answer *why* the two were in her apartment.

"What the hell?" she said once she caught her breath. She put her things down on the coffee table and scowled at her older sister. "I gave you the key for emergencies. What's up? You scared the hell out of me."

Maya had her hand over her heart then raised her pierced brow. "We're family, and I wanted to see how your day went."

"Plus you had food in your fridge," Jake said, a bowl of potato salad in his hands.

"You both have fridges of your own. Go shopping."

He smiled at her, and she sighed. Damn he was sexy. Not as sexy as Decker, but whatever. "I like your food. Maya was telling the truth. We wanted to see you." He plunked himself down in the middle of the couch so Maya was on one side, leaving space on his other side.

She rolled her eyes then sat down next to them. "I was going to have that for dinner and some cold fried chicken I had left over."

"You have chicken? Hold this." Jake handed over the salad then hopped up. He soon returned with napkins, three spoons and a container of chicken. "We'll have a couch picnic, and you can tell us about your day."

Miranda took a spoon and rolled her eyes. She shouldn't have been surprised they were here. All her family came in and out of each other's homes daily because they were always welcome. It was nice to have someone there to ask about her day.

"I got asked out today," she said. Maya's eyes widened, and then she took a bite of her drumstick.

"So? What's his name? Is he hot? When are you going out?"

Miranda laughed and took a thigh. There was just something about cold leftover chicken that made her happy. "His name is Jack. He's pretty hot. And I said no."

"Why? He give you a hard time?" Jake asked. "You want me to beat him up?"

She smiled and patted Jake's shoulder. "You're such a good friend. And he was perfectly nice about it. I'm just not ready to date him right now."

"Because you have a thing for Decker?" he asked, and Miranda choked on her bite of chicken.

Jake immediately took everything out of her hands and pounded on her back. "Sorry. Sorry."

"Dude. You don't just come out and say that," Maya snapped.

Miranda wiped her eyes, her hands shaking. "I don't know what you're talking about."

Maya gave her a sad smile. "Yes you do, honey. I don't think the boys know, but Meghan and I do. We're the M&Ms. We always know when we're crushing on someone."

Considering Miranda had no idea how Maya felt about Jake, she wasn't too sure about that. Maybe it was just a Meghan and Maya thing.

"Um. So. I have no idea what to say," she mumbled.

Maya gave her a sad smile, and Miranda wanted to ask them both to leave. "Honey, you've had a crush on him forever, but I don't think he's ever noticed. He's a guy."

"Hey," Jake put in, "I'm a guy. I noticed."

Maya narrowed her eyes. "No. I told you. There's a difference." She looked at Miranda again. "And I only did because he's Jake. I would never tell the brothers or

Decker. I only spill the beans on things that are actually happening, not about things that *could* happen and end up hurting them in the process. It's up to you to do what you want with Decker, or with Jack for that matter. But remember, if you walk away before you do anything because you're too scared to do it, you might miss out on something."

Miranda nodded, swallowing hard. "I...I don't know. I don't want to talk about it though. Okay?"

Maya reached over Jake and took her hand. "I'm here if you need me. I'm always here."

Miranda sighed and took a bite of her chicken she'd stolen back from Jake. She knew Maya was right. She needed to talk with Decker, let him know. Not about the depth of her feelings, but at least try...something.

She'd regret it if she didn't.

The cost of what would happen if she ruined it all though?

That might be worse.

Much, much worse.

Chapter Three

Austin Montgomery gave a low groan then rolled over, bringing Sierra closer to him. He kept his eyes closed, knowing the feel of her—every inch of her—in his calloused hands. She wiggled back, her bottom rubbing along the length of his cock. He'd say it was morning wood, but with his fiancée in the bed, it was all for her, not just some chemical reaction.

He slowly brought his hand up her side, brushing along the long scars from her past, to cup her breast. Her nipple hardened against his palm, so he rolled the nub between his fingers, enjoying her sleepy gasps.

She turned over so she was on her back, and he opened his eyes to see her smiling at him. Her long, honey-brown hair framed her face and fanned out on the pillow. He brushed it away from her cheeks, caressing her skin in the process. Damn, she did have soft skin.

"We'll have to be quiet," she whispered. That small smile on her face begged for a kiss, so he pressed his lips to the corner of hers, inhaling her sweet scent.

He pulled back, and she licked her lips, arching her back to try to reach him.

He grinned and lowered his lips to hers once more. "You're the loud one, Legs." He settled himself between her thighs and slowly worked his way inside her. He'd been running his hands along her body long enough that she was already wet and ready for him. He loved the feel of her around his length, bare, and all his.

"Then you better kiss me so I don't shout."

He did as he was told, working in and out of her in a lazy, perfect rhythm. He loved waking up by making love to his woman, his fiancée.

He loved that word.

He couldn't wait to call her his wife.

Soon, he thought. *Soon.*

They made love leisurely, and when she came apart in his arms, he took her mouth with his, catching her moans and screams. He followed soon after, emptying himself deep within her.

"Love you," she said once they caught their breath.

He kissed her again. "Love you too."

"Sierra! Dad! We're going to be late!"

Austin rested his forehead against Sierra's forehead, holding back a laugh. "Well, at least I'm awake now," he said quietly to her. "I'll be out in a minute!" he shouted to Leif.

She laughed softly then pushed him up. "Go get your son some breakfast and make sure he has his homework in his bag. I put it there last night, but you know how he takes things out to make sure they're there then leaves them in another place."

Austin rolled his eyes then smacked her bottom as she got up. "Go shower, though I like the thought of me still inside you for the rest of the day."

She scrunched up her nose. "Uh no. The idea of you seeping down my leg while at work is so not what I want to think about."

He smacked her bottom again, loving the way her eyes darkened at the sting. Oh yeah, his baby needed some time under his hand a bit later. He'd find time. Ever since Leif had come into their lives, they had to hold off on some parts of their relationship, but they were slowly finding a balance. He'd have to treat them both to something sweaty and kinky tonight.

"I don't like the look in your eyes, Austin Montgomery."

He licked his lips as he put on his jeans, tucking himself in gingerly. "You will. Now go shower."

She rolled her eyes then sauntered off naked to the bathroom. He loved his life. He made his way out to the kitchen where Leif was going over spelling exercises. Austin snatched the paper away and started quizzing him.

His son huffed but answered and spelled everything correctly. The kid was smart. Austin quickly made up some oatmeal and fruit for the three of them and doctored his and Sierra's coffees. They weren't running too far behind, and since Sierra liked to get to places early and worked fast if she had to, they'd probably get everything done right on time.

Morning sex was totally worth it.

By the time Austin grabbed a quick shower, Sierra was finished getting ready and Leif was on his way to the school bus. The fact that he had a ten-year-old kid still surprised the hell out of him daily. Leif had come into his life late, but there was no way in hell he'd change his future.

He had Sierra and Leif, a wedding to plan, a family that gave him fits daily, a dad getting healthy—at least that's what the old man said—and a job he loved.

Things were good.

He pulled into the parking lot behind Montgomery Ink and leaned over to kiss Sierra goodbye. He loved the fact that her boutique, Eden, was right across the street from his job. Of course, he'd never have met her if that hadn't been the case. Life was funny like that.

"Have a good day, okay?" Sierra said as they walked toward the street.

Austin wrapped his arms around her waist and kissed her again. "I will. Make sure you don't wear panties tonight."

She blinked then blushed. "Austin," she whispered then looked over her shoulder.

He took her chin and met her gaze. "No. Panties."

"Okay," she said softly then smiled. "Oh! And tomorrow we have a meeting at the reception hall for the wedding. I know neither of us want a huge wedding, but with that many Montgomerys, there's no way around at least having a decent-sized one."

"No problem, Legs." He kissed her again then smacked her bottom before she walked across the street. She glared over her shoulder, and he smiled. Oh, she'd pay for that glare with another spanking. She seemed to get the drift from his look and blushed. Yep, she liked it.

Austin rolled his shoulders then made his way into Montgomery Ink. Maya stood by the window and gagged.

"If you were any closer to her, you'd be fucking her against the wall."

He flipped her off then went to the back of the room, passing Decker along the way. He frowned then remembered the date. "Shit, I forgot we moved the appointment. Let me get my stuff ready."

Decker shrugged. "I'm a few minutes early, but I wanted to check the drywall job I did last month."

Austin nodded then went to the office to get his things. When he came back out, Decker was lounging in Austin's station, drinking coffee he must have gotten from Hailey's café next door.

"You get me some?" he asked as he sat down.

Decker nodded then motioned to the cup on Austin's desk. "Yep. It might be cooler now since I didn't know you'd be in late today."

"Eat me," Austin said. "I was five minutes late. If that."

Decker just grinned and stripped off his shirt. "We're working on my back, right? Just want to make sure you didn't change your mind and decide to tattoo something random on me."

Austin snorted. He wouldn't do that to family, though he might joke about it. He quickly got his stuff ready for tattooing, setting out the inks and needles he'd need for this project. "Yeah, Maya did the dragon on your arm, and I did the dog paws, but it's my turn for your back."

"I get his legs!" Maya called out.

Decker chuckled. "Look at you two, always fighting over me. There's more than enough of me to go around."

"Like I said, eat me," Austin said back.

"No thanks. You got Sierra for that."

Austin snorted then made Decker face the opposite way so he could see his back. "We're working on the dead tree today. I'll add more to it, piece by piece."

"Sounds good to me."

"So, speaking of eating..." Austin said as he wiped down Decker's back.

Decker laughed, and Austin grinned. "Yeah?"

"How are things between you and Colleen?"

Decker looked over his shoulder. "We chicks now? Gonna talk about our feelings?"

"Fuck you both," Maya snapped from her station.

Both men flipped her off, not bothering to look over.

"I was just asking. And Sierra wanted to know." She'd mentioned it in passing, but whatever.

Decker raised a brow, totally seeing through his bullshit. "We're casual. I know I keep saying that, but it's the truth. We eat together sometimes, but that's about it these days."

Austin blinked. "You mean you two..."

Decker groaned. "No. You got a problem with that? And since when do we talk about sex?"

"Since we used to do the scene together a couple of years ago. But we're both out of the public part." They both had been into their own type of kink, just like a lot of his family and friends were, but they weren't twenty-four/seven Dominants like a lot of the guys he knew from back then.

Decker shrugged. "I'm good with where I am. I like Colleen and all, but...I don't know."

Austin frowned. "Okay. If you need someone to talk to..." He cleared his throat. "Call Maya."

"Like I said, fuck you both. But he's right. You want to talk about sex? Talk to me. Though I'm not going to do you. Sorry."

"Seriously, Maya," Austin groaned. "Stop it. I *really* don't want to think about any of my sisters having sex."

Decker cleared his throat then turned away, an odd look on his face. *Huh. Wonder what that was about.*

Whatever. He'd figure out what was wrong with his friend. That was his job. He was the oldest Montgomery. He fixed things. And since his life was finally on track to being something fucking amazing, he might as well spread the wealth.

Chapter Four

Why the hell was she wearing such short shorts? Her legs looked fucking fantastic in them, and all Decker wanted to do was see them wrapped around his neck as he ate her out, making her scream his name.

Shit.

That special place in hell now had his name carved on the door. He had a hammer in his hand and one in his pants at the thought of a certain soft brunette who shouldn't be on his mind in the first place. His best friend's little sister wasn't even looking at him, and yet he couldn't get her image out of his brain.

Had she always been that sexy?

Nope.

No, he wasn't going to think of that.

Sex and Miranda Montgomery would only lead to bad things.

Namely, Decker's balls in a vise, courtesy of Meghan and Maya, and his ass up around his ears, courtesy of the Montgomery brothers.

Grif, the bastard, had asked Decker to come over to Miranda's and help her install a few shelves. To do that, he had to measure first since he wanted to build them by hand. Yeah, he was a sucker, but he wanted her to have nice things, not some pressed board crap that would only hold a few books. Considering the number of books the woman had, he was afraid for the walls.

Sure. Keep telling yourself that.

"You don't have to do this, you know," Miranda said again.

"I do," he grunted as he stepped back.

"No, you don't. I know Grif asked you to help with my shelves, and I think it's great, but I can do it myself. Mom and Dad taught me."

Decker smiled at her. "I know they did. All you Montgomerys know what you're doing around power tools. Well, maybe some more than others, considering that one time Grif tried to use a saw."

Miranda threw her head back and laughed. "He didn't cut his finger off, so that's something."

"True. But really, your brothers just want you to have a nice place, so I'm going to help." See? Brotherly. Not *I-want-to-do-you.*

"I'm not going to get you to quit, am I?"

Decker shook his head then went back to hammering in a nail. Since he was there, he put up the large mirror in her hallway. The thing opened up the space so the hallway looked bigger than it was. It had been too heavy for her to do it on her own, and he'd wanted to help. He'd already taken most of the measurements he needed for her custom-built shelves. Once she moved out, they'd be able to take them and put them in her next place. Any place was going to be bigger than what she had now, so it would work.

"Well then. Thank you." Miranda ran a hand down his back, and he stiffened.

Dear dick, calm down.

For the love of God, calm down.

He looked over his shoulder and saw the shock of hurt over her face before she schooled her features. Fuck. He wasn't doing this right. He just couldn't think when she was near him, and when she touched him...damn it.

What he *wanted* to do was put down his tools, press her against the wall, and taste every inch of her.

What he was *going* to do was finish measuring everything and then go to his place to work on her shelves. He couldn't breathe in here without inhaling her sweet scent. She always had a different lotion or spray on, so it was a constant surprise what she'd smell like from day to day.

Today was honeysuckle or something like it, and he hated himself for wanting to see if she tasted just as sweet.

"I'm almost done here," he said gruffly. "Then I'll be out of your hair."

"Oh. Okay. You want lunch or anything?"

"No. I'm good. Got things to do."

"Okay," she said brightly. She didn't sound hurt, but damn it, it wasn't as if she wanted him like that or anything. It was more that he was being an ass to someone he cared about because he cared too much. Wanted too much.

If he'd put the moves on her, she'd knee him in the balls, slap him hard, and then call her brothers to pounce on him.

Or Maya.

He held back a shudder.

He did *not* want Maya on his back.

Or his balls.

"You can go do whatever you need to, and I'll get done faster so you have your space."

"Fine with me," Miranda snapped. "You don't have to be an asshole about it. If you don't want to do this, don't."

Decker cursed then turned around. "I'm sorry. I'm tired and in a mood." A guilty and horny mood, but that was beside the point. "I want to do this. You're family."

She rolled her eyes then walked away, looking over her shoulder as she did so. "Whatever. Thank you anyway. Let me know if you need anything."

"I won't," he whispered. Not anything she'd give him anyway.

He quickly finished up his work and left her with a wave. He needed to get out of her place so he could think clearly again. She lived so close that he could walk to her place easily—something that was a blessing and a curse—so the drive home was quick. His back still ached from the outline of the tattoo Austin had worked on the day before, so he was grateful it was Saturday and he had the day off from work.

He loved his ink. Between Maya and Austin, he had the best of the best when it came to artwork. Each piece meant something to him—not that he told everyone what it meant. The dragon on his right arm had been his first tattoo and was a symbol of the fire and rage he'd tried to overcome to be the adult he was today. The paw prints on his left forearm...well, those were for Sparky.

He leaned his head onto the steering wheel when he parked in front of his house.

Damn it. He did *not* want to think about Sparky today.

He'd loved that damn dog. Loved him so much that the one man who was supposed to take care of Decker had killed the dog because he could.

Because he was a rat bastard with no soul.

Fuck.

He stormed out of his truck and stomped into his house, annoyed he'd let the man he hated more than he thought possible enter his thoughts.

That was another reason he couldn't have Miranda.

The blood that ran through his veins was tainted because of his sperm donor, and he wasn't about to let Miranda anywhere near that.

Not that she'd have him.

Fuck.

He sighed then set his stuff down in the foyer. When he'd saved up enough money, he'd bought a three-bedroom ranch-style house that had a full basement. It probably would have been a money pit for most folks, but he built houses for a living and knew the bones beneath the drab exterior were worth saving.

He closed his eyes and cursed. Today was the day for hidden meanings in his thoughts. Time to put that away and think of something else.

He grabbed a soda from his fridge and then went into his garage. When he'd bought the place, he'd remodeled the garage into workspace so he could build and not dirty up the rest of his house. He loved to work with wood, carving and building things with his own hands. Sure, he worked with drywall, paint, and other things when he worked on buildings with Montgomery Inc., but his favorite part was the wood details. He usually got to do the wooden staircases, carved banisters, and mouldings, while Wes and Storm worked on other things. The fact that they trusted him enough to do so meant the world to him.

Yet another reason he wasn't about to poach on their sister.

Jesus, he needed to get a grip.

He needed to clear his thoughts of sexy brunettes with long legs and fathers with meaty fists and hammers that broke skulls.

Decker paused, swallowing back the bile that'd risen in his throat.

Jesus, he hadn't thought about that in so long.

No, that was a lie.

Every time he looked at a hammer, he remembered the sound of his dog dying at the hands of his father. But every time he saw the paw prints on his arm, he remembered the good times, not just the bad ones.

Maybe he needed to get another dog. He hadn't had one since Sparky. Been too afraid of the memories. They already haunted him anyway, so why not go down to the shelter and pick one out?

Settled slightly, he turned on the radio, took a swig of his drink, and got to work. Miranda had great furniture, soft and relaxing. The dark colors of the wood blended nicely with the creams and bright colors she'd used to decorate. He wanted her shelves to match that so he'd do his best to make sure they did so almost perfectly. He might not be able to have her as his, but she'd have the best things she could.

The best things did *not* include Decker Kendrick.

He'd said yes to Griffin when the other man had asked him for help because it was Miranda. Now, though, he felt guilty. Grif had no idea what thoughts went through Decker's mind. If he did, well, Decker would probably deserve the fist to his face. The Montgomerys had trusted him enough to bring him into their home. He couldn't go back on that and defile their younger sister. Even his thoughts and wants were too much.

He'd just get over it. Make sure she was happy and keep on dating Colleen or someone like her. Someone he liked well enough that he had a chance of maybe making happy. He wouldn't use her, but he wouldn't taint her with who he was, either.

With a sigh, he got down to work, losing himself in the craft. He measured twice, cut once, and carved until his back ached from bending over too long. Still, he pushed through it. He'd rather deal with a little pain and work his ass off than sit for too long, thinking about what he shouldn't.

His cell phone buzzed on the table, and he set his tools down to answer it. When he looked at the screen, he cursed.

Mom.

He did not have the energy to deal with her right then, but like always, he couldn't give up on her. She might not have been the best mother ever, but she'd tried every once in awhile. She'd had her own shit to deal with.

Steeling himself, he answered the call. "Mom."

"Oh, Decker, good, I caught you." Her voice held that beaten-down tone and lack of energy he'd dreaded as a kid. She'd always spoken too soft, too wary, too afraid to speak out.

He ran a hand through his hair then walked into his house. He didn't want to be near anything he was putting in Miranda's home when he had this conversation. It made no sense, but he didn't want to have anything she'd touch be tainted with his past.

That, again, included Decker himself.

He resisted getting a beer from the fridge since drinking had never helped his family anyway. Instead, he leaned against his kitchen counter, willing himself not to ask her if she needed help. Every time he did, it only hurt them both in the end. She had to know by now that he'd be there for her no matter what, but it didn't matter when she ignored it.

"You caught me. What's up, Mom?" He made sure his voice was soft, non-threatening. He hated the fact that if he let his voice go as deep and rough as it normally did, she'd freeze or hang up. He'd never laid a hand on his mother, but he held the same genes as the man who had.

She cleared her throat then mumbled something he couldn't quite catch. A cold knot formed in his belly, but he pushed.

"I didn't hear you. Can you repeat that?" God, please don't be what he thought it was. Please be something good for once.

It was never good.

"Your father is being released tomorrow. Dinner is at five thirty tomorrow night, and we'd like for you to come."

The buzzing in Decker's ears increased, and he gritted his teeth, forcing himself to not scream into the phone, hang up, or crush it in his hand. His mother didn't deserve his anger, as much as her lack of spine killed him. She'd been beaten into who she was, and he couldn't fault her for that. He could only try to help her—like she hadn't helped him growing up.

Fuck.

He needed to get off the phone, or he'd freak the fuck out.

"I thought he was in for another year," he said, his voice low, emotionless. Jesus, hell, why was the old man getting out? His body broke out into a sweat, and he sucked in a breath.

No, he had to be calm. He wasn't that little boy anymore. He was a fucking man, a man with big hands and bigger arms. He didn't need to be afraid anymore.

For himself anyway.

"Oh, Decker, you know he usually finds a way out." She whispered that last part, and Decker's heart ached again. Damn it.

"What was the excuse this time?"

"Overcrowding, I think. It doesn't matter, honey." She paused, and he had to hold his breath. "He's coming home, and you need to come to dinner. He wants you there."

And whatever Frank Kendrick wanted, Frank Kendrick got.

Well fuck that.

"No. I'm not coming, Mom."

"Decker, you need to. He...he said you needed to be here."

He closed his eyes at the catch in her voice. His fist clenched, but he held himself back. Violence from the threat of violence wouldn't help.

"You don't have to let him back in, Mom. You can leave."

"We've talked about this, honey." An uncomfortable silence filled the line, and Decker sighed.

"Mom."

"Everything will be different now."

She always said that.

It never was.

"I'm not coming to dinner. I'm not going to see him again. Ever. You need to leave him, Mom. You're welcome here. You're always welcome in my home." *Please, Mom. Please leave him.*

"I'm sorry to hear you won't be making it. Call me if you change your mind, honey."

She hung up then before he could talk her out of it, say he loved her...do anything other than stand in his fucking kitchen with the phone seemingly glued to his hand.

He'd never felt more useless.

He set the phone on the counter and ran a hand over

his face. He'd been trying to help his mother since he was big enough to fight back against his father. No matter what he did, it was never enough. He'd finally—after the second time his nose was broken—had walked away from the house. He tried to get his mother out, tried to make sure she knew he was there, but it wasn't working.

She'd never leave her husband.

She'd taken her vows, and that's how things were.

He wouldn't give up on her though. She was his mother. No matter the fact she had been incapable of raising him—even when the old man was in jail—because she was too weak.

He couldn't give up.

The thought of that beer filled his mind when the doorbell rang. For the love of God, he hoped it wasn't his mom wanting him to come to the house for dinner. Maybe she'd been on her cell phone and had been lying in wait. She never came by his place, but there was a first time for everything. He didn't know if he had the guts to say no to her face and those tired eyes.

When he opened the door, he held back a groan. Today was not his day, and his control just kept being tested.

"Miranda, what are you doing here?" He didn't growl out the words, but he was damn close.

She'd changed from those short shorts of hers into an even shorter purple dress that made her look sexy as all hell. It looked soft, like cotton, and he wanted to run his hands up and down her sides, up her dress, and all over her damn body.

Fuck, he was for sure going to hell.

Instead of looking annoyed at his unwelcome response to her presence, she tilted her head and smiled. His dick twitched, and he took a deep breath.

Mistake.

He could smell that sweet goddamn fragrance, and now he had to deal with that on top of everything else going on inside his head.

How was a man supposed to drink alone and deal with all the shit going on?

He'd rather pound on his punching bag or beat a shelf into shape.

"I need to talk to you for a minute. Can I come in?" She sounded nervous, yet oddly determined. He had no idea what to make of that.

He stepped back, not knowing what to say. He didn't like feeling like he was out of his depth, but that's what happened more often than not when he was near Miranda Montgomery.

She brushed past him, leaving that honeysuckle scent in her wake. He closed the door behind her and tucked his hands in his pockets. That seemed the only place safe for them.

He didn't want her here. Didn't want her in his space. It was hard enough to keep her out of his thoughts when they were out in public or with the Montgomerys, but now she'd leave her scent in his home, and he'd never get it out. He didn't want her near anything that had to do with what he was, where he'd come from. Now she was in his home, and he had his dad on the brain.

Fuck he needed her out of his space.

"What do you want, Miranda?" he ground out. She needed to leave. Now.

She licked her lips—fucking A—and he ground his teeth. "I..."

She didn't look as sure as she had a moment ago. What did she want? Already angry about his father and what his mother was doing for the old man, he didn't have the energy to deal with Miranda. It was nothing she'd done; it was all *how* he dealt with it. Another reason he wasn't fucking good enough for her.

"I wanted to see if you wanted to get dinner." She blinked at him and looked as though she was holding her breath.

"Dinner?" he asked stupidly.

"Yeah." She cleared her throat. "Dinner. You know. A meal, at night, out in public since I'd like to go out. What do you say?"

"With who?" Dear God. He was a fucking idiot. He could usually string more than two words together, but right then, it didn't seem like it. The vein at his temple pounded, and he knew he was at the breaking point. Images of his father's fist mixed with Miranda's smile, and he had to take another deep breath.

She smiled at him in that special way of hers, and he fisted his hands in his pockets. "With me, silly. You and me. Dinner."

"Why?" Why did she want to go out with him? "Is there something wrong?" Shit. "Is it Harry? You want to talk about him? Did something happen and no one told me?" He walked past her and checked out his phone. No missed calls, so it wasn't an emergency. Or maybe they'd called when he'd been on the phone with his mom and it hadn't gone through. "Maybe we should go over there to make sure."

She cringed when he looked up, and he frowned. "What? What is it?"

"Dad is fine." Her mouth wobbled, but she held together. He always thought Miranda was stronger than her brothers and sisters gave her credit for. She might cry more than the others at bad news, but it didn't make her weak. It was something he liked about her.

She huffed out a breath and threw her hands up in the air. "Damn it, Decker. I'm usually better at this. It's not like I'm a newbie when it comes to dating."

"Dating?" he growled. Who the hell was she dating, and what did it have to do with him?

"Yes. Dating. I want to go on a date. With you. Out to dinner. Not to talk about my dad, though that might come up because he's important to us both. So. What do you say?"

She was asking him on a date? Him? Jesus. What the

hell was she thinking? He wasn't fucking good enough for her. So what that he wanted her. So what that he'd dreamt about having her under him at night and by his side during the day. It wasn't ever going to happen, and this little girl dream of hers was idiotic.

Maybe she wanted to live out some fantasy of being with the foster kid from the wrong side of the tracks, but he wasn't about to let that happen. Miranda Montgomery was too good for the likes of him.

Still angry over the fucking justice system and his old man, he didn't bother to keep his words in check.

"Is this some kind of joke?"

Her smile fell, and the light went out of her eyes. He felt like a shit for being the cause of it, but better she knew that now than later when she regretted it.

"No, Decker. It's not a joke. I came over here to ask you out to dinner. You don't have to be an asshole about it."

He prowled toward her, and she took a step back. Good. She should be afraid. She backed up until her body was against the counter, and he caged her in, his palms flat on top of the counter.

"I *am* an asshole, little girl. You'd best remember that. I'm too much for you and your first time looking for a good, hard night." Because it would be damned good. But it wasn't going to happen.

She narrowed her eyes, that Montgomery fire scorching. "Fuck you. I've had a few hard nights of my own, thank you very much. You wouldn't be my first, so you can get off your high horse. And stop trying to fucking scare me."

She'd been with someone else? His hands fisted on the counter. Whatever little fucker had touched her was dead. That wasn't the point then, though. "It's good that I'm scaring you. We're family, Miranda. You don't go fucking with family because you have an itch to scratch." Hell, he was being a fucking bastard, but if he didn't push her away the right way, there'd be a chance she'd come back. He couldn't let that happen. Better to hurt her feelings now so she could go on with her life than risk something worse later.

Tears filled her eyes, but she blinked once, twice, and they were gone. "Damn it, Decker. What is wrong with you? Why are you acting this way? If you think I'm too young or not enough for you, then just say it. Don't act like you're not good enough. We both know that's not true."

He narrowed his eyes at the lie. "Honey, that's the lowdown. I don't know what you're looking for, but you're not going to find it here." She didn't look like she was backing down so he did the only thing he could do.

He kissed her.

He cupped her face, her skin soft under the roughness of his hands, crushing his mouth to hers. She gasped before opening up for him. Damn, he wanted more, *craved* more, but that wouldn't be happening. Their tongues clashed, their teeth nipping, scraping. He rocked his body against hers, pushing her harder into the counter. His cock pressed against her belly, hard, waiting.

She moaned and her body shook.

He gripped her hair and pulled her head back so he could deepen the kiss, fucking her mouth with his tongue even though he knew he needed to stop.

Before he could take it further, he pulled away and pressed his forehead to hers. His breath came in pants to match hers. He needed to scare her away. "Fuck, little girl. You feel that? That's me being easy on you. You can't handle what I have. You better go back to Mommy and Daddy and forget about playing with the man from the wrong side of the tracks. Got it?"

"What?" She pushed at his chest, and he stepped back. No matter how much he wanted to scare her into keeping her distance, he'd never do anything to harm her.

The contradiction in his actions didn't escape him.

"Go home, little girl." He didn't beg, but he was well on his way to doing so.

She licked her bruised, swollen lips, confusion in her eyes. She had beard-burn on her jaw and neck, and her hair looked as if he'd run his hands through it, pulling hard.

He had.

If she'd gone to any of her brothers or sisters right then, they'd kick Decker's ass.

And he'd deserve it.

"What's wrong, Decker?"

"You need to go, Miranda. That's what's wrong. I don't want you here."

She shook her head. "No. I'm not going anywhere. You wanted to scare me? Fine. You did it. I won't ask you out again. I'm not going to make a fool of myself again. But, as you put it so eloquently before, we're family. You were wound up before I even walked through the door, and I was so focused on my own worries, I ignored yours. What's going on?"

He ran a hand over his face and tugged on his beard. "Just go, Miranda." He sighed.

She put her hands on her hips. When she got that look in her eyes, he knew it would be hard as hell to make her do anything she didn't want to do.

Fuck.

"Fine. You want a beer? I need a fucking beer." He walked past her and grabbed himself one.

"Yes. I could use one. It's been a weird day. That's for sure."

He got her one as well and opened them both. She took hers, and they both took long pulls from their bottles before taking another breath.

"Tell me," she whispered then stood on her tiptoes and rubbed the spot between his eyebrows. He closed his eyes, inhaling her scent, calming at her touch. When Colleen had done that, touched him that way, he'd felt weird, like the other woman was trying too hard.

But Miranda?

Damn it.

He took a step back, ignoring the hurt in her eyes.

Better just tell her so she'd go away and leave him with his own shit to deal with.

"My mom called today. I guess Dad's getting out of jail tomorrow, and they want me over there for dinner."

Miranda didn't know everything that had gone on in his house when he hadn't been with her family, but since she was a Montgomery, she knew enough. Not even Griffin knew everything, and back in the day, Decker and Grif had been closer than twins.

Her face softened, even as a spark of anger flared through her eyes. "Oh, Decker. I'm so sorry. I hate your dad. I know it means nothing that I do, but I wish there was a special place for him where he couldn't hurt you anymore."

He didn't believe there was anything she could do, but the fact that she cared? That had to be something...something he'd ignore because he couldn't go on like this.

She looked down at his tattoo on his forearm and frowned. She couldn't know what it meant...could she?

"I hate him," she whispered, her fingers trailing over the paw prints.

His hand fisted. "Why are you looking at my tattoo?"

Her wet eyes met his, and he cursed. "No one told me...but I overheard Mom and Dad talking about it when you got it. Don't be mad at them, but they knew what happened to your dog and why you got paw prints inked on your arm. I'm so sorry that we couldn't be there to stop it."

He swallowed back the bile at the memory and shook his head. There was no way he would have wanted Miranda to be part of that, and no way he wanted her entangled with the memory of his dad's violence.

"It was a long time ago," he said, his voice rough. Her gaze told him she didn't believe him, just as he didn't believe himself.

"Is there anything we can do? Anything we can do to keep you safe?" She put her hand on his arm, over the ink, and he let her keep it there. She'd touched him before, and he hadn't burst into flames. He'd try not to let it happen now.

"Nothing we can do," he grunted. "Just move on and try to ignore the fucked-up way my family is."

"You have a family, Decker, and it's not them. And if what I did today screwed it up, I'm sorry. I'll do my best not to let it happen again."

He sighed and shook his head. "We'll forget it." As if he could ever forget her taste on his tongue, but that was another matter.

She winced, but then gave him a small smile. "Okay. And I'm sorry, Decker. So sorry that they're letting him out of jail, and there's nothing we can do about it. I wish I could go kick his ass or something, but that wouldn't solve anything."

Miranda understood.

She always understood.

That's why he couldn't be with her.

She knew too much and saw it all.

Or at least most of it.

He wasn't good enough for her, and one day, she'd see that too.

Chapter Five

S he'd thrown herself at him.
Dear. God.

She'd walked right over there and had taken the biggest chance of her life...only to find out she'd done it for nothing.

How much more of an idiot could she have been? She banged her head against her bedroom wall and cursed herself. She just hoped she hadn't ruined what she had with him. He was her friend. The person who knew her— or who she'd been—just as well as any of her family. If not more, if she was honest with herself. Sure, it was going to be horribly awkward at family functions, but she'd get over it. She *had* to.

What she'd known from the start was that Decker was part of the Montgomery family even if he wasn't blood, and she wouldn't let him walk away from that. She'd seen first-hand what happened to him when his old life tried to claw at him, pulling him back in as he fought against it with all his strength. She wouldn't let him pull away from the only family he knew.

Damn it.

She quickly stripped and got into her shower, wanting to wash away the day. A small part of her—okay, a larger part of her than she'd wanted to admit—would like to have kept his scent on her skin, but she didn't want to cross the stalker line into obsession. Water slid down her skin, and she closed her eyes. This feeling of...inadequacy? Loss? Whatever it was, it would pass. She was made of stronger stuff than a wallowing little girl, but it was sure as hell hard right then.

It had been important to her to take that leap and talk to Decker. If she'd stayed away and yearned from afar, she'd have regretted it. Regretted *not* knowing, even if knowing ached. She rubbed a hand over her heart between her breasts. Yeah, it hurt like hell he didn't want her, but now she knew.

Oh yeah, he'd kissed her.

Truly *kissed* her, but it had been a demonstration.

She moaned aloud at the memory. He'd been so rough, so in control, so *powerful*, that she'd almost climbed up his body like it was a tree. The man was absolutely built, and she'd felt his hard erection pressing into her belly. He'd been huge. Long, thick, and so ready to be inside her. Maybe her pussy, maybe her mouth, maybe even between her breasts. She whimpered slightly, letting her hand fall between her legs.

Just one more time.

Just one more time, and she'd never let herself come again just thinking of him.

This was so, *so*, bad, but she didn't care. Not right then.

She let one hand cup her breast while the other fell between her thighs. Decker had revved her up so fast, so hot, that even after talking with him for twenty minutes about things that had nothing to do with her needs, she still felt his presence. She could still smell him on herself, still feel the rough scrape of his beard on her neck.

God, what would it feel like to have that beard scrape along the inner silk of her thighs, as he ate her out, licking and sucking along her pussy, nibbling at her clit? What would it feel like to have that other edge, that other pleasure?

She rolled her nipple between her fingers, tugging and twisting to get that slight pain she always loved when she made herself come. No man had ever found that edge for her, but she had a feeling Decker would have found it quickly.

She lifted her hips so the hot water slid between her fingers and over her pussy. The moan escaping her grew louder as she imagined Decker's fat cock sliding between her legs to press into her in one hard thrust. She pumped her fingers in and out of her channel, mimicking what she wanted Decker to do to her. He'd set the pace, and she'd let him. God, how she wanted to give up control and just *feel*.

She imagined Decker licking down her neck and biting down on her nipple. Hard. With a flick of her wrist, she pressed down on her clit and came. Her legs shook, and she slowly slid down the shower wall until she sat on the floor, water pouring around her. God, how she wanted him. Wanted more of him.

She'd never have him though, and that was something she'd have to learn to be okay with. No one got everything they wanted, and Miranda knew that she had to stay positive.

Even though it hurt and she'd always love him, yearning after a man who would never love her would only make it worse.

She got up and quickly washed her hair and body, trying to push Decker out of her mind. She'd done what she'd said she'd do and asked him out. It hadn't worked, and hopefully, she hadn't ruined what they had. It didn't make her fickle to want to keep what she had even if she'd scratched the surface of it. It only made her protective of her heart and her connections.

Now she'd take the next step on her plan and make sure she was happy before she found someone else. She didn't plan on living her life alone, nor did she want it to revolve around a man. It would be nice, though, to find a happy medium.

It just wouldn't be with Decker Kendrick.

And that would have to be okay.

Eventually.

"YOU LOOK LIKE YOU'RE GETTING THE HANG OF everything."

Miranda looked over her shoulder at Jack and smiled. It had been two weeks since she'd opened herself up for heartache, and the world hadn't ended. Fourteen days of her growing up and being an adult.

Things were going to be okay.

Things *were* great.

"I'd like to think so," she replied as she closed her take-home folders. The end of the day bell had rung about twenty minutes before, and she was so ready for the weekend. Maybe even more than the students.

The semester was in full swing, and the first set of exams were looming the next week. She hoped her students were ready, but there was only so much she could do. At some point, her kids would have to learn to study on their own, with their parents, and show Miranda what they had.

God, had it always been this stressful when *she'd* been a student?

"You look like you could use a drink. What do you say to dinner tonight?"

She blinked up at Jack, surprised he'd asked her again.

He hadn't asked her since that one afternoon in the parking lot, so she figured he'd given up or hadn't thought about her in more than a co-worker sense. For a moment, she considered saying no politely and moving on, but for some reason, she wasn't quite ready to do so.

She knew she needed to get over Decker, and dating would be one way to do that. Plus, Jack wasn't an unattractive man; in fact, he was downright good looking. She could do worse than Jack. The school wouldn't have a problem with it unless she made it a problem. She'd looked up the bylaws just in case even asking her out had crossed a boundary, and it hadn't in the least.

Which was why she knew she had to try.

"You know what. That sounds great. Where were you thinking?"

Something like satisfaction washed over his face, and he smiled full-out. He did have a nice smile. Not as nice or dangerous as Decker's but...

Nope. That was enough of that. There would be no more comparing the man in front of her, who wanted to date her, and the man who would have to remain her friend and only her friend.

"Let's go to this piano bar I know near my place. They have great food, better drinks, and even better entertainment."

She'd never been to a piano bar, but there was always a first for everything. "That sounds great. What time were you thinking?"

Jack picked up her bag from her desk and slid the strap over his shoulder. She sighed inwardly but kept a smile on her face then took it back from him. She was more than capable of holding her own things. Jack raised a brow, but let her have her bag back.

"Seven works for me. How about I pick you up then?"

She shook her head. "I can meet you there at seven if you give me the name or address." There was no way she'd just give her address to a man on the first date. She was smarter than that.

Something washed over his face for a moment before he smiled again, rattling off the name of the bar. "See you at seven, Miranda. I can't wait to see you in a dress."

Apparently he wanted to see her in a dress that night. Well, that was okay since she'd been planning to wear one anyway, but for some reason, it annoyed her a bit that he assumed he'd get his way. It was like the bag thing when they'd been in the parking lot. Little things that put up red flags for no apparent reason. Maybe she just needed to push that to the side since it probably had to do with Decker. She was just looking for things to nitpick, and she shouldn't ruin something before she even had a chance to see how it went.

"See you then."

He walked her out to her car, his body brushing slightly against hers. She moved to the side a bit, making sure they kept as much distance as possible without looking like idiots. Even though it was okay that they went out on a date, she knew it wouldn't be smart to flaunt it at work.

"SEVEN SIBLINGS? THAT'S CRAZY."

Miranda rolled her eyes and took a sip of her one glass of wine for the night. Jack's response to her number of family members wasn't a first. These days, that many siblings was something of an oddity. She knew that, as did her family, but she wouldn't have had it any other way. She liked the way the eight of them had grown up. She liked the noise, the constant in-your-face connections, and the worries that came with that many people being in her business.

She'd grown up with two parents and seven older siblings who seemed to know everything she got into. Sometimes it got to be annoying as hell since she'd never been able to sneak out of her house and party like some of the girls in her class, but she'd had enough of that in college. Between her immediate family, her numerous cousins, and Decker, she'd always had someone to hang out with, so she'd never been lonely. Not many people could say that outside her family.

And that was going to be the last time she thought of Decker, darn it.

"It was loud, always busy, and what I grew up with, so I loved it," she finally said. She played with the stem of her wineglass. "I don't really know what it's like to *not* have a large family. I'm the last, so I've always had that many siblings. The others at least had time with less before the rest of us came along."

Jack shook his head. He had smile on his face that didn't make her tremble, but at least looked really pleasing.

Pleasing?

Dear God, she needed to try harder at this.

"I can't believe your oldest brother is what, fifteen years older than you? His name's Austin, right?"

She smiled then, thinking of her big brother who had never been a parent to her like some other siblings in big families had been. Her parents had somehow found a way to make the age difference work so the older kids never had to raise the younger ones.

"Yes, his name is Austin. And now the age difference doesn't seem to matter much." Well, the older ones still babied her a bit, but that was waning. Some.

"I've never known what it's like to have so many siblings. Do you have any nieces or nephews?"

He seemed genuinely interested instead of just talking to fill the time, so she smiled. "Yes, I have two nephews and a niece."

Jack's eyes widened. "That few for so many of you?"

Miranda shrugged. She wasn't about to get into the whole secret-baby thing that happened to Austin, or the fact that Alex didn't have any children with his wife though she thought he'd always wanted them. Some things weren't meant to be shared unless the other person was truly part of her life. Jack wasn't there.

"Only a couple of us are married or engaged. I think we're right at the stage in life where more weddings and babies are coming though. Or at least I like to think so."

Jack winked at her, and Miranda blushed, mortified. "I meant with the others. Dear God. Sorry. That came out all wrong. I totally didn't mean that I was looking for marriage or anything. Please. Just shoot me now."

Jack threw his head back and laughed. "No worries. I figured out what you meant." He raised a brow. "Or at least, I hoped I had."

Miranda took a sip of her water, liking the fact he hadn't freaked out. She might not have meant what it sounded like at the time, but she *did* want to get married and have children. Eventually.

"So I know you're a teacher and some of your siblings work in construction. What about the others? What does Austin do?" Jack asked as the waitress set down the appetizer between them. They started munching on calamari while the man on the piano played a little Billy Joel—of course.

"Austin and Maya own a tattoo shop. Montgomery Ink? It's right off 16th Street Mall. Austin's fiancée, Sierra, owns Eden, which is across the street. That's how they met actually."

Jack tilted his head, a frown marring his face. "A tattoo shop? That's...interesting."

Miranda did her best to keep the smile on her face. God, she hated when people judged without knowing what ink meant. Most of those people just thought that if someone had tattoos or worked in a shop, they were unintelligent, degenerate criminals. Sure, the landscape of art and the new generation—her generation—had more ink, and it was becoming more accepted, but those who *did* the art themselves still had that stigma.

Maybe Jack would be different.

Maybe.

"Yes. It *is* interesting. Austin and Maya are two of the most sought-after artists in the west outside of LA. Even people in LA come out to get inked by the two of them. They started their little shop with nothing, and now they have six full-time artists and people who come in to work in shifts when they're in town."

Jack nodded, that frown leaving his face. He didn't smile, but he didn't look like he was judging either. That was something, she supposed.

She also knew what the next question would be.

"So, do you have any tattoos?"

See? A predictable, but not an unwelcome, question. Her ink might be hidden due to her job and the way those people might react, but she wouldn't have let anyone ink her skin if she wasn't proud of it.

She had to remember, though, that this was a date, not an inquisition. Jack was just curious, and she had a tight string when it came to people judging her family. She was a Montgomery. Sue her.

Instead of being annoyed about the questions, she let them roll right off her. At least she tried to. She tilted her head and smiled, brushing her hair off her shoulder. Jack's eyes darkened as his gaze traveled down the long line of her neck to the bare skin of her shoulder.

Look at that, she still had it.

"I might. But that's not something I usually reveal on the first date," she said, flirting a little.

Jack grinned and reached over the table to take her hand. She flipped her hand over casually so he could play with her palm.

"I like that. I never thought of tattoos as sexy...but... well, this *is* a first date after all." He motioned toward the waitress, and by some hidden cue, the woman nodded back. "Dance with me," he said to Miranda when he faced her again.

"But what about dinner?" she asked, surprised at the turn of events.

"When we came in, I told her to wait to put in our order in case we wanted to dance. She'll put it in now so we can dance a song or two and have our meals ready when we get back."

Wow. He'd planned all of this really well. Yet it seemed a bit...contrived. No, that wasn't the word, but it felt like he'd surely done this before.

Get a grip, Miranda. It wasn't like she'd never dated

anyone before. For cripes sake, she didn't know why she was acting this way. Well, she did, but she wasn't about to think about *that* name.

Jack stood up, his hand still on hers, so she got up with him. He led the way to the dance floor and put his other hand on the small of her back once they reached the center.

"You look gorgeous tonight."

He danced well, not like he'd taken lessons, but like it came naturally to him. Jack seemed like the type of man that many things came naturally to. And there she went again, judging because she was in a funk.

"Thanks," she replied. "You don't look too bad your-self." He pulled her closer so they were pressed together the length of their bodies. She could feel his erection against her belly, but again, it didn't turn her on. Instead, she moved back slightly so she wouldn't feel so boxed in. The thing was, she'd had years to feel that spark with the man-who-would-not-be-named, so the fact that she didn't feel the exact same thing with the man in her arms wasn't Jack's fault. It was just poor timing.

She wouldn't give up though. It wasn't a chore to dance with Jack, to eat with him, enjoy his presence. Just because she didn't feel a huge spark to end all sparks with him didn't mean it wasn't there at all. Maybe it would be just a slow burn.

He twirled her smoothly on the dance floor then made her laugh when he did a little jig, as if knowing she needed to smile more. After a couple of dances, their food arrived, and they made their way back to the table. They talked of work because it was something they had in common and, frankly, a passion of hers, and more of her family. They didn't delve too much into his life other than the fact that he was an only child and both his parents had passed on years before. Her heart hurt for him at the loss, and she'd held his hand, even though it looked as though he'd wanted to brush it off. She didn't know what she'd do if she'd lost her family.

She swallowed hard at the harsh reminder of what her father was going through. She hadn't told Jack about it, and wouldn't. Not on their first date. It was deeply personal, and unless he knew her family and her dad, she wasn't sure he'd get the deep ache and brutal cut along her heart at what was going on.

She hated not knowing, not having things in her control. But that's why she made lists and plans when it came to things she *could* control. Or at least things she *thought* she could control.

Dating was just one of those things she'd put on her list. Hopefully it wouldn't crash and burn.

AFTER DINNER AND DESSERT, JACK WALKED HER OUT to her car. Unlike the time at the school, this held a little more anticipation. She loved kissing. Loved sex.

When they got to her car, she turned to face him.

With her in heels, the top of her head came right up to his forehead so it wasn't that much of a distance in case they wanted to kiss goodnight. Though she hadn't felt the sparks she'd craved, she'd enjoyed herself so that had to count for something.

Jack stood in front of her, his hands on her arms. She smiled, and he lowered his head. She tilted up her chin and let his lips brush hers before letting him deepen the kiss slightly.

He wasn't a bad kisser, far from it. He just wasn't... Decker. Or maybe she was thinking too hard and needed to just live in the moment.

She pulled back and gave him a small smile. He didn't seem disappointed, but she couldn't hold back the emotion on her end. It'd been fine. Good. Not great. But good.

"Well, I guess I'll see you on Monday then," she said pleasantly, trying not to get into her car too quickly. He was a nice guy; he just didn't make her hormones dance. The fact that she wanted to run away and get in her sweats with a tub of ice cream didn't make him a bad man.

"I'd like to take you out again, Miranda."

She held back a sigh. There really wasn't a reason to say no other than the fact that she didn't want to crawl up his body and feast on him like a starving woman.

It wasn't his fault.

After all, she wanted to get over Decker.

"That sounds good," she said.

"I need to grade papers this weekend and do other

things, so maybe next weekend?" Jack asked, his smile bright again.

"We can plan once we know what our workload is. How's that?" *Boring, Miranda. Downright boring.*

Jack traced his finger along her jaw. Nothing. No tingles. No sparks. Maybe with more time...

"We can do that. See you on Monday, Miranda." He kissed her again, and she sighed when he pulled back. His eyes warmed at her sigh, but she didn't have the heart to tell him that it wasn't passion.

Just because Jack wasn't Decker didn't make him wrong for her.

She just had to remember that.

And get over a certain bearded, broody, tattooed man.

Easier said than done.

Chapter Six

"**H**is name is Gunner, and he's three years old."

Decker looked down at the cage, his hands in his pockets. "What breed is he?" He honestly couldn't tell from the big ears, brown and black patches, and feet too big for its body. Since the dog was three years old, Decker figured it was finished growing. Too bad it never grew into its feet.

"A shepherd mix, we believe. It's hard to tell with some of the mixes, but he's housebroken. He does like to chew, however, so you'll have to make sure you have rawhide bones on hand, and maybe keep your shoes out of the way until he gets used to you."

Perfect. A dog that might pee outside but liked to eat anything in its path. Huh, sounded familiar.

Honestly, the ugly thing had a face only a Montgomery could love.

Decker wanted him.

There was nothing like being a stray, begging for scraps. He'd never be that boy again, and he damn well would make sure this dog wouldn't have to do it either.

"I'll take him," Decker grunted before kneeling in front of the cage. Gunner put his paws on the metal separating the two of them and barked. His tongue rolled out of his mouth, and he panted. It looked like the damn dog was smiling.

A pang of grief slid over him as a memory of Sparky doing the same thing filled his mind, but he pushed it away. There was nothing he could do for the pet he'd lost, but he'd damn well take care of the one in front of him. He wouldn't let the old man touch this one. Decker's fists were larger, his body taller. He'd protect what was his just like he had since he'd been able to.

With that pleasant thought coming back to him, he stood up and put his hand on the door of the cage. "Let's get the paperwork done so Gunner here can get out of this cage."

The shelter worker smiled up at him and then at Gunner. "I think we have a good match." She fluttered her eyelashes at him, and he held back a snort. *Sorry, honey, you're even younger than Miranda. No thanks.*

Fuck. He needed to stop thinking of Miranda.

"Paperwork?" he grunted again.

Her smile fell, but she bounced around the room anyway. She was like one of the smaller dogs she was trying to find a home for. All perk and no worries. Well, she could keep that up as long as he got to get out of there fast. The sounds of barking and lost causes were starting to grate on him. He could take only one pet home, and he knew if he stayed any longer, he wouldn't last.

Damn, if he'd brought Miranda, she'd probably have wanted to adopt every single one. Even going as far as to gift one or two to each of her siblings. She was always like that, saving every little thing when she was growing up. She'd tried to save him just by being herself. He knew that much.

Damn. Okay, enough of Miranda.

He filled out the paperwork, paid the fees that helped keep the shelter open, and had Gunner on a leash within thirty minutes. It hadn't been spur of the moment to come and get him since he'd prepped his house some. But it had been in the back of his mind for far longer than a few days. Ever since he'd kicked Miranda out of his house after spilling his guts and forcing his kiss on her, he'd been in a bitch of a mood. This might help.

Maybe getting over what his father had done—or at least trying to—would help in the long run. Who the fuck knew, but now he had a dog to throw in the mix.

He got Gunner settled in the passenger seat of his truck then closed the door before walking around to the driver's side. Gunner stood stock-still, as if he didn't know what was going on, or maybe it was that he couldn't trust that what was happening was a good thing. Decker had been there.

He really needed to stop seeing himself in this dog. It wasn't doing good things for his already piss-poor mood.

Before starting the car, he looked over at Gunner, who stared back at him, those big eyes of his filled with...hope? He couldn't tell, but at least it didn't look like fear. He didn't know if he could deal with some dog being scared of him right then, not when he'd done his best to scare Miranda away.

"So...you're coming home with me." The dog didn't move. "I haven't had a dog in a long while. In fact, I haven't had anything I've had to really take care of other than myself so we're going to learn how to do this together."

Gunner tilted his head, studying Decker.

Weird.

"I'll make sure you're fed, watered, and have a place to run around. I'm not going to coop you up in the house all day. In fact, if you behave, then I bet you can come to job sites with me. Wes and Storm would get a kick out of that." He grinned at the thought of Wes trying to figure out how to organize a dog's life while organizing his own. Yeah, that would be worth it. "Now, I'll do all that, but don't piss in my house and don't chew on shit. I know you're going to want to so we'll figure it out, but try not to. Okay?"

Gunner lowered his head then raised it.

No shit. That couldn't have been a nod, but he'd take it as one. The damn dog smiled again, and Decker almost smiled back.

That was until he smelled it.

"Jesus Christ. You trying to gas me out of my own truck?" He coughed then opened the windows. "Damn it. That smells rank, Gunner. What the fuck were you thinking?" Gunner just put his head out of the window and let out a little sigh.

Nicely done. A perfect family. Decker started his truck and headed home, his eyes watering. "I have no idea what you ate to give you that stench, but we're going to find something better at home because fuck, dog..."

Gunner looked over his shoulder, barked, then went back to trying to catch air or bugs or shit outside the window. Well, the dog looked happy, so that was something. When Decker pulled into his driveway, he saw he wasn't the first one there.

He stopped the truck and opened his door. "You have a key, dumbass. What are you doing just sitting in your car?"

Griffin looked over his passenger seat out the open window. "Huh? Shit. I didn't realize I was out here that long. I finally figured out how to fix this one chapter and needed to write it out. My car seemed as good a place as any."

Decker rolled his eyes at his friend. Some things never changed. "At least you weren't driving."

"Hey, I'm not an idiot." Decker didn't blink. Grif sighed. "Fine. That was one time, and since you were in the passenger seat, you kicked my ass. I haven't endangered another person with my daydreams in a long time, thank you. And if I had needed to, this time I would have pulled over." Grif frowned. "Dude. You know you have some kind of ugly dog thing in your truck, right?"

Decker grinned then looked over his shoulder at Gunner. His new dog hadn't left the truck, though he'd left the door open. Good thing. He was lucky Gunner hadn't run off since Decker had given him the opportunity. Next time he wouldn't be such an idiot.

"Hey, Gunner. You can get out now. Come to me." He held out a hand, and Gunner jumped readily. Decker took the end of the leash he'd left attached and looked over at a surprised Grif. "Good boy. Grif, meet Gunner. Just picked him up at the shelter. Gunner, meet Grif. He's an idiot, but he's a good guy."

Grif flipped him off then got out of his car. "Damn, Decker. I didn't know you wanted a dog. Nice." He walked around the front of his car and held out his hand. Gunner looked over at Decker, and Decker nodded. The dog went over to Grif and smelled him before allowing himself to be petted.

"Hey, he's pretty well behaved. Nicely done."

Decker shrugged. "Got lucky I guess. I just saw him in the cage and figured he'd be good."

"Well, he's ugly enough that no one would have

wanted him for their little kid or whatever." Griffin smiled brightly. "I guess this mug would fit in with your ugly face nicely."

"Suck me," Decker said, flipping his friend off.

"Later, baby. You'll need to shower first."

Decker snorted. "Jesus. Don't put that image in my head. Fuck. Now I'm going to need to shower to get clean since you're a creep." It wasn't the idea of a man with him that creeped him out; it was the whole brother thing.

"I do my best. You got beer?"

"Of course I do. I had to restock after you cleaned me out last time you were here." He ran a hand over Gunner's head. "Come on, boy. Let's show you your new home."

"But I already have a home."

Decker punched Grif in the arm and opened the door. "You can go on in, Gunner. Shit." He looked over his shoulder. "Will you get that bag of dog things and food I put in the back of the truck?"

"How big a bag of food are we talking?" Griffin asked, running a hand over his arms. The man wasn't as built as the rest of his brothers, but he lifted just like the rest of them. Sitting on his ass for hours a day writing didn't seem to hurt him. "Take two trips. Let me show my dog around. I'll get you a beer."

Grif grumbled then stomped away. He'd have gotten a beer anyway, but this way, Decker would watch to see what Gunner would do. The dog shuffled around the house, smelling and brushing against everything he could.

Decker ran behind him, catching a lamp before it fell to the floor since Gunner's tail wagged like it was a life or death situation.

He heard Grif huff behind them then walk to the kitchen, a twenty-pound bag of dog food over one shoulder and a bag of bowls, toys, and other things in his free hand. Decker got two beers out of his fridge then leaned against the counter. He had already put a dog bed down in the kitchen since he didn't usually make impulsive decisions. He'd known he was getting a dog that day. He just hadn't known which one he'd get.

Gunner sniffed around the bed then laid down on it.

Looked like it was a good fit.

"Give me that." Griffin took one of the bottles from Decker's hands and opened it before taking a sip. "God, that's good."

Decker raised a brow, and after opening his own drink, took a sip. "It's only like four o' clock. Why are you in need of a beer?"

Griffin rolled his eyes. "It's beer. Duh. Plus, that scene about killed me. It took me four days to get past this one chapter while it usually takes me maybe a day. I hate when I have to pull words out of me like pulling teeth."

Decker ran a tongue over his own teeth and winced. "Yeah, I don't want to think about that. Glad you pulled through. Now, not that I mind you being here, but is there a reason you were camped out on my driveway?" Decker put his beer down then started to take everything out of the bag. He filled a water dish and set it down next to Gunner, who happily slurped it up, making a mess of himself and the floor. Well, at least he'd put in hardwood with numerous coats of lacquer. Small mercies.

"What? Oh, yeah. My house is a mess."

Decker raised a brow. "Yeah? Tell me something I don't know."

"Yeah, well, it's always been a mess, and unless I change something, it's going to *stay* a mess. I can't help it. Once a deadline hits, everything like housework and grocery shopping gets pushed to the side. If I didn't have Meghan coming over every once in awhile to make sure I ate something, I'd die."

Decker snorted then took another pull of his beer. "You're a spoiled ass. Meghan has two kids and a husband that's a fucking prick, and she still spends time to take care of you. Spoiled."

Griffin lifted his lip in a snarl. "I know I'm lucky. Maya and Miranda take turns checking in on me too. Actually I think the others come over to check on me as well, but they end up eating whatever food I have. Austin has long since given up taking care of me. Not that I've ever asked him to take care of me in the first place."

Decker pointedly ignored the mention of Miranda. "Damn straight. You're twenty-nine, Grif. Grow up."

Griffin threw up his hands. "I know. I have a job that tends to take my brain away. I get it. That's why I need help."

Decker picked up a ball from the bag on the counter and walked to the backdoor to let Gunner know where he could take a leak and run. The dog followed him, leaning into his leg when he could. They were lucky Decker didn't trip and flatten them both.

"I'm not going to be your maid, Grif, so get that out of your head right now."

"But you'd look hot in a French maid costume."

"Fuck you." Decker threw the ball to the other end of the yard but still on his side of the fence. "Go get it, Gunner, and bring it back to me." The dog looked up at him with that smile and long tongue then ran at full speed to the end of the yard, tripping over his feet in the process.

Damn dog.

"I don't need a maid. I need...organization."

"Organization," Decker repeated. Gunner ran back with the ball and deposited the drool-covered thing at Decker's feet. "Good dog." He picked it up and threw it again, slobber and all. Gunner ran off after it.

"Yes, organization. I have a lot of books."

That was an understatement, but Decker had a feeling Griffin knew that. "True."

"I need bookshelves."

Gunner left the ball in the middle of the yard and proceeded to chase his tail. Well, it took all kinds apparently.

"Bookshelves."

"Yes. Bookshelves. And stop fucking repeating me."

"Sorry. But how are bookshelves going to keep the rest of your house clean and shit?"

"It'll help."

Decker nodded, agreeing at least on that. It wouldn't help much, but it would be a start. "You want me to build you some bookshelves so you can keep your house clean."

"Yes. I need help."

"Well, that goes without saying," Decker said with a grin.

"Eat me."

"Not my type," Decker said pleasantly, doing his best to keep thoughts of exactly who was his type out of his head. "And yeah, I'll build you some shelves. You tell me what you want, and I can get it done. Why didn't you ask Wes or Storm?"

Griffin shrugged. "I would have, but you came to mind first. And since I'm not allowed to use saws anymore, I couldn't do it myself."

"You're not allowed to use saws anymore for a good reason," Decker put in.

"I didn't lose my finger," Griffin snapped.

"That's not exactly the most promising endorsement to allow you to use a saw, Grif. Come with me to my workshop, and I'll get some ideas down for you. Gunner! Come on in, boy." Gunner rolled around in the dirt a minute more then stormed inside. He skidded along the floor, leaving dirt and leaves in his wake.

"Nice," Griffin said with a smile. "Looks like I won't

be the only one with a messy house." He leaned down and gave Gunner a good body rub. "You know, I'm surprised he's so well behaved and trained."

Griffin crouched down and petted Gunner's head. "Yeah, me too. But who knows what'll happen in storms or even when he gets more comfortable. The lady at the shelter didn't know where he'd come from other than the fact he'd been dropped off one morning. So I don't know how he is around kids or anything. I'll call Austin and Meghan and give them a heads-up so we don't scare the kids or Gunner. You know?"

"Smart. You'll figure it out. You always do."

"I hope so. Come on. Let's go. While we're there, I'll look into what I can do for a doggie door or something. I don't want to force him inside all the time. I don't know how he'll do with the sounds of the saw and construction equipment, and I don't want to freak him out the first day. Stay here, Gunner." Hopefully his furniture wouldn't get beaten up with Gunner alone in the house, but he had to leave him alone for a bit eventually.

"Aww, look at you being a good doggie dad," Griffin teased then ducked when Decker threw a weak punch at him. "Too slow, old man. Fuck!" He winced and rubbed his shoulder when Decker's fist connected that time.

"Don't taunt," Decker said casually as they made their way into the garage.

"Hey, look at these shelves," Griffin said when they walked in. "I like them. They for Miranda?"

Decker swallowed hard. Damn, if Griffin ever found out about what had happened in Decker's kitchen just a couple days before...well...Decker would be dead, that's for sure.

"Yeah. Almost done with them." Then he'd have to install them in her home. Hopefully he could do it when she wasn't there because he wasn't sure he could handle close proximity and short shorts again.

"They look good. Maybe I'll go with you when you install them so I can grill her over her new guy, Jack."

Decker froze, the ringing in his ears amplifying. He must have heard wrong because he was pretty sure Griffin had just mentioned some soon-to-be dead guy named Jack was dating Miranda.

"Huh?"

Griffin gave him an odd look. "I want to grill Miranda's new boyfriend, Jack. He apparently works with her. He's a teacher or something like that. I don't know much about him, so I'll need to make sure I get every detail out of her while I can. You can distract her with the shelves, and I'll wheedle the information."

"She's dating? Dating a teacher named Jack?"

Griffin's brows rose. "Yeah, buddy. Keep up. Anyway, no one has met him, and I hear they've only gone on one date so far. At least that's what she told Maya. Maya wouldn't tell us anything else since they have that sister bond or some crap."

Well hell, it looked like Miranda hadn't wasted any

time moving on from putting the moves on him in his kitchen. He couldn't blame her, not with the way he'd acted. But hell, he wished his plan hadn't worked so well, so quickly.

He didn't have much room to speak since he was still technically dating Colleen. Sure, he hadn't talked to her in a week and hadn't slept with her in six months, but still. He didn't own Miranda and didn't have anything to do with her.

He needed to remember that.

"You okay, Deck?"

He cleared his throat and nodded. "Yeah. Just trying to come up with a way to grill her," he lied. Well, maybe that wasn't much of a lie, but still.

Griffin smiled. "Knew I could count on you."

No, bro, you really can't.

His phone buzzed, and he answered without looking at the read-out. Mistake.

"Decker, honey, thank God you answered."

He cursed and set his beer down. Griffin raised a brow and did the same, folding his arms over his chest.

"What is it, Mom? You okay?" He couldn't help the question that popped out. Damned if he was crazy for wanting his mother out of a situation she refused to run away from, and refused to protect him from.

"Yes, of course." He could sense the lie but didn't call her on it. Not this time.

Griffin cursed under his breath and gripped Decker's

elbow. He let himself be led back into the house and into the living room while his mother talked about random goings on in the neighborhood. He sat down on the couch with Griffin on one end. Gunner jumped on the sofa between then, and Decker let him. It was a bad habit, but fuck, it wasn't like he had top-of-the-line things anyway. A man needed his dog, and a dog needed space to lie.

"Mom." He interrupted her talk about jam or some other shit he didn't care about. It wasn't why she was on the line anyway. They both knew that. Hell, Griffin knew that.

"Oh, honey. You need to come to dinner," she said in a small voice. "Your dad wants you here. And you know how he can get."

Yeah, he knew how the old man got. Hence, why he wasn't going. Fuck, he couldn't just let his mom stay there alone, but he'd told himself long ago he wouldn't let that man win.

"Mom, I'm not coming. You know why I can't. As long as he's there, I'm not stepping foot in the house. Once he goes back to jail, because you know he will, then I'll be there for you. You want to come over here to eat? I'll make something, or we can go out. Just the two of us."

"You know I can't do that," she whispered.

"Mom." He closed his eyes, willing the memories to fade. They never would. "Please."

"I can't. If you're not coming to dinner...then I'll let him know." She hung up, and Decker screamed.

Fuck. Once she told him that he'd said no, then the old man would take it out on her. If they were lucky, Frank would only yell and scream. He was still close enough to his jail time that he might not use his fists.

Yet.

"It's not your fault, Decker."

"The hell it isn't. He's going to beat the shit out of her eventually because I won't go to dinner. I should just suck it up and deal with it."

Griffin cursed. "No. You shouldn't. It's not your fault. You get that? It's not your fault that your dad is a fucking drunk and cheats on her. That's all on him. The fact that your mom won't leave him even when you try to pull her out, well, I don't know as I can say that's on her, but it's all on him no matter what. It's not your fault."

Decker ran a hand over his head while Gunner put his head on Decker's lap. The dog shook, and he sighed. Great, now he was scaring dogs too. "Sorry, buddy." He petted Gunner and ground his teeth.

"You're not going to listen to me, and I get it. But what you will do is get in your truck and follow me to Mom and Dad's. I was going over there anyway for dinner to see how Dad's treatment's going, so you're coming with me." He looked down at Gunner. "The dog too. They'll be glad to have you both."

"I'm not fit company, Grif." He just wanted to be alone and forget all the shit around him. Maybe he'd pound on his punching bag some more. It hadn't helped to get Miranda out of his head, and his scraped knuckles hurt like a bitch, but he'd take that over this pain any day.

"So what? You're family. So get off your ass, dump the rest of your beer, and let's go. I'll call ahead and let Mom know. That way she's not surprised. But hell, Decker, come to dinner with us."

Decker rubbed the bridge of his nose. "I didn't want to go to dinner with Mom. Why should I come with you?"

"Because we're family," Griffin said simply.

Decker sighed, knowing he'd go with Grif tonight and be welcome like he was their son, brother, and friend. Hell, even Gunner would be accepted as one of them without a second thought. That was another reason why the Montgomerys were the best people in his life. He wouldn't change them for anything. Without that relationship, the one with Marie and Harry, well, he wouldn't be the man he was today. They'd opened their arms for him and never let him go.

He'd needed that more than they'd ever know.

Hell, he *still* needed that.

Yet another reason he couldn't be with Miranda Montgomery.

The reasons were piling up, yet he couldn't get her out of his head. He'd find a way though. There wasn't another option.

Chapter Seven

G etting older sucked.

Feeling old at twenty-nine was hell.

Sierra Montgomery rubbed her hip and winced. The accident had happened a decade ago, and yet she still hurt every morning and in the evenings after a long day. Sometimes she even hurt in the afternoons too. There was no escaping the damage from a motorcycle accident—externally or internally.

With a sigh, she turned so she saw her scars in all their puckered glory. She'd just gotten out of the shower, so rivulets of water trailed over the damaged skin and the bloom of daisies Austin had inked carefully on her skin. Her fingers danced along the petals, knowing her fiancé had touched each, softly, roughly, purposely.

She stretched her arms over her head, ignoring the ache. Her breasts rose, her nipples hardening in the cool air of the bathroom. Austin thought her body was perfect, *his*, and after finally giving in, she agreed with him. She was perfect for herself. Perfect for him. The evidence of their rough lovemaking from the night before dotted her skin. Beard burn on her inner thighs, along her neck. Bite marks dotted her breasts, her stomach. She could see the faint outline of Austin's hands on her hips from where he'd gripped her hard, pummeling into her pussy. She'd clamped around him, begging him for more. Her wrists had been tied to the bedpost, so she hadn't been able to reach for him.

Her body shivered at the memory.

Austin knew exactly how to love her, *make* love to her, and just let her be her.

That's why she loved him so freaking much. Scary to think that she'd almost lost it all because she'd been afraid to take that chance, afraid to let herself love again. When she'd lost her first fiancé in the crash, she'd figured she'd had her one shot. She'd lost him and the baby she was carrying. She hadn't known she was pregnant at the time. No, that had come as an awful surprise later on in the hospital.

Now because of that day, that horrible memory, her joints ached like an eighty-year-old's, and she had to talk to Austin about their future. She was going to marry him. That wasn't going to change. But she was so freaking worried she'd never conceive. It wasn't like they'd been trying in the first place, but it was something that had been tumbling in the back of her mind for far too long.

Sierra was only twenty-nine years old, so if she hadn't been in the accident, she'd have a good five to ten years of possible childbearing time left in her. Now, though, she wasn't so sure. The accident had bruised her heart, as well as many organs. It wasn't going to be easy. The doctor had broached that subject years before. So now she had to talk to Austin about what would happen if—no, when—they tried for a baby.

They had plenty of time before their small—as small as a Montgomery event could be anyway—wedding. Austin, however, was turning forty within the next year, and she knew he wanted to be able to run with his kids and not feel like an old man. He'd never be an old man to her since he was damn sexy at thirty-nine, and she knew that wouldn't be changing any time soon. They both wanted his son, Leif, to have siblings nearer to his age though.

Leif had just recently come into their lives after being hidden away with his birth mother for the first ten years of his existence. After a few bumps, he'd fit into their new family nicely. He called Austin Dad and her Sierra. It didn't hurt her in the least that he didn't call her Mom. He'd had a mom who had cared for him—even as she'd hidden the truth of his birth from Austin for all those years. But now Maggie was dead, and Sierra was raising Leif at Austin's side.

Sierra might have been an only child, but Austin came from a huge family. They wanted to meet in the middle.

If only her body would cooperate.

Sure, she knew she was freaking out and worrying before anything actually happened—or didn't happen, as the case might be—but she couldn't help it. She refused to hide things from Austin, so she'd have to tell him her worries. Yes, they'd be able to adopt if she couldn't conceive. She wasn't opposed to that in the slightest. In fact, if they wanted a larger-than-average family, she thought adoption would be a fantastic way to have that. She just couldn't nudge the annoying part of her that told her that if she couldn't have a baby on her own, there was something wrong with her.

How stupid was that?

Idiotic.

Untrue.

And horribly misguided.

Hence why she needed to talk to Austin. If she could have a baby on her own, then great. If not, then she'd find another away. That's what options were for, and making herself sick over what she couldn't change wouldn't help anyone.

"Knock, knock," Austin said from the other side of the door. She ran a hand over her face and sighed.

"I'm naked in here."

The door opened, and Austin barged in. "Naked?" His eyes darkened. "Mmm. My favorite outfit of yours."

She rolled her eyes, warming at his words. His arms came around her middle, and she leaned into him. "You're a dork. I thought you liked that little black number I wore the other night."

Austin growled and gripped her ass. She sighed, loving his rough hold. "That's one of my favorites too. I seem to have a lot of favorites when it comes to you." His fingers played with the crack of her ass, dipping lower until she shivered at his teasing.

"Austin," she gasped. "I need to go meet the girls at Taboo and then go to work." He worked his fingers in and out of her slowly, taunting.

He nibbled at her lips, her neck, and she angled her head so he could have better access. Since she knew they both needed it, she undid the button of his jeans and took him in hand. He hissed out a breath then bit down on her neck.

"Fuck, make me come, Sierra. Make me come on your belly, your breasts. Do it."

She shivered and worked him, gripping his cock in her hand while going on her tiptoes so he could finger her at the same pace. They both panted, her vision going blurry when his thumb pressed against her clit.

"Austin."

"Come, baby. Come on my hand. Make me wet."

She did as he commanded, arching her back as she came. His mouth latched onto her nipple, sucking it into his warm heat. She didn't let her hand stop moving, using her own thumb to rub the liquid at the tip of his dick. He pumped his hips, helping her along, and then shouted her name as he came. He spurted on her belly with some splashing on her breasts.

He kissed her softly, cupping her face. "I suppose we'll both need another shower," he said gruffly once he pulled away.

Sierra smiled then rolled her eyes. "I suppose we both will. Separately." He groaned, and she snorted. "Go into the guest bathroom and use that one. We'll never leave if we're all naked and wet."

He growled then kissed her again. "Damn, woman. Stop making me want you. I need to go into the shop and do a seven-hour piece. I can't do that with a fucking hard-on."

She laughed then swallowed hard. God, her head hurt, and her joints ached worse than normal. Maybe she was stressing herself out to the point of getting sick. Not fun.

Austin cupped her face. "You okay, Legs?"

She nodded, leaning into his touch. "Yes, just a little sore."

Concern marred his features, and he ran a hand over her back. "I'm sorry. Was I too rough?"

She shook her head. "You never could be. You know our limits. I'm just tired, and now I need to shower. Again."

He searched her face then nodded before giving her a kiss. "As long as you're sure. I'll go shower in the guest bathroom. Alone. Then head into work. If you're free, stop by to say hi at the shop later."

She nodded, kissed him again, and then watched him walk away. Damn, she loved the way he looked from behind.

Well, she loved the way he looked from all angles, but that was a given.

Her bearded tattoo artist was one sexy man.

With that pleasant thought in her head, she took another quick shower and got ready as fast as she could. She wasn't running late, but she wasn't going to be early. Oh well, a morning orgasm was so worth it.

By the time she made it into Taboo, Callie, Miranda, and Hailey were already there. Hailey worked behind the counter, making up drinks for other customers while Callie and Miranda were sitting on the other side, talking and laughing. Hailey owned the place that was connected to Montgomery Ink through a side door, and because of that, Sierra had quickly become friends with the woman. She was smart, beautiful with that bleach-blonde sharp bob, and knew how to tell it like it was.

Callie was a new tattoo artist at the shop and had been Austin's apprentice for over a year or so before Sierra had moved to town. The woman was younger than Sierra, around Miranda's age, and had the energy of twelve twenty-year-olds. That boded well for Callie's forty-year old fiancé, Morgan.

Though technically Sierra was closer in age to Maya

and Meghan than Miranda, for some reason, she'd really gotten closer to Miranda. Sure, she had meals with Meghan when she could, and she hung out with Maya often, but Miranda was the one she felt closest to. Maybe it was because they were both starting new phases in their lives at the same time.

"Hey, you," Callie said with a smile then narrowed her eyes. "You got morning nookie. Nice."

Sierra blushed while Miranda trilled a laugh. "Oh God. I do *not* need to be thinking about Austin getting laid. Thanks for that."

"My pleasure," Callie said then smirked. "Or was that Sierra's pleasure?"

"Stop," Sierra said on a laugh as she sat on the other side of Miranda. Hailey immediately placed a caramel latte in front of her. "Thank you, honey. Business going well?"

Hailey wiped her hands on her apron and nodded. "Very busy this morning, and we're just hitting that lull that makes it easier for me to actually talk with you guys. So, nookie? Was it good?"

Sierra rolled her eyes and took a sip of her drink. Perfect. "Of course it was good. It was Austin. Now please stop before we give Miranda a heart attack."

Austin's sister just grinned. "I guess I need to get over the fact that my brothers have sex. I mean, I have sex. Not recently, but it has happened in the past, so I should just put that connection out of my mind."

Callie looked over Miranda at Sierra. "Not recently? So you're going slow with Jack?"

Sierra perked up. Jack? "Who?"

"Oh! You don't know. Apparently Miranda is dating a coworker named Jack. A blond, golden god according to Maya."

Miranda closed her eyes and groaned. "I'm going to kill Maya."

"If it wasn't Maya, it would be someone else," Hailey put in. "There are no secrets between the Montgomerys."

"That's true," Sierra said. "So, Jack?"

Miranda nodded and smiled, but it didn't seem that bright. Odd. "We've gone on one date and have another planned for the weekend. It's not a big deal."

Callie patted Miranda on the shoulder. "Ah, so no spark? That sucks."

Miranda sighed. "There might be sparks. I'm just in a funk. Jack's a great guy, so I'm going to try another date."

Sierra nodded along as the others talked more about Jack and then about Morgan and other things in their lives. Miranda didn't look too happy with this new guy in her life, but it was early yet. Odd, because Sierra could have sworn she'd seen sparks between Miranda and Decker. Not that she thought Decker would act on those sparks. That might have been the point. Bro codes and family connections made things like that difficult. While it was sad the brightness Sierra had seen might never come to fruition, at least Miranda was trying something out. Trying something new.

She sipped her coffee and let the voices of the people in her life she'd come to love settle her. Things were changing every day, and with the Montgomerys, nothing ever seemed to remain the same. She'd just hold on tight and go along for the ride.

Chapter Eight

Date number two would prove to be better. Right? Miranda fixed her lip stain while trying to drum up the excitement that should have come with going on a second date with a handsome man. She honestly didn't know why she was forcing this. She should have just said no to Jack when he'd asked her to dinner over the phone earlier this week. Or even said no to him when they'd been standing in the parking lot outside the piano bar.

Now she was stuck going on a date she didn't want to go on with a man who might be nice, but wasn't the man she wanted. God, she was a picky bitch sometimes. The whole reason she'd said yes in the first place, other than her habit of not wanting to hurt people's feelings, was to get over Decker and try new things. Fretting over something that hadn't happened yet wouldn't be helping anyone. Least of all her.

As she applied her lip-gloss over the stain, she thought up reasons to not call off the date at the last minute. One, it would be horribly rude. She had to work with Jack daily, and begging off would make things awkward. That brought her to number two, the fact that she *did* work with Jack. Not going out with him when she'd said she would might hurt her work relationship with him. They hadn't done more than kiss twice and dance, so it wasn't like she'd be breaking his heart, but it still wouldn't be easy. That was her fault though, for agreeing in the first place. Three, she needed to get over Decker. That sounded stupid when she thought about it, but she couldn't help it. Going out with Jack, at least once more, would help pave her Decker-less path. The man who'd been in her life for as long as she could remember didn't want her the same way she wanted him—kiss or no kiss—so she had to get over it and move on.

This was her moving on.

Too bad it had to be with a man who was nice, but wasn't for her.

Against her better judgment, she'd agreed to have Jack pick her up for their dinner date. It was their second date, and since they worked together and, as it turned out, lived only a couple neighborhoods apart, having him drive seemed like the most realistic thing to do. There wouldn't be any inviting him in that night after he dropped her off, though. Even if she hadn't been having second thoughts about the date itself, she wasn't ready to sleep with him. She didn't have the zing with him, and though she truly loved sex, she wasn't about to jump in bed with a man because it had been awhile.

Now if that man was a certain bearded...

Nope.

Stop it, Miranda.

Things were going well for her. Most of her students had passed their exams, and those who hadn't met with her at her urging. She was considering meeting with two sets of parents to see if that could help the situation, but other than that, she was on her way to getting them ready for the next exam and set of chapters.

Austin and Sierra's wedding was on its way to being halfway planned, or at least that's what Miranda hoped. Her friend, Callie, was engaged to a wonderful and sexy man named Morgan, and Meghan had smiled and joked with her today when she'd stopped by for lunch with the kids.

Things were going to be okay.

Her phone rang, and she picked it up as her pulse raced. It always did that whenever she saw her parents' number on the screen. "Hello?"

"Hi, honey, I was just checking in." Her mom didn't sound frantic or as if the world had ended, so Miranda calmed a little. God, she needed to stop doing that, stop thinking of the worst-case scenarios. But she couldn't help it. Not when her dad was sick and the world had kept turning despite it.

"Mom, is everything okay?" She couldn't stop the question popping out.

Her mother sighed, and Miranda bit her lip. "He's tired, baby, but he's doing better. He's taking a nap right now, or I'd put him on the phone. Your dad might be sick, but he's not down for the count. You don't need to worry about each phone call. Sometimes I just want to talk to my youngest child."

Miranda sat down on the closed toilet seat and took a deep breath. "I love you, Mom."

She could practically hear the smile in her mother's voice. "I love you too, baby girl. Now I hear you're going on a date tonight, so be safe and enjoy yourself."

Miranda blushed straight to her roots. "I swear I'm going to kill Maya." Were there no secrets in her family?

Well, no one knew she loved Decker—other than that damned Maya—so that was something.

"Don't threaten your sister. You know how I hate it when you all threaten to kill and maim one another. Anyway, have fun tonight, and if you really like this young man, we expect to see him at dinner soon."

Miranda rolled her eyes. Oh yes, the Montgomery interrogation would work wonders with him. Just what she needed.

"Goodbye, Mom. And tell Daddy I love him."

"I will, honey. Have fun."

She ended the call and rubbed her temple with her free hand. The fact that her father was sick made her want to cry and curl into a ball sometimes and then scream and fight with all her might at others. There was nothing she could do but pray and help her dad when she could.

And tonight was about her and Jack, not about worries and aches that would never go away.

She quickly finished up her makeup and was just about to finish packing her small clutch when someone knocked on her door. With a quick look at the clock—on time—she zipped up her clutch and made her way to the door.

Jack had said he was taking her out to one of the upscale restaurants in downtown Denver. He had some family money from his parents, so that had to be how he could afford it on his teacher's salary. Miranda, for sure, could not afford anything like that on her own. Sure, her parents might be able to after years of working themselves to the bone with Montgomery Inc., but she wasn't her parents.

She brushed a piece of lint off of her lacy black dress and rolled her shoulders. She would have fun, damn it. It didn't matter that he wasn't the one man she wanted. She was getting over *that* man.

When she opened the door, Jack stood there in a suit and an open-necked shirt. His blond hair was slicked back, making his cheekbones stand out even more and his blue eyes pop. Even if she didn't feel that zing, he was still hot. That had to count for something.

Now *that* was shallow.

Okay, then at least she'd try to have fun. She could be friends with Jack.

"You look amazing," Jack said, and his gaze traveled over her body.

She'd worn a short lacy dress that had an empire waist and thick straps. At first glance, it looked almost like a baby doll dress, but a little more regal. She'd paired it with a cute shrug and sexy heels—because, come on, sexy heels made everything better. She'd let her dark brown hair fall in soft curls around her shoulders and knew she'd done well by the look on Jack's face. She'd dressed up to please herself, but if he liked it too, then that was a bonus.

"Thanks, you don't look too bad yourself."

He held out a hand, and she took it, crossing the threshold and walking outside. She let go of him to lock up behind her, and then they made their way to his car. He was a perfect gentleman, opening the door for her and helping her get in the low car with her short dress.

When he walked around the car to get in on his side, Miranda took a deep breath. Date number two would be okay. Better than staying at home alone and eating chocolate. Though she did love chocolate.

They made their way to the restaurant, talking about work and her family yet again. While she loved both, she figured she might actually like Jack more if she talked to him about *his* life, rather than just hers.

"So, did you always want to be a teacher?" she asked when they pulled up to the valet. He gave her a look then got out without answering. Weird.

She let him help her out of the car since it would have been awkward in her dress. She probably should have worn pants, but nothing beat a little black dress to knock out weird moods.

"So? Did you?"

Jack frowned, and Miranda elbowed him playfully. "Did you always want to be a teacher?"

"Yes, I enjoy enriching lives. I'm sure you're the same way. It's not like your other siblings and their...odd career choices."

Whoa. Red flag right there. She stopped in her tracks on the way to their table, but Jack pushed her at the small of her back. Rather than make a scene like she really wanted to freaking do, she let him lead her to the table.

"Excuse me?" she whispered after the hostess sat them.

"I'm just saying, your brother and sister and their odd job of tattooing. While it's nice that they're able to do that with the types of people that come to their establishment, I don't know that it's appropriate for a teacher to have connections like that. People talk."

Miranda blinked. People talk? What the ever-loving hell? He'd been a little off when she'd mentioned on their last date what Austin and Maya did, but this was so crossing the line it wasn't even funny.

"You know what? I'm going to call a cab. I'm not in the mood for you to dismiss my brother's and sister's lives because you don't understand it. You're judging people and their lives because you can't seem to think outside the box and figure that, hey, your opinion, while it's yours, doesn't really matter. You don't get to dictate how people live their lives." She stood up, but he gripped her wrist. Hard.

Her pulse picked up, and she tugged. Thankfully, he let her go. "Don't leave, Miranda. I was wrong to say that. I'm sorry."

She didn't know if she saw truth in his eyes, but she knew she wouldn't be dating this man again. "I'm not sure if you mean that, Jack."

He traced a finger down her arm, and she pulled away. "I'm sorry, Miranda. That *was* judgmental of me. I apologize profusely. Please sit down, and let's start the evening over."

She wanted to go home and take off her heels that were now killing her. Apparently thoughts of a good night helped women persevere through high-heeled death traps.

"Please," he said again.

Miranda sighed then sat down. She'd eat a good meal, try to salvage their working relationship since, right then, she wanted nothing to do with the man who judged her family without meeting them, and then go home.

"Thank you," he said, his hand on hers. She pulled it back. This would be a dinner between two co-workers. Not a date.

The waiter came over, and Jack ordered for her without asking her input. She raised a brow. She'd already had her speech for the night and wouldn't be making another unless she needed to. She didn't particularly want the Cornish game hen, but she wasn't in the mood to slap that smile off his face in public.

"You'll like the hen," he said when the waiter left.

"Will I?" she asked casually. "I suppose I might, though it would have been better if I'd been able to choose my own meal."

Jack gave her a condescending smile that set Miranda's back teeth on edge. Who the hell was this man? "I was being a gentleman. You'll like the hen," he repeated.

"Just a heads-up, women these days don't like to have their choices taken away. Whether it be dinner or family members."

Jack merely took a sip of his wine. "Some women do. You'll understand."

Oh no, she didn't think so. She took a sip of her water. She wouldn't be drinking her wine that night. She needed to keep all her wits since she didn't trust this creep one bit.

Why the hell was she doing this?

"You know what, Jack? I think I'm going to leave. I think it would be best if we remain merely co-workers. We clearly don't have much in common." She stood up, put some cash on the table—don't call her a mooch—and strode toward the front, where they would hopefully call her a cab. If not, she'd just walk the two blocks to Montgomery Ink. It was early enough that Sloane or one of the other artists would still be there.

Jack was on her tail, and she turned on her heel when they reached the lobby. "Miranda. Don't go. Let's salvage this night."

She shook her head. "No, I don't really think we can, Jack."

"Don't be petty. We enjoyed ourselves last time."

"Petty? Seriously? No, I'm sorry. That's not who I am, and you're an ass for thinking that."

Jack looked over her shoulder and pulled her closer to the wall. She pulled from his grip. "Don't manhandle me."

He put both hands up. "I'm sorry. I was just moving us out of the way so we wouldn't make a scene."

She wasn't too keen on making a scene, either, since she didn't want to ruin anyone's evening, but fuck this man and his attitude.

"I want to go home, Jack. We clearly don't suit. You don't like my family even though you've never met them, and you're a little too happy with taking everything over."

"Miranda, you don't understand."

"No, I'm afraid I do."

He sighed, and she turned around, only to come to a complete halt. Decker stood there in a suit with Colleen on his arm.

Of course he did.

Because fate was a fickle bitch.

While he wore a similar, if not thriftier, suit to Jack's, he looked nothing like the man behind her. Where Jack was all smooth lines and slicked-back hair, Decker looked...dangerous. He'd kept his beard, but had trimmed it so it looked groomed rather than like he'd just gotten up and left the house. Miranda loved both ways. His hair curled around his ears, too long and in need of a good cut, but it still begged for her fingers to tangle through. He'd left the top two buttons undone on his shirt so she saw tanned, golden skin. His shoulders filled his suit jacket like no other man could. Broad, sexy, and built.

She swallowed hard then blinked when his gaze met hers. He frowned when he looked over her shoulder.

Jack put his arm around her waist, and because she'd been frozen at Decker's appearance with Colleen at his side, she hadn't moved quickly enough to get away.

Damn it.

Colleen looked amazing in a red dress that hugged her curves, but Miranda barely noticed. All her attention was for Decker. He gave her that chin tilt of hi, then followed the hostess to his table. Colleen looked over her shoulder and frowned, but kept going.

Well then.

Jack moved his hand from her wrist to her arm and tugged her outside. Hard. She winced and pulled away. "What the hell was that?" he snarled.

She rubbed her arm, sure she'd bruise the next day. "Um. Excuse me? You don't get to touch me. Ever. Again."

The valet walked over, his eyes wide, and the sneer on Jack's face smoothed out to a smile. "You're with me, darling. Don't look at other men like that. It annoys me."

She lifted a lip in her own snarl. "You know what annoys me? Your possessiveness. Don't call me. Don't talk to me. I'm taking a cab and going home."

She stomped away as Jack yelled her name. Luckily, a cab was waiting right at the edge of the restaurant, and she got in, thanking God she'd brought enough cash for the ride.

Where the hell had that side of him come from? She rubbed her arm and sucked in a breath, trying not to cry. He'd hurt her sure, but he'd hurt her pride more. He hadn't seemed the type of man to push and pull at a woman to get his way, but he'd sure crossed those boundaries tonight. Now she'd go home, lock her door, and take a bubble bath or something. Work would be fucking awkward, but there was no way she'd be able to see him without remembering the feeling of his hand on her arm.

When the cab pulled up to her place, she paid him and looked around for Jack's car. She never could be too sure.

The cabbie looked like he wanted to get out of her neighborhood and get another fare, so she got out and ran to her door. She wasn't too scared, but she wasn't about to be an idiot either. She had her keys in her hands, ready to get inside, when someone rammed her into the wall.

Her body shook, and her lungs stopped working. The right side of her face hit the brick wall outside her door, and her eyes stung from the impact.

"You don't get to just leave me, Miranda."

Frozen, she tried to turn around, fight back. Something. Her brothers had taught her how to protect herself, but it was different when it was actually happening to her. Maybe someone would hear him and come outside. She couldn't count on that though. She only had herself.

"Let me go, Jack. You don't want to do this." She wiggled, and he pulled at her arms, turning her around, before slamming her back into the wall.

"I don't want to do what? Show you that you're mine and you don't get to fucking leave me? You embarrassed me, Miranda. That can't happen again."

She wouldn't cry, wouldn't give him the satisfaction. She fought at his arms, and he slapped her on her right cheek. Hard.

Tears slid down her cheeks, and she thrashed against his hold.

"Don't scream, or I'll make it worse."

She didn't scream, afraid he'd hurt her where she couldn't move, but she kept fighting. He hit her again. She tasted blood on her tongue, and her vision grayed.

"You're going to stop fighting me, and you're going to know that we're meant to be together, Miranda."

No, this couldn't be happening. This *wouldn't* happen. He leaned closer, his breath on her neck.

She brought up her knee and rammed him in the balls with all her strength. He cursed, breaking away from her to clutch his crotch. Her keys in hand, she opened her door and slammed it closed. Her heart raced, and she dug out her cell phone from her bag. She should have had that in her hand the whole time. Damn it.

She called 911 and shook as she told them what happened.

Yes, she was inside.

No, she didn't know where he was now.

No, she didn't feel safe.

Yes, there was someone she could call.

Yes, she could wait for the police to come.

She crawled to her landline and hit the first speed dial that came up—Maya. Her cheek ached, and so did her back. Her arms hurt from his hands, and her body shook. She wanted to cry, weep, or scream, but she did none of that. Instead, she calmly told the operator that she was calling her sister and to hold.

"What's up, buttercup?" Maya asked when she answered.

Miranda opened her mouth to speak, but nothing came out. She didn't know if Jack was out there. What if Maya came over and something happened to her?

"Miranda? What's wrong?" Her sister's tone sharpened. Miranda took a shuddering breath into the phone.

"I need you," she whispered.

"Jake and I are going to be right there. What happened?"

"Jack...hit..." She couldn't finish her words and she hated herself for it.

"Fuck. Did you call the police? Talk to me, baby girl."

Miranda nodded then remembered Maya couldn't see her. "I'm on the line now, and they're coming."

"Okay, honey. Do you need me to stay on the phone with you too?"

Miranda took a deep breath. She shouldn't break down. Not yet. "No. The police are coming."

"I'm on my way. Stay inside. I love you."

"I love you too."

She hung up and listened to the operator tell her the police would be there in two minutes. When someone knocked on the door, she screamed then shook her head.

"Police! Ms. Montgomery? Are you okay? Can we come in?"

On shaky legs, she stood up and looked through the peephole. She saw only the police and their badges and didn't see Jack. She let out a breath and opened the door.

WHEN MEGHAN, MAYA, AND JAKE CAME TO THE DOOR, Miranda had already been through a series of questions, observations, and had an ice pack over her eye. Miranda tried not to wince at the look of pure rage on not only

Maya's face, but Jake's as well. Apparently, Maya had called Meghan as soon as she'd gotten in the car. The three M&Ms needed to be together. When the officers had the nerve to hold Jake back since they thought he might be Jack—one had dark hair and the other was blond— Miranda didn't blame the man for the frozen posture.

Meghan came to Miranda's side and wrapped an arm around her shoulders. Miranda wouldn't break. Not until the cops left and she was able to breathe again.

"So, you're sure he was just a little rough with you? You sure it wasn't part of your date?" The older cop looked down at her short dress and high heels with a look Miranda wasn't quite sure she liked.

"Excuse me?" Maya snapped. "Did you just ask if my sister got beat up by a man she did *not* ask into her home because she wanted it?"

"I wasn't asking you, miss. I was asking the woman next to you. Since that one book came out, we've needed to be sure that this wasn't part of one of those...games."

Miranda stiffened then lowered her ice pack. She didn't know what she looked like, but from the curse that left both Jake and Maya's lips, it wasn't good. "No. I didn't ask for him to throw me into the wall and then to slap me."

"What's your badge number?" Jake asked. He took his phone out and snapped a photo of the cop.

"You're going to want to put that phone down," the cop said slowly.

"No, I really don't think so." Jake snapped another

photo while Meghan wrote down the number. God, Miranda just wanted everyone to leave and let her sleep. "You're going to leave now, and let us take care of her."

"Is she your girlfriend, or is the other one? Or is it both? Maybe all three?"

"Sir," the younger cop whispered.

Fucking idiots.

"Thank you for coming to take down my statement," Miranda said woodenly. She stood up, Meghan and Maya at her sides. "I'd like to ask you to leave now. Please let me know if you need me to come down and make another statement or when you arrest Jack."

The older cop raised a brow. "We're still collecting evidence." He stood up anyway. "We'll let you know how it pans out."

The asshole cop and his little minion left, and Miranda blinked once. Twice.

"Baby," Maya whispered.

She'd had enough. A whimper escaped her, and then she let it all out.

Miranda broke down, gut-wrenching sobs forcing her body to shake.

"Oh, honey." Meghan brought her into a tight hug while Maya hugged her from behind. She felt Jake's hands guide them to the couch, and then he left the room to give them privacy.

She cried into her sisters' arms, her head aching, her

privacy and security broken. God, how had this all happened so fast?

"We've got you," Maya whispered, and Miranda hiccupped another sob.

They did. She knew that. No matter what happened with the cops and subsequently Jack, she knew her sisters had her. When her brothers and parents found out, she knew that all of the Montgomerys would have her.

She was blessed.

And one day she'd feel it again.

Chapter Nine

Montgomery dinners were always loud, boisterous, and full of drama. Usually, the drama wasn't too deep and had more to do with family squabbles or dealt with work, but sometimes it was more.

For some reason, Decker had a feeling this time there would be more.

It was his first Montgomery dinner since he'd kissed Miranda.

His first one since he'd seen her out to dinner with that slick guy who must have been her boyfriend, Jack.

His first one since he'd dumped Colleen and now had no one holding him back from Miranda.

No one other than himself.

And said Montgomerys.

Harry had been through another round of treatments,

but his energy was on the rise. Marie knew what she was doing when she planned these things. She wouldn't have invited the rest of them to dinner when Harry was truly feeling down, but this way, the head Montgomery would have his family around when he was starting to feel better. And the kids would see a little bit of their old dad again, rather than the fragile man he was fast becoming.

Austin and Sierra were talking in a corner with Wes and Storm about some addition to their house while Leif played outside with Gunner and Meghan's kids. The dog had fallen in love with the three kids at first sight, and with the adults watching, the four of them had forged a friendship made in heaven quickly. Meghan and Maya were huddled in another corner talking about something serious. Something he wasn't sure they were ready to talk to the family about. They'd all know soon enough since no one ever kept secrets in this family. At least not for too long.

Griffin was in the middle of a conversation with Harry that made them both smile and laugh. Grif was always good at telling stories that fit the person who was listening, or more often, that the people fit the stories he told. That's what made him a great writer.

Meghan was on her phone, frowning and trying to whisper, though Decker had a feeling it was her prick of a husband on the other line. The loser hadn't come to dinner, though Decker knew for sure the man had been invited. In fact, now that he thought about it, Alex's wife wasn't there either. Instead, Alex stood by the window, a frown on his face and the ever-present drink in his hand. Shit, the man looked paler than usual, and the dark circles under his eyes looked even starker with the combination of the expression of loss and rage on his face.

Decker knew it was none of his business, but he made his way over to Alex, knowing that no one should be drinking alone in a room full of people. Everyone but Miranda was there and ready for dinner. The other two-thirds of M&M had said she was running late and would be there soon. Their cagey expressions told him that something was up, but he was sure he'd figure it out soon. He always did. Or he at least tried to.

"Hey, man." Decker spoke causally as he came to Alex's side. He had a soda in his hand rather than a beer since he was driving soon and hadn't wanted to risk it. Alex, on the other hand, had an amber liquid in a glass. Again.

"Hey," Alex grunted but didn't look at him.

"What are you doing here all alone?"

Alex looked over slowly and blinked. "I'm not alone. You're here. Plus the fifty Montgomerys in the room make it hard to be alone."

Decker frowned. "You okay?"

Alex sighed then took a drink. "I'm fine. I wish everyone would stop thinking there's something wrong with me and asking if I'm okay."

Decker lifted his brows. "Maybe if you stopped

growling and acting like an asshole, we wouldn't stop to wonder if you were okay."

He was just brimming with tact today.

For a moment, Decker was worried the other man would throw a punch. Instead, Alex threw his head back and laughed. The others quieted, watching the man they loved laugh, though it wasn't a happy one. No, this one bordered on the edge of manic.

"I am an asshole, Decker. That's not going to change anytime soon."

Decker sighed and put his hand on Alex's shoulder. He was lucky the other man didn't brush it off. Or punch him.

"What's wrong, Alex?"

Alex met Decker's eyes with glassy ones of his own. "Notice anyone missing?"

Miranda.

But he didn't think Alex was talking about her.

"Where's your wife?"

"She left me."

"No shit," he said softly then cursed when Alex's eyes went blank.

"She did what?" Marie Montgomery came quickly to her son's side. "Alex, honey, why didn't you tell us?" She framed her son's face with her hands and did a valiant job of hiding her wince when he pulled away from her.

Alex shrugged, and Decker sighed. "You all saw it

coming, so don't lie." He raised his glass in a toast. "It's over, and I don't want to talk about it. Got it?"

Marie shook her head and Harry pulled her closer. Alex's brothers patted his back, murmuring the usual condolences, but not really anything important. What was there to say when a clearly unhappy marriage had ended? It just reinforced what he knew in the first place.

Marriage no longer meant much. Divorce was an easier way out than the effort it took to make a marriage work. In any event, when it ended, by choice or circumstance, someone was left to suffer. He refused to look at Harry and Marie, knowing if they saw him, they'd see too much.

Instead, he focused on Meghan, who looked shaken. Her pale face made her eyes look wide, scared. Decker didn't know what that was about, but he knew it couldn't be good. She and Alex were the only two married Montgomery kids, and neither had good marriages. Yeah, Meghan was still married to that asshole, but anyone could see things were rocky.

As if she knew he was looking at her, she blinked at him then put a pleasant expression on her face. "I need to check on the kids. I...I'm sorry, Alex." With that, she walked outside, leaving the rest of the family standing awkwardly around a man who clearly didn't want to be there and didn't want to deal with his family.

The fact that Alex was there, though, spoke of the

underlying strength of the Montgomerys. He just hoped it was enough to pull Alex out of whatever funk he was in.

And Miranda still wasn't fucking there.

God, he didn't want to see the look on her face when she heard about Alex and Jessica. She cared about her family, but she was a fixer. She wanted to make everything right for everyone. It didn't matter that she couldn't, but she always insisted on trying.

His phone buzzed, and he looked down at the screen. With a curse, he hit ignore then sighed. He couldn't stand in this room with these people for too much longer. They might call him family, but he wasn't. No, the family he had kept calling him, wanting to suck him back into the abyss he thought he'd clawed himself out of years before.

Grif gave him an odd look, and Decker lifted his chin toward the front door. His friend frowned, but Decker just mouthed "two minutes", before walking out the door, taking his leather jacket with him. He just needed some damn air, and he wasn't going to get it in the house, not with so many people around him going through their own shit. Austin and Sierra were getting married. The twins had their own problems at work most likely. Maya looked like she was hiding something. Meghan had her asshole husband, and Alex was drinking in a corner. Harry and Marie were dealing with Harry's illness, and Griffin was starting to see too much.

They all saw too much.

Decker walked out to the big tree on the front lawn and stuck his hands in his pockets. He wasn't going to leave before dinner. That would hurt Marie's feelings, and she'd been dealt enough blows recently. Leaving without a word would only make it worse.

He didn't know why Miranda was late, but she should be there soon. She'd get there, find out part of her world had crashed, and he'd be there to pick up the pieces. He always had. When she'd found out about her dad's illness, he'd been the one to hold her. He'd been the one she'd leaned toward. Maybe it was because of her crush or whatever the hell she had, but that couldn't be all of it. She'd always been part of him, close to him, even when they were growing up.

He just wasn't sure he could handle it anymore. Not after that kiss. Not after scaring her out of his kitchen. Scaring her right into Jack's hands. Damn, the couple had looked perfect together in the restaurant, all long lines and smooth features. The fucker had put his hands on Miranda like he knew he was welcome there. Miranda hadn't pulled away, hadn't looked like she'd rather have someone else. It hadn't helped that Colleen was on his arm and hadn't liked the look on Decker's face when they walked in. He thought they'd both known the score, and considering they hadn't slept together in months, she shouldn't have been surprised when he ended it. In fact, he wasn't sure there *was* anything to end other than a few dinners here and there. She'd been fucking pissed, but now it was over, and he was free.

At least free of her.

The virtual shackles and confused thoughts were due to another long-legged brunette.

The one who was just pulling up to the Montgomerys' street. He stayed where he was, his hands still in his pockets. He wasn't a nice man, and she needed to see that. He wouldn't open her door and help her out or lead her into the house with his hand on the small of her back. She'd be fine on her own, and so would he.

She had on big sunglasses, but those didn't hide it all.

What. The. Fuck.

Ignoring his earlier thoughts, he took his hands out of his pockets and stormed toward her. She made it to the sidewalk and squeaked when she saw him. Her hand came up to her throat, and he cursed. He hadn't meant to scare her, not this time, but shit.

This was why she was late?

"What the hell happened?"

"Decker..." She put a hand out, but he didn't touch her. Couldn't right then. He was so fucking pissed he was afraid he'd hurt her more. He was his father's son, and he couldn't trust himself.

"Who do I have to kill? Who the *fuck* put their hands on you? Was it that fucker, Jack?" He dug his keys out of his pocket, and she put her hand on his wrist.

He stilled at her touch, so soft, so small.

"Mir, tell me."

With a shaky hand, she took off her sunglasses. She hadn't bothered with makeup, as it wouldn't have hidden the swelling and bruises on her face anyway. He could see every single inch where someone had hurt her. He took in each bruise, each cut, each mark on her perfect face. He'd beat the bastard bloody, making sure to replicate the bruises and add a few more.

After all, he wasn't a nice man.

"I took care of it." She spoke softly, but she was clearly unbowed. Holy hell, this woman was strong.

He took her by the shoulders gently and brought her to his chest. Fuck whatever was going on in his head. He needed to touch her and feel that she was still there, still okay. She stiffened for a moment then melted into him, gripping the front of his shirt.

"Of course you took care of it," he murmured. He wouldn't expect any less of Miranda—and Maya and Meghan, if their earlier looks were any evidence. He ran his hand through her hair and over her back to soothe her. "Tell me what happened so I can take care of it, too."

"If you go in and beat someone up, you'll only make it worse. I just want it to go away."

He growled softly, squeezing her tight until she protested. He loosened his arms and rested his cheek on the top of her head. They stood out in the middle of the sidewalk where anyone could see, but right then, he didn't give a flying fuck. People could think what they wanted for the time being. He needed to make sure she was okay, and then he'd deal with the others.

"Jack did this, didn't he?"

She nodded against him, and he struggled not to curse or growl.

"What happened?"

She shivered, and he took off his beat-up leather jacket and wrapped it around her shoulders. She sighed and nuzzled closer.

She told him about the date and how she hadn't truly wanted to be with Jack in the first place. He would process the fact that she hadn't wanted to be with the man and yet had pushed herself to do so later. When she got to the part where she'd called a cab, he stopped her.

He pulled back and lifted her chin with his knuckle. "I was right there in the restaurant, Mir. You could have come to me, and I'd have given you a ride."

She shook her head. "Could I? After what happened in your kitchen, could I really?"

He closed his eyes and cursed inwardly. He'd done a great fucking job there. "Yeah, Mir. No matter what happened in that fucking kitchen, I'd have taken you home. But let's move on from that."

She looked at his face and saw something she must have understood in his eyes because she nodded. "I got as far as my front door. I had my keys out and everything because I was scared, you know?"

His grip tightened, but he nodded. "Go on," he bit out.

She sighed. "He knocked me into the wall." She pointed to her face. "I think that's where most of this comes from. Then he scared me a lot. Turned me around, hit me once."

He growled, straight up growled. "I'm going to kill him."

She shook her head. "He didn't hit me again, because I kneed him in the nuts and somehow got inside my place and behind a locked door."

He grinned then. Yeah, it wasn't a pleasant grin, but Miranda sure knew how to surprise him. "Good for you. Hope you kneed him hard."

She grinned with him, just as menacing. "I think so. He screamed a bit, and I used all my force to do it." Then she shrugged, and he knew that, although that bit had made her feel better, there was still a long while to go until she would feel like herself again. Fuck if he knew how to help her with that. "I called the cops then Maya. Actually I sort of did it at the same time. Thank God Dad made me keep my landline."

"True." For some reason, he wished she'd have called him, since, out of all of the Montgomerys and friends, he lived the closest. But he hadn't been home, and they weren't speaking.

Well, fuck him.

"So, Maya, Jake, and Meghan showed up and took care of me since I had a minor breakdown when the cops left."

He raised a brow. "You're allowed to have a breakdown, minor or not. That little fucker had to have scared the shit out of you, so if you want to cry again or punch something, you let me know."

"You're going to let me punch you?"

He snorted. "Smartass. If that's what you want, you can try. I meant the punching bag I have at the house." He frowned. "In fact, you might want to try it out anyway so I can make sure you can protect yourself. I know the brothers taught you some moves, but I want to see them."

She sighed. "I thought I knew them too, but it's different when you actually have to use them. You know?"

Sadly, he did know, but he didn't tell her that.

"What did the cops say?"

She narrowed her eyes and shook her head.

"What the hell? What did they say, Mir?"

"Well, other than the older one pretty much blaming me because I'm a woman, not much."

"You've got to be fucking kidding me. You get his badge number? Fuck that idiot."

"You've said fuck like ten times in the past two minutes. Calm down, Decker."

"Fuck that." Despite his best effort, his mouth twitched. "Mir."

"Deck," she said in his deep tone. "Jake got the badge number and took a photo of the guy. Made the idiot even angrier, but whatever. As for Jack, well, they said so far since there isn't much evidence and no witnesses, it's a case of he said/she said. I don't know what's going to happen, but Jack has a lot more money than me if he fights it or whatever."

Considering he'd lived a life where, no matter the evidence, his dad always got his way because his mom had been too scared to say anything, sadly, this didn't surprise him. There were good cops out there, great ones, but they never found Decker most days.

Something occurred to him. "I'm a witness. Well, not to what happened, but I saw him with you at the restaurant. I can tell them that."

She shook her head. "You're welcome to try, but even the valet couldn't help, and he saw us arguing."

Decker ground his teeth. "Anything I can do, Mir, name it. If it takes me beating the shit out of that little fucker so he understands exactly who he messed with, then I'll do it." And enjoy it, but he didn't mention that part.

"You can't do anything, Decker. Besides, I took care of it," she repeated.

"I'm damn proud of you for doing what you did, but it doesn't matter that you took care of it. I want to take care of it, and you sure as hell know your brothers are going to want to take care of it too."

She winced then. "I know. Damn. I didn't want to come today since, well..." She pointed to her face, and he nodded. Yeah, there was no hiding that. "I don't want to tell the whole story again and again, and that's what I'm going to have to do if I *don't* go in. This way everyone is there, and I can get it over with. Then I can go home or something."

Decker knew it was a mistake, but he'd help. He couldn't help himself. "How about this...I go in with you. You tell your story, and then I get you out of there. Come home with me, and I'll make sure your face is okay, and you can meet Gunner."

"Gunner?"

"Hell, I forgot you didn't know. I got a dog. Gunner. He's in the back now hanging with the kids. So, you in?"

She searched his face. "A dog? This I've got to see. I'm in."

Yep, he was a glutton for punishment.

He took a step back, and she put her hand in his. He swallowed hard then pushed that feeling away. He'd help her because he couldn't help himself, and then he'd find a way to get over her. If he didn't, he wasn't sure how he'd make it through the next few years.

They walked step by step toward the door. When he put his hand on the doorknob, she squeezed his hand.

"You ready?" he asked.

"No, but I need to be."

"I'll go in first," he said, knowing it would only delay the inevitable.

The family saw him first, curiosity on their faces. Then one by one, he saw them focus on Miranda.

The room exploded.

"Oh my God, baby." Marie ran to Miranda's side and took her daughter's face—the unmarred side—in her hands. "What happened?"

Miranda hissed out a breath, and since his hand was still holding hers, he pulled her away.

"Everyone calm down," Decker said, his booming voice over the fray. "She'll explain everything, but you need to step back."

"Really?" Austin bit out. "I need to fucking step back?" His gaze traveled down to Miranda's and Decker's clasped hands. "Mind telling me what the fuck is going on?"

For a moment, Decker thought the man he'd called a friend, a brother, thought that he had been the one to put the bruises on Miranda's white-as-milk face. He shook it away, though, because that couldn't be it. They wouldn't think that...though they had all the right in the world to. After all, he'd come from that type of man, that blood. It wouldn't be a stretch to think he'd been the one responsible, although he'd never hit a woman in his life.

"Mind telling all of us?" Storm asked. The man glared while his twin at his side didn't say anything. The murderous expression on his face said it all.

Alex stood against the wall, not saying anything. At first, Decker thought the man was too drunk to care, but the anger in the man's eyes was the first real emotion he'd seen in a long while.

That was something.

Griffin, too, didn't say anything. He just stood next to his father with a look on his face that Decker couldn't quite decipher.

"Stop it. Stop it, all of you!" Maya yelled, and the room quieted.

"If you're done yelling like a bunch of Neanderthals, I'm going to take Cliff and Sasha home," Meghan put in. "It's been a long day already, and I think it's time for everyone to sit and talk." She came to Miranda's side and kissed her sister's temple. "Be well, and call me when you get him."

Cliff and Sasha quietly hugged Miranda, sensing the mood in the room.

Sierra and Austin shared a look, and with Austin's nod, she took Leif back outside with Gunner. Decker was sure she'd hear it all from her fiancé later, but this was not the time for the kids to be about.

"It seems to me that the girls knew what was going on before all of us," Griffin said smoothly. "Now Decker does. I don't like being left out of the loop. I especially don't like it when it looks like someone used my baby sister as a punching bag."

"Quiet," Harry said softly. He walked carefully up to

his daughter. Decker didn't release her hand. He wasn't sure he could in the first place.

"Is the person who did this to you dead?" Harry asked.

Miranda shook her head, tears filling her eyes. Damn it. "No, but I took care of it." She told them the story just as she'd told Decker minutes before. She was right in thinking she wouldn't want to tell it over and over again. This way she got it out in one fell swoop and she could move on. As much as anyone could anyway.

Harry traced the bruised side of her face with his finger, barely brushing it so Miranda didn't even wince.

"I don't want my sons in jail, nor my daughters and wife, because they took the law in their own hands," Harry said smoothly. "You say you have this under control, I believe you. But know this, baby girl, if you need us, we're here." He kissed her forehead then looked over at Decker. Decker tilted his chin up, and Harry nodded.

Yeah, the man knew some of the score. Decker would help and wouldn't back down. Sometimes it took another person outside the den of a family by blood to find a way through another's shields and help.

If only they all knew *exactly* what was going on between him and Miranda.

Which was precisely nothing, he reminded himself.

Miranda wasn't his.

He'd help her out, make sure she could take care of herself, and then let her be on her way.

She met his eyes, and he saw the plea in them. He gave

her a nod. "I'm going home," she said softly. "I know I just got here, but I only came to... well..." She pointed to her face. "You saw, you know as much as I do, and now I want to rest."

"I'll make sure she gets home." Griffin's eyes met his, a question in his gaze. A question Decker wasn't ready to answer—if he even knew the answer to begin with.

"Stay here and say your goodbyes. I'll get Gunner," he whispered in her ear. She smelled of roses today.

She nodded then started the long goodbyes that came with any Montgomery family event. There were just too many people to make it easy to leave. He went out to the back yard and took a frolicking Gunner away from Leif. Sierra put her hand on Decker's arm, but he shook his head. It wasn't his story to tell, and from the looks of it, Austin would need to vent and get everything off his chest.

"You're a good man, Decker," she said softly then kissed him over his beard.

He didn't agree, but he let her think that. It was what he was good at.

He put Gunner's leash on then made his way back into the house. Marie had loved the dog at first sight and let him roam around her clean house. Gunner was another Montgomery-by-claim just like him. It would do well for Decker to remember that.

Miranda saw him coming then looked down, her face breaking out into a smile.

"Oh, he's adorable." She got down to her knees and let

Gunner come up to her. The dog sniffed around her then nuzzled her neck softly. Gunner seemed to know that Miranda was the kind of fragile that made hearts ache and took care not to push her down—unlike when Maya had met him.

"Adorable?" Storm gaffed. "Miranda, honey, how hard did you hit your head? Ouch!" Storm rubbed his own head where Wes smacked it.

Miranda just laughed and shook her head before standing. "I will see all of you soon. Thank you for understanding."

They said their goodbyes, and he walked her to her car. "I'll follow you," he said.

"It's your place. Why don't I follow you?" she asked, tugging his jacket closer.

"I want to make sure I see you at all times," he said. "Bear with me. Just for today."

He cupped her face and felt her suck in a breath. He brushed her lip with his thumb, and she opened for him, her tongue darting out to lick the tip. He swallowed hard, meeting her gaze. This was stupid, oh, so fucking stupid. But he was going to do it, let go and live.

If only for a moment.

"See you at my house," he said softly.

"Decker," she whispered.

"Later, Mir. Later."

God, he was a selfish man. He knew that no matter

what happened next, even if he never touched her again, he'd need to see her in his place, and see her safe.

He wouldn't be her future. No, that couldn't be, but maybe, just maybe, he could live to be her present. Maybe he'd take a glimpse of her happiness before she saw the truth.

Before she found out who he was.

Chapter Ten

M iranda finally relinquished Decker's jacket once they made it to his place. She hadn't wanted to part with it, but it would have been beyond obvious if she kept it on while they were inside and then ran away with it. She hadn't been to his place since she'd made a fool of herself in his kitchen, but even though not much time had passed, things were different.

She wasn't sure how, but she'd felt the shift in front of her parents' house.

She didn't know what it meant or even what she was doing there. He said he'd show her how to protect herself, but she hadn't thought it would be right then. No, he'd made sure she was safe but also free to breathe again. Though she loved her family with every fiber of her being, it was difficult to not worry about how to protect them from what had happened when she couldn't even protect herself.

"You want something to drink?" he asked, his hands again in his pockets. She'd like to think it was because he couldn't keep his hands off her, but she wouldn't bet on it.

Despite the fact that she knew Decker, knew his ticks, knew his past, she didn't *know* him as well as she thought she did.

Yes, she still loved him, was still *in* love with him, but maybe if she knew him better, she could find a way to live with that love.

God, now she sounded like a pathetic, lovesick fool.

Open, honest communication would be the only way to deal with that.

That or smiling through it and ignoring her feelings.

Either way.

Gunner came to her side and leaned into her leg. She looked down at the adorably ugly dog and scratched behind his ears. His tongue rolled out, and he gave her an adoring smile.

Then she gagged.

"Dear. God."

"Fucking dog," Decker grumbled. "Come out here with your smelly self. Don't you know not to stink up a room with a girl there? Have you no decency?"

Miranda's eyes watered, and she couldn't help the laugh bubbling from her throat. Decker took Gunner outside then came back into the room, a smile on his face.

Gunner and his horrible bad case of doggie gas had broken the awkwardness between them for the time being. If only it hadn't been such a putrid way to do it.

Decker took Miranda's hand and brought her to the kitchen. The rough feel of his calloused hands felt like home in hers. Damn, she was an idiot. But she'd take it. For now. "You never answered if you wanted something to drink or not. I'm thirsty, and we need to get out of the living room, or we might die due to lack of oxygen."

She laughed with him and leaned against the kitchen counter when he went to the fridge. "I'll take a soda if you have it."

"I have Coke. No diet."

She rolled her eyes. "You've known me for how many years, and you think I'd drink diet?"

He looked over his shoulder. "No, but you could have changed when I wasn't looking." He wasn't talking about the soda, and they both knew it.

"I don't drink soda often since it's horrible for you, but if I'm going to indulge, I'll go with the sugar rather than the aspartame."

"Sounds logical to me." He held out a can then frowned. "You need a glass and ice or something?"

She let out a breath, took the can, and popped the top. "No, I'm not fussy. It's cold, so that's all that matters. Decker, what's wrong? Why is this so awkward?"

Decker met her gaze, and her stomach clenched. She

wasn't sure if it was the good kind or the bad kind. Wasn't sure if she wanted to know.

"Last time we were in this room, I pushed you against the same counter you're leaning on right now and kissed you. Hard. Last time you were here, I had my hands in your hair and my tongue down your throat. Lot's happened since then. Yet not enough."

She held back a shiver at the memory of his touch, his taste. She wanted it all again, wanted more. That didn't mean it was going to happen though. Especially when she remembered who she'd seen him with the last time she'd seen him.

"How's Colleen?" she asked, her voice as casual as she could make it. Meaning not that casual.

Decker raised a brow. "Not here."

She gave a little growl. "Ass. That's not what I mean. You were with her that night."

"Yeah, and that's the last time I was with her. We weren't serious before. And we're not anything now."

She licked her lips, annoyingly pleased at that fact. Yet... "So you just tossed her aside?" Maybe he was right, maybe she didn't know him at all.

He sighed. "No, I didn't. We were casual. We weren't really friends because we didn't have much in common."

"Then why were you with her?" She could have bitten off her own tongue. Of course there was a reason he'd been with her. Not that she wanted to think about that particular reason in any way.

His lips twitched. "It's not what you're thinking." He sighed again. "We hadn't slept together for months, Mir."

Her eyes widened. "Seriously?"

"Not that it's any of your business, or maybe it is your business if there's a reason we're talking about this. Colleen and I hadn't slept together for months, like I said. I don't even think we were truly dating since we didn't do much but eat together every once in while. I hadn't planned on having her come to the Montgomery thing that one time, but she sort of invited herself. She's a nice woman, but not a woman I really wanted to be with." He met her gaze, and Miranda sucked in a breath.

"Decker."

"Miranda."

She laughed softly. "I don't know what I'm doing here." She pressed her hands to her face then cursed.

Decker came to her side, his unopened Coke in his hand. He put it on her bruises and searched her face. "Don't hurt yourself, Mir."

She closed her eyes. If she took this step—and oh God, how she wanted to take this step—she might not be the one to do the hurting.

"I forgot about the bruises," she said instead.

He took her chin in his hand and raised her face to his. "I didn't," he said, his voice low. "I could kill him for doing this to you." From the promise in his voice, Miranda believed him.

"It's over," she said, hoping it was true. Monday

Carrie Ann Ryan

morning at work would be uncomfortable and horrible, but she'd push through. She was a Montgomery.

He traced his fingers down her face while still keeping his other hand on her chin. "Not yet, but soon. I won't let him hurt you again."

"What are we doing?" she asked, her voice annoyingly breathless.

Decker searched her face then took a step back. She hated that she felt cold at the distance. "We're going to drink our drinks, and then we're going to talk."

"About?"

"About the fact that, though I pushed you away, I can't seem to keep you away."

She narrowed her eyes, stung. "You make me sound like a bug you just can't squash."

He popped open his drink and took a sip. "Come sit with me."

It didn't escape her attention that he hadn't corrected her bug description. Jerk. Hot jerk, but still a jerk. She followed him to the living room anyway, grateful Gunner's earlier gift had dissipated.

She sat down next to him on the couch, leaving enough room so that they weren't touching, but she could still feel the heat of him. Torture much?

He met her gaze then winced.

"What?"

"Uh, I forgot you missed the first part of the evening. Shit. I don't know how to put this."

She frowned. "What? What happened? Is everyone okay?" She'd been so centered on herself she hadn't noticed the others. Damn it. That wasn't like her.

"Everyone's physically okay." He let out a breath. "I don't know the whole story, nor has he told it to anyone it seems, but Jessica left Alex."

Miranda set her drink down on the coffee table. "Seriously? Oh, poor Alex. I mean, we all hated Jessica even though we tried not to because she was his wife. He's not taking it well, is he?"

Her heart ached for her big brother. He was the closest to her in age, though he was a full five years older. He'd gotten married too fast, too young, and now he had to deal with the fallout. It didn't matter though. He was her brother, and she'd do whatever she could to help him through it. Even if he didn't want her to be part of it.

Decker sighed and set his drink down next to hers. "No, he's not, but he's got enough of you guys to make sure he stays on track." His look told her they both were thinking the same thing.

It might not be much, but she'd try her hardest to make it happen.

"I know they were having issues. It's still hard to hear. You know?"

Decker shrugged.

"What?"

"It wasn't too surprising, and things like this were

bound to happen." There was an edge in his voice she didn't understand.

"What do you mean?"

"It's nothing, Mir. Don't worry about it."

She shook her head. "Don't treat me like that. Don't treat me like a little girl who doesn't understand."

He mumbled under his breath and sighed. "Fine. They got married too young. Or maybe they just married the wrong people. Whatever happened, they didn't know each other well enough, and now Alex is in hell. Sometimes you don't know the person you're with until it's too late."

At that bitter comment, Miranda let out a curse of her own. "That's a very cynical view on relationships."

He raised a brow. "I come by it naturally."

Bullseye. "Be that as it may, if you're using this as a not so clever way to talk about us, then you're way off mark."

He snorted. "There is no us, Mir."

She put her hand on his arm, thankful he didn't brush it off. "Yeah, there is. There might not be a relationship us, but there's an us. We just need to be clear about what that means."

He met her gaze. "You want me. I want you. Clear enough?"

She swallowed hard, warm at his words. "I'm surprised you said it aloud."

He cupped the uninjured side of her face. "I'm not going to lie to you. Not about this. But Miranda? You want me? You'll have to deal with all of me. Me being with you is a stupid thing to do."

Struck, she pulled away. "Excuse me?"

"Fuck, that's not what I meant. See? I'm screwing things up. You're too young for me. You're family. You're my best friend's little sister. We do this and we end it? We ruin everything we had and hurt more than just you and me. You get that? You get that we could throw it all away for a chance that could mean nothing?"

"It won't mean nothing," she whispered. It couldn't. Not her and Decker.

"We aren't the people we were before. We aren't the same people we grew up with. We've grown up, and we've moved on. We've had lives. We're not those shells. You aren't the little girl I saw all those years ago, and I'm sure as hell not the boy I was then. If we do this, it will be much different. We need to get to know one another. I'm not the man you think I am. You've got to understand that. I'm not the dream or whatever the fuck you have in your head. You really don't know me."

She closed her eyes and took a deep breath. She would not get angry. You know what? Fuck that.

"Of all the condescending bullshit," she snapped.

"What?" He looked genuinely confused.

"I'm not some young kid, Decker. You want to get to know me? Fine. I want you to. I want to know more about you, too. I want to see how we fit. I know we were good together as...well, whatever we were before, and I want to

165

know what it will be like when we're more. People change when they're together." She held up her hand. "I'm not saying that's a bad thing, far from it. Those little changes happen when people blend into a relationship. I'm not as young as you think I am, and I think you need to learn that. You're also not some guy I need to put on a pedestal. I'm not that dreamy-eyed girl, and we both need to know that."

"Mir."

"Deck."

His eyes crinkled, and she sighed. "Decker, you don't get it, do you?"

"Get what?"

She cupped his face, his beard tickling her palms. "I like *you*. I want to get to know *you*. I want to know the man, not the boy I grew up with. I'm not starry-eyed." She pointed to her face. "I've already seen that past the smiles and angelic looks, men can be assholes."

Decker growled. "I'm going to kill him."

She patted his cheek. "Stop threatening to kill people."

"See? I'm not good people. I'm not good enough for you."

"You just said you don't know me, and I don't know you. Well, that means you don't know me well enough to know that you're not good enough."

He closed his eyes and sighed. "Miranda. I'll hurt you."

Her heart fluttered, and she had a feeling he just

might. But it would be worth it. If she didn't try, she'd regret it.

"Kiss me."

He opened his eyes and met her gaze. "We do this, there's no going back."

"I don't want to go back."

He pulled her into his arms and onto his lap. Before she could take her next breath, his mouth was on hers, and she was lost. He nipped and sucked on her lips, her tongue. She framed his face with her hands, his beard scratchy, yet oddly titillating. His hands were tangled in her hair and holding her tight. She could feel his cock between her legs, hard, ready where she straddled him. She rocked her hips, wanting more.

He tore his lips from hers, panting, and put one hand on her hip, steadying her.

"Decker."

"Damn, at least we know that part is good."

She grinned, pleased. "Oh really?" she teased. "Maybe we should do it again. Just to make sure."

"Temptress." He leaned forward and bit her lip. Hard. The thrill that shot through her surprised her more than she thought possible.

"Good to know," he murmured.

"What's good to know?"

He shook his head. "Just something on my mind."

She tilted her head. "Cagey."

"True. Now I'm going to follow you home to make

sure you get there, and then I'm coming back home to eat and go to sleep. Alone."

She blinked. Surprised. "Really?" She wiggled on his lap until his fingers tightened on her hip.

"You want this?"

She smiled like the Cheshire Cat. "Yes."

He rolled his eyes. "I mean this, as in us together. You want that? We go on an actual date first. We figure out what we want before I strip you down and taste every inch of you."

She swallowed hard. Shivered. "You're dictating how we'll be together?" For some reason, some part of her wanted that. The other part wanted to slap him for his high-handedness.

He kissed her softly. "If that's what comes of it. I'll pick you up at seven a.m. tomorrow. If you still want to be with me, all of me, then be ready." He paused. "Wear jeans and an old shirt."

Her mind whirled. It was really happening. How on earth had it happened? One minute she was alone and in pain, the next she was sitting on Decker's lap, listening to him talk of seeing her the next day. Maybe he was right and she needed the night to think, to comprehend.

He tapped her chin. "See? You need to think. Wear the jeans. The sexy ones with the hole in the knee."

She raised her brow. "You know what jeans I own?"

"Yes. And I know that they're sexy." He stood up with her in his arms, and she let out a squeak, wrapping her arms and legs around him. His hands cradled her ass, and she sighed. Seriously. Hot.

"What are we doing tomorrow?"

"You'll see. Oh, and wear your old hiking boots."

She frowned. "I'm not sure you know what dating means, Decker. This sounds a little grungy."

He grinned then, and she held back a girly sigh. "I'm taking you out. That's all you need to know." She slid down his body as he set her down, slowly. When he let out a curse, she grinned.

Decker was right, at least *that* part worked between them.

She just hoped everything else did too.

"HIKING?" SHE ASKED, UNBELIEVING. THEY'D DRIVEN to the foothills.

"Hiking," Decker repeated. Gunner bounced around their feet, apparently ecstatic at the turn of events. "I figured you usually do the dinner and movie thing, and that's good, but not as fun as this. We'll see wildlife and just enjoy what's out there without having to deal with others." He turned toward her and took her chin between his fingers. "This way, we can hang out and not have to deal with people staring at you or thinking that they need to call the cops because the big dude next to you must have hit you or something."

She sighed and leaned into him. "Screw them for

thinking that." Though it had been on her mind. She'd noticed the few people who'd walked by and given Decker a wide berth. He *was* a big guy with tattoos and a beard that hid his smile unless you were close. And her face currently looked like someone had sprayed five different colors of paint on it with all the bruising. She kind of liked hiding behind the mask.

He leaned down and kissed her, and she melted. She *really* liked this Decker. He wasn't affectionate in the weird way guys were when they weren't comfortable with public displays of affection, or worse, were trying to mark their territory.

He touched her just enough to heat her up—she couldn't get enough of him—but not enough to make either of them uncomfortable. She still didn't know how they'd ended up here, together, with his lips on hers. If she thought about it too hard, she'd scare herself, afraid it wasn't real.

Gunner pressed into her side, and she shook her head.

"You still here?" he asked, and she nodded.

"Sorry, got lost a minute there. I'm better now."

He smiled then took her hand. "If you get tired, just let me know. I have a pack with the essentials, and we're not taking the hard trail. No rock climbing or scary treks."

She nodded then took a deep breath. Hiking wasn't number one on her list of things to do, but it was a Sunday, and she'd caught up on her grading the day before. This way she could hang out with Decker and get to know him.

He took her hand and started up the trail with Gunner leading them, scenting everything he possibly could. Thirty minutes in, she knew he'd taken the easy trail for her. She didn't complain. She'd rather not sprain her ankle trying to prove herself.

"Do you come out here a lot?" she asked.

Decker squeezed her hand and nodded. "Yeah, enough I guess. I used to come out here with Griffin." He winced. "Fuck."

She winced with him. "He'll understand."

Decker raised a brow at her. "Sure, Mir. Sure he will."

With that, they kept to safer topics. Like work—without actually mentioning the fact that he worked with her family, and she worked with the asshole who'd hit her. They talked about her apartment and how she liked it for now. She wanted to move eventually, but it was good enough for where she was in life.

They hiked for another two hours, with a break for a granola bar and water, and then made their way back to his truck. Before they got in, she looked back at the mountain range and smiled.

"God, I love living here," she said. Her muscles ached, and her jeans were dirty, but she felt like she'd gotten a second wind.

Decker came from behind and wrapped his arms around her. "Yeah?"

She sighed and leaned into him. "Yeah. Where else

can you just go on a hike and see deer, a river, birds, and other things?"

"Plus that bear."

She screamed and jumped into his arms. Decker fell back against his truck, laughing his ass off.

"I can't believe you fell for that," he said through his laughs. Gunner barked and trotted around them, playing.

She set her feet down and glared, her mouth twitching. "So not funny."

"Yeah? Then why are you laughing?"

She rolled her eyes then scratched Gunner behind the ears. "Let's get back to your place for lunch. I'm starved, and now I'm scared to look too closely at that big shadow."

He snorted, kissed her, and slapped her ass. She swallowed hard. Was it wrong she liked that? Nope? Okay then.

"Get in the truck. That shadow is just a shadow. Of a tree."

When they got to his place, they piled out and chugged water in his kitchen. Miranda looked down at herself and winced. "I think I brought a good chunk of the forest with me."

Decker grinned. "Well, you're the one who ran into that tree."

"You distracted me!" She blushed. She hadn't realized he'd seen that.

"You were checking out my ass."

Well, that was true, but he didn't have to point it out

like that. "Whatever. Can I use your shower?" Her gaze traveled over his body, and she swallowed hard. "You could use a shower too."

His mouth twitched. "I have two showers, Mir. We can each take one. We're going slow. Remember?"

She sighed. "Sure. Though, so far, the only thing we're doing different than normal is kissing."

He lifted her chin. "Yeah. And while I like the kissing, because, woman, you're fucking phenomenal at it, I'm not going to push you. We change the dynamics too fast, we ruin it all. Got it?"

She pulled away, lest she jump him. "Fine. I'll go shower. You have anything for me to wear?"

His eyes darkened, and she hoped he was imagining her naked. She'd imagined him naked enough times.

"What's that blush about?"

She coughed. "Oh, nothing. So, clothes?" No way was she going to admit her dirty, dirty fantasies. At least not then.

He cleared his throat. "I have something for you."

She showered quickly then toweled off, looking at the old shirt and sweats he'd given her. The sweats would be too big and would probably fall off. It would be best to leave them off altogether. After all, the shirt reached to the middle of her thighs anyway. She just needed to wear that and her panties and she'd be fine.

Decker wouldn't know what hit him.

She quickly undid the bun on the top of her head so

her hair fell around her shoulders in waves. She stepped out of the bathroom, only to run smack into a very hard, very naked, very sexy male chest.

Decker cursed then looked down, his eyes wide. "Fuck, Mir. Didn't I give you sweats?"

Her eyes wouldn't leave his chest and the water droplets making little trails down his small patch of hair, all the way down to his belly button and the happy trail that led to very, very good things.

He tugged on her hair, forcing her head back and her gaze to his. "Mir. Baby. Look at me. This isn't a good idea."

"Stop trying to make my choices for me," she said softly. He frowned, and she continued. "I get it. You want to protect me, but telling me what I'm thinking and what I want, that won't cut it for me. You know me well enough—even though you claim not to—to know that I won't stand for someone doing that to me. If you don't want to make love to me, fine." Well, not fine, but that was another topic for another time. "But if that's the case, then you need to just lay that out. You can't put it on me when I'm the one saying I want you. I was the one who took the first step in your kitchen, and now I'm doing it again. If you want me, then take me. Take me as I am. Putting barriers down that don't exist in the first place doesn't help anyone."

He ran his hand over her hair a few times and sighed. "I don't know what to do with you, Miranda Montgomery."

She put her hand on his chest then brushed his skin,

lower and lower until she gripped his denim-covered cock. "I know what I want to do with *you*," she purred.

She wasn't the little girl he thought she was, and from the look in his eyes, he was just now seeing that.

Good.

"We do this, there's no going back." His voice had gone low, dangerous.

"There never was any going back, Decker. You know that."

He licked his lips then gripped her hips, his hands scrunching up the shirt, pulling it up slightly. "You know about my past, know about my life, but you don't know how I fuck, baby girl."

"Yeah? Then show me."

"I'm not easy," he said as he leaned down, trailing his mouth over her neck. He didn't kiss her but breathed warmth on her skin, sending goose bumps all over her body. "You know what I used to be part of."

She nodded. "You used to be part of the scene. Like Austin." Her knees shook, but she didn't fall, not with Decker holding her up.

"Yeah, like Austin. And not like him." He pulled away, and she frowned. "I'm not a true Dominant in the sense that you might think, Miranda. I'm just me. It took me a long time to figure that out. I like being in control, in and out of the bedroom, but I'm not into most of the things that come with kink."

She nodded. "Everyone's entitled to what they want,

Decker. I..." Well, if he was going to be honest... "I like it when you tell me what to do," she whispered. "I like it when you pull at my hair and kiss me. I feel...empowered because you want to do that to me in the first place. Does that make sense?"

He grinned, and she relaxed. "I get it. And I think we can accommodate both of us. It's just you and me, Mir. No family, no ties, no exes, no rules other than we please each other. You get that?"

"I do. Now kiss me."

He snorted. "You telling me what to do?"

She winced. "Uh, no?"

He smacked her ass. Hard. She yelped then sighed when he rubbed the sting. "I'm going to like finding out what you like, Mir. Going to like it a lot. Why don't you walk back to the bedroom? Do it slow so I can see how my shirt rides up when you walk."

She swallowed hard then did as he ordered, very conscious that his gaze was right on her butt. Each time she moved, she felt his shirt ride up. She could picture the peek of upper thigh, and if she hadn't been ready to just strip right there, she might have teased him more.

When she got to the bedroom, she wasn't sure what to do next. Did she lie on the bed? Did she keep her clothes on? He really should have given her more direction. As it was, she inhaled his scent in the room. He had large, masculine furniture and had done the room in dark colors.

The fact that the room was so Decker calmed her and revved her at the same time.

"I like the look of you in my shirt."

She turned on her heel to see him standing in the doorway. He looked dark, sexy, and so hers. At least for the night.

Nope, not going to think about that. Not going to think about a future, what everything meant, or anything that could hurt. She'd live in the moment and enjoy every bit of it. This was finally happening, and she would take it as it was. If they parted tomorrow and that was it, then she'd at least have tonight.

She wouldn't let what happened between them now hurt what they already had. She'd thought she'd done that before, and now she'd protect her heart—and his.

Decker offered no promises, and she would offer truth.

He prowled toward her, and she leaned her head back so he could take her mouth. Damn, the man could kiss. He licked and sucked on her tongue, her lips. She let her head fall back as he trailed his mouth down her neck. He bit down gently on the juncture between her neck and shoulder, and she shivered.

"Decker," she whispered, panting.

This was really happening. She was going to sleep with Decker. She'd fantasized about it sure, but she'd never thought it would really happen. Now that it was, she didn't want it to end.

Decker tugged on her hair and forced her gaze to his.

"Mind on me, Mir. You want this? I get all of you. You understand?"

He didn't mean that though. He didn't mean all of her, nor did it mean he would give all of himself to her.

She nodded anyway, breathless.

"Say it."

"Yes. I understand."

"Say my name. Say my name while I strip you down, eat your cunt, then fuck you hard. Say it."

She pressed her legs together at his words, her clit throbbing. Dear God, the man could talk dirty. She wasn't a fan of it usually, but with him? Hell yeah. He didn't make it sound like he was a boy learning to speak to a woman because he could say the words. No, he was a man who said the words because he wanted to. Because he knew *exactly* what the words did to her. What they did to both of them.

"Decker. I get it. Please. Do all of that. Can we do it now?" She smiled as she said it, and his lips twitched.

He trailed his fingers down her side, over her shirt, until he met skin. She sucked in a breath as he slowly lifted the hem over her hip. When he tugged higher, she lifted her arms so he could pull the shirt over her head.

She stood in front of him in only her panties and had never felt sexier. His eyes darkened, and he let out a little groan.

He licked his lips and brushed her nipple with his thumb.

"God, please. Touch me."

"You'll take what I give you, when I give it."

Yes, please.

She swallowed hard and let him study her. Had anyone else looked over her body in such a fashion, it would have made her feel uncomfortable, but Decker made her feel like a queen. He looked at her like he wanted to taste every inch and enjoy it.

"I've seen you in that fucking bikini out at the pool before, and I always had to leave early or jump in the fucking cold water because I'd tent up my shorts. Getting a hard-on with your brothers around? Not a good idea. I didn't want you to know. I'm still in awe that you know. Back then you were all curves and sex appeal, and yet right now? Right now I feel like I was missing out on so fucking much because I've never seen a woman like you. You're gorgeous, baby. So fucking gorgeous. I want to lick up each inch of you until your taste lingers on my tongue forever."

She blushed, remembering those days at the pool when she'd watched him out of the corner of her eye. She'd done her best not to look at him too hard when she was sunning herself or playing water polo. When their bodies had touched in the water, sliding against one another when they'd been on opposite teams, she'd had to swim away fast or she'd have done something stupid, like pull him under with her and kiss his brains out.

He frowned at her then traced her stomach. "This is

new. I didn't know you had a belly ring, babe. I like it." His fingers played with the bar, and she held back a giggle. She was ticklish, but laughing probably wouldn't be the sexiest thing to do right now.

"It's sort of new," she said, and then she sucked in a breath. God, his touch did wicked, wicked things to her. "Maya did it after she got her piercing certification."

Decker grinned. "It's fucking hot. And I'm glad you didn't have it when you were wearing those tiny pieces of fabric back then. I wouldn't have made it."

She licked her lips, aching. "Should I mention that I bought the little black one for you?" she asked casually.

His gaze shot up to hers, and he smiled slowly. "Oh? Well, you tortured me, Mir."

Powerful. That's what he made her feel.

"You tortured me too, you know. All tan and built. I had to go take care of matters myself a couple times after I saw you in your suit."

She closed her mouth tight, her eyes wide. She did *not* just say that out loud.

He smiled then, his eyes dancing. "Oh, you shouldn't have said that, baby. Now I'm going to want to watch you put your little hand down those panties of yours and watch you make yourself come."

She shivered. Could she do that? Touch herself while Decker watched?

She met his gaze.

Yes. Yes she could.

He brushed his thumb over her other nipple, and she bit her lip. "Next time, Mir. Next time we'll do that. Maybe I'll even jack myself off while watching you." She sucked in a breath. He nodded and smiled at her reaction. "Oh yeah, you'll like that. I've come thinking about you countless times, honey. You're not alone."

"Thank God," she teased.

Decker brought her closer and crushed his mouth to hers. She sank into the kiss, into him. His hands went down her back and over her ass.

"You have such a luscious ass. God, I want to fuck it one day, Mir. What do you say to that? You want my dick in this sexy ass of yours?"

"Uh..."

He chuckled roughly. "Too fast?"

She shook her head. "Not fast enough. Please, I need you in me." She narrowed her eyes. "In my pussy for now, if that's okay."

"I like the sound of that word coming from your prim and proper mouth. If you want me to fill you, I can do that. Turn around for me."

She scrunched her brows but did as he wanted. He sucked in a breath, and she swallowed.

"I forgot you have your Montgomery tattoo on the small of your back."

She laughed at that. "Yes, I have the tramp stamp one. I couldn't figure out another place to put it that would be hidden under my clothes and still feel like me. You know?"

She looked over her shoulder and saw the need in his eyes. Not just the need for her, but the need for the ink she wore. Each person in her family had the tattoo, and yet, as far as she knew, Decker did not. He should though, and she'd make sure to tell him.

Later.

Right now, though, she wanted to get this party going a little faster.

She wiggled her ass then faced the bed. With her head still turned over her shoulder so she could see him, she bent over, pressing her chest to the bed and tucked her hands in the sides of her panties.

Decker's gaze darkened, and he gave her a nod.

She slowly pulled her panties over her ass and then down to right at the top of her thighs. It was the farthest she could reach at this angle, and it left her open for his gaze and completely at his mercy.

She freaking loved it.

The way the fabric bunched under her ass, it felt as if it lifted her up a bit, like it was on a shelf and framed for him.

His large hand cupped her ass and squeezed. "You leave me breathless, Mir."

She sighed, loving the feel of his hands on her. "Ditto."

He chuckled again then moved down so he was crouched right behind her, his face really close to her pussy. She tried not to squirm and feel so exposed, but she couldn't help it. She *was* exposed. Plus, she liked him being there.

A lot.

"I knew you'd be this pink, this blush." His finger gently traced her outer lips, and she sucked in a breath. "So pretty," he murmured then leaned down.

"Decker!"

He clamped his mouth on her pussy, nibbling, and sucking. God, his mouth. His fucking mouth. She wiggled, trying to get closer. His tongue kept missing her clit, and knowing Decker, he was doing it on purpose, teasing her until she couldn't breathe.

He smacked her ass then caressed, and she shuddered a breath. "Don't move, Mir, or I'll spank you harder."

Without thinking, she wiggled again.

"Damn, Mir. You want my hand on you? You want to have me redden that sweet little ass of yours?"

She sucked in a breath, and he smacked her other cheek.

"Use your words." His voice was a drug all on its own, so deep, so rough, so *Decker.*

Fine. If he wanted the truth, wanted it all, he'd get it. "Yes. Yes, I want you to spank me. I want you to eat me, make me come, spank me, fuck me, tie me up. I want all of it. Okay?"

She looked over her shoulder again to find a pleased-as-sin Decker grinning at her. Was it wrong she thought the beard made him look sexier?

"I like the way you think, baby. I'll do all of that. Maybe not all right now, but all of it. Now let me get these panties off you. I'm going to eat this juicy cunt, and then I'm going to fuck you. You ready?"

She let out a moan, unable to speak clearly. He seemed to be okay with that non-verbal answer because he didn't spank her again.

He stripped her bare then spread her legs wider. The cool air on her body did nothing to lower the heat blazing inside her. God, she wanted him, wanted to come.

When his mouth latched onto her clit, she gripped the bed covers, biting her lip. Her fingers dug into the fabric, and if she wasn't careful, she'd tear it altogether. God, that talented tongue of his should come with a warning. The rough scrape of his beard between her thighs was even more erotic and sensual than she'd thought. He licked and sucked at her clit then fucked her with his tongue.

When he speared her with two large fingers, she cried out, clamping down on him. The orgasm hit her hard, bucking her back so she pressed against his face. Her limbs shook, and her vision grayed.

Before she could take another breath, Decker had her on her back and his lips on hers. She could taste herself on him, and she almost came again. He still wore only his jeans, and the rough feel of the fabric on her over-sensitive skin sent her into another tail-spin.

She pulled her mouth away, needing to catch her

breath. "Please, for the love of God, lose the pants and get in me."

He grinned then and stood up. With his gaze on hers, he undid the button on his jeans and lowered the zipper. When his jeans fell to the floor, she lost all ability to think.

Her Decker went commando.

Holy freaking shit.

He was long, thick, and ready. And dear God, he was pierced. He had a Prince Albert that looked like it would feel freaking amazing when he pressed deep inside her. His cock throbbed, which looked almost painful, the blue vein underneath stark against the redness of his length. The head was round and had that little drop of fluid at the tip around the piercing that left a trail on his belly when he moved since his dick slapped against his skin, tight and ready.

"You keep looking at me like that, and I'm going to blow before I even get inside that tight pussy of yours."

She blinked. "You're...uh big." *Good one, Miranda. Clever.*

His smile was almost wicked. "You say the nicest things." He walked around the bed to the nightstand, pulled out a little foil packet, and then sheathed himself maneuvering the condom carefully over the ball of metal at the tip.

She'd tell him that she was on birth control and clean another time. They'd have all those talks another time.

Right then, they were safe, and she wanted him inside her. Now.

He knelt on the bed then got between her legs. With his forearms on either side of her head, she felt caged in, but safe.

His fingers played with her hair, and she sighed. "You're so fucking beautiful, Miranda."

Her eyes stung, and she swallowed hard. She couldn't cry just then. She wouldn't. The man she loved was being so freaking sweet she wanted to weep, but she wouldn't. She could do that later.

He lowered his head to hers, kissing her softly. She ran her hands up his back, digging her nails in while she deepened the kiss. He let out a groan then moved his hips so his cock pressed at her entrance. She lifted her hips slightly so he could have better access then pulled away from his lips so she could see his eyes.

When he thrust in slowly, her mouth fell open. He was so thick, so...Decker. She felt so full, stretching, waiting. It seemed like forever, and then he was deep inside her, his body still as he waited for her to stretch to accommodate him.

He groaned then pulled out partway before slamming back in to the hilt. "Jesus Christ, Mir, you feel so good."

She smiled then arched her back, wrapping her legs around his waist. "You're so freaking big, you're going to make me come just from that." She licked her lips. "Fuck me, Decker. Fuck me hard."

"Seriously, baby, you say the nicest things."

He grinned then kissed her before he started to pump into her over and over, increasing the pace with each thrust. His piercing hit her at the right spot, and she shook. She threw her head back onto the pillows and screamed as she came. He didn't stop though. No, he just put his hand between them and played with her clit while latching onto her nipple.

God, the man had talented hands to go with that sinful mouth of his.

Well, pretty much talented everything.

When she fell over the crest again, Decker kissed her, capturing his name on her lips. He came right after her, filling the condom, yet still pumping. They were slick with sweat, their bodies twined together and spent.

He gave her one last kiss then pulled away to take care of the condom. Though she felt empty at the loss of him, he was back before the sheets cooled completely.

When he came back, he picked her up, surprising her. "Decker?" Seriously, the man made her swoon sometimes.

He kissed her temple, held her with one arm, and then fixed the covers. "You're going to get cold," he said softly and tucked her in.

When he spooned behind her, she let out a sigh. "I..." No. She couldn't say that. "Do you want me to fix us something to eat?" she asked. It was still relatively early in the day, but she liked cuddling. She just didn't want to become dependent on it. Not when she didn't know what Decker wanted.

His hand played with her hip, and she licked her lips, happy. "We can cook together in a little bit. Just relax, Mir. We're not going anywhere."

She sighed, letting her mind relax because he'd said to. She'd worry later about what would happen next and how she'd deal with it. Right then, she would cherish this time in Decker's arms. She didn't know what would come tomorrow, and that thought scared her enough to push it away and deal with it later. She had Decker now. That was good enough. It would have to be good enough.

Chapter Eleven

"Why am I not allowed to go find this asshole and kill him?" Austin growled. He paced his bedroom and mumbled to himself. It had been a week since he'd seen his precious baby sister bruised and cut up by that bastard, and he hadn't been able to do anything about it. The fucker had gotten off too easy, and Austin wasn't sure he could hold himself back much longer. Miranda was the softest among them, and he'd be damned if he'd let her be in pain like that.

"Honey, no, you can't kill him. If you end up going to jail because you killed a man, it would put a damper on the wedding. I don't think an orange jumpsuit will go with our color palette."

Austin paused then looked over at his fiancée. She sat in the middle of the bed, her tablet in her hand, and a sly smile on her face. Her honey-brown hair tumbled around her shoulders, making her look young and tempting. She wore one of his old shirts and nothing else. He grinned. Yeah, that's exactly how he liked her.

Well, he liked her any way he could get her, but that was beside the point.

Her words came back to him, and he shook his head. "Did you really just say I couldn't kill the man who hit my sister because my jumpsuit would clash with the wedding décor?"

She let out a breath and ran a hand over her face. She'd been doing that a lot lately. In fact, she looked like she could use a good nap. He'd been trying to keep his hands off of her since she was so tired all the time. At first, he'd thought it was just the stress of opening a new business, planning the wedding, and learning to raise Leif with him, but now he wasn't so sure.

He'd have to make sure he took special care of his woman.

"I'm just saying that Miranda, and Decker for that matter, seem to have it well in hand. You beating someone to death isn't going to help matters." She held up a hand. "Yeah, I know it sucks. God, I want to beat the shit out of that little asshole too for daring to touch one of us, but there's nothing we can do. We just have to pray the justice system works."

He gave her a long look, and she sighed. They both knew that sometimes, no matter how hard they tried, they got screwed over by the way the law worked...and the way others got around it.

"Has she said anything to you about work?" he asked as he sank into the mattress next to her. She leaned into him and shook her head.

"Not really. He's leaving her be, though the police haven't done anything yet. There were a lot of questions from the teachers, students, and I bet the parents, but other than that, Miranda has kept her chin up."

He growled softly then pulled Sierra closer. "I don't like it."

"I know, Austin. I know. But she'll be okay. She's learning to take charge and take care of herself. And she has Decker. She'll be okay."

Austin froze. "What do you mean she has Decker?"

Sierra pulled away and shrugged. "Decker's taking care of her. You know, making sure she feels safe as well as actually is safe."

He narrowed his eyes but couldn't tell what was bothering him about that. It was nice that Decker was taking care of his sister, but something was...off.

Before he could think much more about that, Sierra groaned then took off to the bathroom. He sprang off the bed and followed her.

"Fuck. What's wrong, Sierra?"

He held back her hair as she vacated her stomach, her body shaking. He got out a washcloth and ran cool water over it before patting her face.

She took a shaky breath. "I don't know. I think it's the flu. I've been achy. Or at least achier than usual."

He ran a hand down her back then held her when she leaned into him. "I'm sorry, baby. You want me to take you to the doctor?"

She shook her head. "No. I'm okay, I think. If it doesn't go away soon, I'll go to the doctor, but I'm sure I'll be fine."

Austin rested his cheek on the top of her head. He never thought he'd care about a person as much as he did Sierra. Here he was, holding his fiancée while sitting on the bathroom floor after she'd puked up her guts. He wouldn't trade it for anything.

"I'm here, Legs."

"Stop calling me Legs." She said it so softly he knew she didn't meant it.

"You just tell me what you need, and I'm here."

She moved her head to smile up at him. "I know. That's why I know Miranda will be okay. She has all you Montgomerys looking out for her. We're family, Austin."

He kissed her temple. "Yes, we're family."

And if anyone tried to hurt his family again, he'd find a way to fight back.

Chapter Twelve

Decker ran his hand over Miranda's face, loving the way, even in sleep, she turned into his palm. Her mouth opened slightly, and she sucked on his thumb. He held back a groan, lest he wake her, and slowly removed his hand. She whimpered then burrowed back into the pillow. He stood beside the bed, dressed for work, his jeans old, his boots older, and felt oddly out of place in her room. Yeah, he'd stayed the night, but he felt like he should have worn cleaner jeans or something.

Miranda didn't seem to care, though.

How the fuck had he gotten so lucky?

It had been over a week since he'd broken his promise to himself and let in an ounce of happiness. They'd spent four of those nights together, mostly at his place since he had Gunner and the large house. Last night, though, they'd spent the night at her place since Austin had kept the dog at his place so Leif could practice caring for a pet. Decker hadn't mentioned where he'd be sleeping since Gunner wouldn't be there and because Austin would probably punch him for letting him know that.

He and Miranda didn't talk of futures and commitments but, rather, what they normally did, only now they'd added sex to the mix. Now he didn't feel like he would blow because he was holding himself back. He didn't have to bite his tongue when he wanted to tell her she looked fucking hot. He didn't have to put his hands in his pockets when he wanted to touch her, hold her.

Fuck, he was a damn lucky man.

At least for now.

Once the Montgomerys found out what he was doing to their baby girl, well, his life would be forfeit. Or at least the life he'd had with them.

She was worth the pain, but he hoped that she never found out that he wasn't worth the same.

He had to head to the job site early, so he left a sleeping Miranda in bed. She'd be up in an hour for work and needed her sleep. He'd kept her up late the night before. He grinned at that despite himself.

"Decker?"

He cursed. He hadn't meant to wake her since she needed the sleep. He looked over his shoulder at a sleepy Miranda standing in her doorway. Her hair looked like someone had run their hands through it for hours—*guilty*. She'd put on the shirt he'd worn the day before, and the long T-shirt brushed the top of her thighs. Damn, she looked fucking amazing. He turned around, and his cock filled, pressing at his jeans. Fuck, he did *not* need to have his zipper permanently engraved on his dick. He adjusted himself then crooked a finger.

She gave him a sleepy smile and walked toward him. He opened his arms, and she sank into his side. When he kissed the top of her head, she tilted her head back, her mouth open. He kissed her softly, brushing his lips across hers in the gentlest of caresses.

She moaned and trailed her hand down to the front of his pants. When she gripped him, he sucked in a breath. Pulling back, he gave a rough chuckle.

"You touch me, we're going to end up naked, and I need to get into work."

She gave a sleepy sigh but didn't touch his dick again. Disappointment filled him.

Later.

"Have fun at work today. Did you need coffee?" She shuffled toward her coffeemaker, and he held back a smile. She was *not* a morning person, but then again, neither was he. He'd much rather bend her over the counter and eat something sweet for breakfast, but he had to go to work.

And he needed to keep at least some distance. The more he stayed here, the more he let himself become ingrained in every part of Miranda's life, the worse it was going to be when they broke things off.

This was temporary.

A distraction.

It was best to remember that.

"Decker? Coffee?" She waved an empty mug at him, and he shook his head.

"I'll get some at the job site. Have fun at work." Rather than kiss her goodbye, he lifted his chin then headed out. If he didn't leave soon, he'd make a mistake and stay.

That couldn't happen.

The sun hadn't risen yet, but the air smelled of morning and rain. Miranda's apartment building was tucked against a copse of trees that gave some shade during the hot months but faced the mountains. Even though the place was small, it was worth it for the view.

He wasn't sure he wanted her there for much longer, though, considering that's where Jack had attacked her. Call him a caveman, but he'd rather drag her back to his place where he could keep her safe.

Just as he made it to his truck, a car that looked suspiciously like Maya's pulled into the parking lot.

Well fuck him.

Rather than jump in his truck and speed out of there like he had something to hide, he stood there, his arms crossed over his chest.

Maya got out of her car, her brows raised. For some

reason, she didn't look too surprised to see him there. He knew Miranda hadn't said anything to any of her family since they were so new and getting to know one another as a couple or whatever the fuck they were, but that didn't mean that Maya didn't clue in real fast.

The woman knew things that no one else should know, and Decker was never sure how she found out.

"Decker." Her voice was cool, but the laughter in her eyes confused him.

"Maya," he said, equally as cool. There was no laughter in his eyes though.

"Have fun at work," she said slowly.

"You're going to tell the rest of them, aren't you?" There really wasn't any doubt.

"I have to," she said simply. "She's ours, Deck."

He nodded, knowing that was true. Sucked, but nothing he could do about it.

"You're ours too. You know that, right?"

He didn't say anything, just lifted his chin and got in his truck. When this all went south—it would because he was a Kendrick, and they always fucked things up—he'd be alone. He'd known that going in, but Miranda had been too much of a draw to pull away any longer.

He was good at being alone.

It just sucked he'd have to leave the Montgomerys because of it.

He made it to Austin's, picked up Gunner from a

sleepy Sierra, and hightailed it out of there before Maya had time to call anyone. He didn't blame Miranda's sister for wanting to protect her, nor did he blame her for sharing the news. It was bound to get out anyway, but he needed coffee before he dealt with the blows.

When he got to the job site, he let out a sigh. This wasn't going to be pleasant. He lived with these people. Worked with them. They were his fucking family, and he'd ruined it all because he wanted Miranda.

Wanted.

Needed.

Craved.

Loved.

No, not the last one. He couldn't afford the last one. *She* couldn't afford the last one.

He just prayed that when it all came crumbling down —because it would—he had enough of himself left to pick up the pieces.

With that unhappy thought, he got out of his truck and Gunner followed him to the trailer. Gunner would be safe in the trailer for the day until Decker took him for walks around the property. Then the dog could follow him outside the construction zone. The damned thing loved the noise, the traffic, and the people. Decker needn't have worried it would be too much for him. Gunner fit right in with the Montgomerys and all that that entailed.

Their current job was restoring an old inn. Since they were out west, none of the buildings were as old when compared to some of the jobs he'd seen out east. Denver was a relatively young city, and its buildings and roads reflected that. However, all that didn't mean there wasn't history when it came to building, and the people for that matter. Storm had worked his ass off on the architectural plans, blending the old with the new while Wes led the team. Decker was Wes's right-hand man. The two of them did most of the grunt work on the project.

He fucking loved it.

Loved working with his hands, loved making something look like it was cared for rather than neglected. He just hoped he didn't lose his job because he slept with their sister.

Jesus, Decker was a fucking selfish idiot.

"What crawled up your ass and died?" Wes asked before taking a sip of his coffee. He cringed then took another sip. "Tabby's out for the week since I forced her to actually take a vacation, so the coffee tastes like shit." Tabby was Montgomery Inc.'s administrative assistant. She ruled the company—and the men—with a manicured fist. Decker was pretty sure she and Wes had a thing going on, or at least had at one point. If not, they were just damn close and knew how the other worked. The result worked well for the company, and Decker didn't care as long as he could keep his job and work the way he wanted.

He probably ruined all of that by finally giving into temptation, but Miranda was worth it.

God, she was so worth it.

Decker poured himself a cup of coffee and took a sip, shuddering as he swallowed. The bitter taste would probably give him more chest hair, but whatever. "You suck at making coffee, Wes. I thought you'd be better."

"Eat me. And why the hell did you have that look on your face when you walked in? Something wrong with the paneling you put up yesterday?"

Decker shook his head. "Nothing's wrong," he lied. Well, lied about himself. The paneling was fucking perfect. "Just not awake yet, and this coffee sure as hell isn't going to cut it." He dumped the cup and shuddered.

Wes gave him a look that said he didn't believe him, but he'd let it pass.

"So, what's on the docket for the day?"

They went through their plans for the day, and after grabbing a bear claw—he already missed Tabby and her jelly doughnuts—he headed out to his section of the inn. Gunner stayed back in the office, content to snooze the day away.

Decker went over the paneling he'd put in the day before, happy with the progress, and then went back to the other side of the building where he needed to work on some of the support beams. When he picked up the hammer, he had a quick flashback of his dad and cursed.

No. He wouldn't be thinking about that man right now. Not ever if he had a choice. His mom had called two more times, and Decker had answered. He'd told himself not to, but he hadn't been able to help it. She wouldn't help herself, and she wouldn't accept his help, but things could change. He couldn't risk not listening.

That didn't mean he'd face Frank though. That was something he could never do.

If that made him a bad son, then so be it.

After a couple of hours of hard labor that left a good sheen of sweat on his body, he went outside to check on a couple of things with his workers. He ate lunch with the crew then worked a few more hours. Wes and Storm were working on other things, so he didn't have to deal with hiding from them. It sucked to have to face them day after day and not mention the fact that he was with their sister, but he couldn't do it. Not yet. Soon though. Because Maya, if she hadn't already, would spread the news because that's how families worked. Other than the fact that he was hiding shit from his family, it was a damn good day. They got tons of work done on the place, and when he wasn't thinking of support beams and drywall, he was thinking of Miranda.

Good fucking day.

A car door slammed, and he ignored it since it could have been anyone.

"You fucking asshole!"

Decker stiffened, set down the hammer in his hands, and then turned to see Griffin striding up to him. He let the fist hit his face, knowing it was coming. He blinked twice, slowly, and then rubbed his jaw. He deserved it after all. He ran his tongue over his teeth and checked to see if any had loosened. Luckily they were in good shape, and he also didn't taste any blood.

He didn't think that would last for long, not with the look of murder in Griffin's eyes.

"You're just going to stand there and take it?" Griffin asked, his chest heaving. He shook his hand then lifted a lip in a snarl. "We trusted you. We fucking trusted you, and you're sleeping with Miranda?"

Wes and Storm ran up from behind Griffin and stood on either side of their brother.

Well then. At least he knew where he stood.

It wasn't like it was a surprise.

"What the hell is going on?" Storm asked. He looked between the two men like they'd gone crazy.

Maybe they had.

"Why did you punch Decker?" Wes asked. "And why the fuck did you take it? Damn it. This is a job site. Work. If you have issues, get the fuck out of here and deal with them. Don't bring it here."

Decker sighed. That was true. "Fine. I'm calling it a day." He met Griffin's eyes. "You want to deal with this some more? Follow me to my place. Let's not do it here." He'd already tainted the Montgomerys with his presence, and now he was doing it again by bringing his shit to work.

Their work.

"You don't want to tell them?" Griffin asked, murder on his face. "You don't want to tell them why I hit you? You're going to try and hide it for as long as you can, aren't you?"

"What is he talking about, Decker?" Storm asked, his voice smooth. The man didn't blow up as quickly as Wes or the others, but when he did, he lived up to his name.

Decker met Wes's and Storm's gazes and raised his chin. "Miranda and I are seeing each other."

There. He'd said it. It wasn't like they weren't going to find out on their own anyway, not with the way Griffin looked like he was ready to blow.

Wes's eyes bugged out. "Seriously?"

Storm didn't say anything. Instead, the man looked thoughtful.

"Yeah," Griffin sneered. "How long has it been going on?"

"Griffin, stop it." Storm sighed. "This will take getting used to."

Wes just blinked a few times and shook his head. "Didn't see that coming."

"How long?" Griffin asked.

Decker sighed. "Not too long, and now we need to leave so we're not here at work. I don't want to hurt Montgomery Inc."

"By taking advantage of Miranda, you already hurt the Montgomerys."

It was like a hit to the solar plexus. Decker swallowed hard, his head pounding.

"Whoa, man, what the fuck?" Wes said, turning to Griffin. "He's our brother. You don't fucking say that."

While Decker appreciated what Wes was saying, it wasn't the truth. It also didn't soothe the deep cut from Griffin's words. His best friend's words. He'd known it would hurt. He'd known that he'd lose everything because he'd taken a chance on the one woman he truly craved, truly loved.

But he hadn't known it would hurt this bad.

"He's not our brother," Griffin said slowly. "He's the man we took in. The man we grew up with together. Now he's the man who took advantage of Miranda."

Decker's hands fisted at his side. "I let you get away with one punch. I let you get away with saying shit about my loyalties. But don't say I took advantage of her. She's an adult. She had choices. So did I. It's mutual."

Griffin tilted his head. "Yeah? And you just swooped right in, didn't you? Right after that asshole beat the crap out of her, hey, here you are, fucking our baby sister."

Decker lost it.

He slammed his fist into Griffin's face, pissed off he'd let Grif bait him in the first place.

"Whoa," Storm called as he reached for Decker.

Decker slid out of the way and came nose to nose with Grif. "Watch what you say about her. She's everything, you asshole. Don't you make it sound like I took her when she didn't want it. Don't you make it sound like she's something I picked up off the street. You know better than that." He took a deep breath. "Or at least I thought you knew better than that."

Fuck, of all the brothers, he thought Grif would have understood. Or maybe that was just the thing. Of all the brothers, Grif was the one who knew him best.

He was the one who knew for sure Decker wasn't good enough.

"You hid it, Deck." Grif shook his head. "You fucking hid it. What am I supposed to think? Maya sees you coming out of Miranda's place early in the morning and you didn't tell us. If it was something you were proud of, you wouldn't have hidden her like a dirty secret."

Decker punched him again and, this time, took Griffin's punch as well. Wes and Storm had apparently given up on keeping them from knocking each other down.

Good.

Griffin got in a good punch to Decker's kidneys, and he cursed. The two of them hit the ground, punching and kicking at each other like they were kids again—only this time it wasn't for fun. The blood and bruises would be real, and he wasn't sure they could heal from the ones that would be left unseen.

He'd have taken the hits if Griffin hadn't disrespected Miranda. As it was, he had to hold back from hitting harder. The rage he felt over the past few months of not being able to do anything about his mom, about

Jack, about most things, slid through him, and he kept hitting.

Grif hit back, though he was smaller than Decker, and if they didn't stop soon, Decker would regret this more than he already did.

He pulled back, his chest heaving.

"We're new. So fucking new we wanted time to ourselves." Truth, but not all of it. "You think I would have risked everything I had, everything that I am with you guys, for something I'm ashamed of?"

Griffin's face shut down. "I don't know what to think anymore, Deck. It's like I don't even know you."

"I'm the same guy I always was." They were just seeing him clearly now.

"She's my baby sister, Decker. You didn't tell us. You *hid* it. I just...I just can't."

Decker stood up, his body aching, his knuckles bleeding. He dusted himself off and offered his hand to Griffin. When the other man didn't take it, but stood up on his own, Decker nodded. He shouldn't have been surprised. It was over.

His mouth hurt like a bitch, and he was pretty sure his face bled, and he'd have a black eye to match Miranda's. Fuck.

Miranda.

She was *not* going to appreciate this.

But what else was new. He'd fucked up, and he'd keep doing so because that's who he was.

"I'm sorry," he said softly. "I'm sorry I didn't come to you first."

Griffin shook his head. "I need some time, Deck. Don't hurt her, or I'll kill you." He met Decker's eyes. "You get that? You get that I just said that to my best friend because he's going to hurt my little sister?"

"It's not all about you, Griffin," Storm put in, his voice devoid of emotion.

Griffin sighed. "It's about all of us. And I need to get out of here." He stormed off, leaving Decker bloody and broken open.

Wes shook his head then followed his brother, not saying anything to Decker.

"Why don't you take the rest of the day off?" Storm said softly.

Decker stiffened. "I'm not going to let this affect my job." He'd be damned if he ruined it all.

Storm sighed. "You're bloody, bruised, and people saw it all. I don't care about that since we're guys and we do that. But this is a place of business, and now people are going to talk. They'll deal with it. We'll deal with it. It's what we do. But you need to go clean up and cool off." He put his hand on Decker's shoulder. "For what it's worth, I like you and Miranda together. She's always had a thing for you anyway. And I've seen the way you look at her."

Decker's mouth dropped, and Storm shrugged.

"It wasn't my place. I don't necessarily think it was Griffin's either, but that's on him. And you. She's ours,

Deck. She's also the youngest of us, so we've all had a hand in being overprotective when it comes to her growing up. You'll figure it out. So will she. Despite the fact we try to forget it, she's an adult and can make her own choices. Just don't hurt her."

Decker swallowed hard and nodded. He didn't promise he wouldn't hurt her; he couldn't promise that. He'd do his damn best not to, but that didn't mean much when shit happened all around them.

He went back to the office, got Gunner, and made his way to his truck. By the time he got home, his hands ached, and his soul felt like someone had ripped it open. He'd fucked up. He'd broken the code or whatever the fuck people called it. He *should* have told Griffin, Austin, and the rest. By hiding what he had with Miranda, he'd made it seem seedy. He'd done a disservice to them both, as well as to the family that had taken him in. He'd been just so damn scared of their reactions.

He looked down at his bruised and bloody knuckles.

He'd been right to expect the pain and the beating.

He saw the blood on his hands and remembered the feeling of his fist hitting Grif, his best fucking friend.

Those weren't his hands. No, those were his father's hands. The hands that had beaten Francine Kendrick for thirty years and had broken Decker's arm.

The sins of the father had nothing on him.

Despite pulling away and doing his best to deny his nature, he'd turned into the old man anyway.

He'd fought back to protect Miranda's name, though she hadn't needed it. Was she worth him losing everything?

Yes.

Hell yes.

She was worth so much more than him anyway.

It just meant he wouldn't be able to keep her.

Chapter Thirteen

S ierra was late.

Well, that was the understatement of the year.

She'd stayed too long at work because she'd felt she'd needed to make up for missing the morning. Since she'd been at the doctor's office dealing with her flu-like symptoms, she'd missed opening and had to have her girls take care of things for her. It wasn't that she didn't trust them to do it, far from it. It was just that Eden was her baby, and she wanted to have her hand in everything.

The doctor had wanted her to stay for extra tests due to her medical history, so it had taken longer than she'd planned on. So that had cascaded into her being late for every consecutive thing scheduled in her day. She *hated* being late. She was the kind of person who needed to be fifteen minutes early, or she felt like she wasn't on time.

Austin made fun of her for it but changed his schedule around to accommodate her.

That was love.

Or her being mildly OCD.

With a sigh, she pulled up to her home and grabbed her things to head inside. A wave of dizziness hit her, and she sucked in a deep breath. She leaned against her car door and closed her eyes. Everything would be okay. Everything *had* to be okay. Damn, she really needed to start feeling better. She didn't have time to be sick. She had a wedding to plan, a fiancé and stepson to love, and a business to run. Not all in that order either.

Austin opened the door before she got there, an odd look on his face.

"What's wrong?" she asked before he could speak.

He shook his head. "Nothing. I just feel like something's off, and then I come out here, and you look pale, baby."

He leaned down and kissed her, despite the fact that she probably contained way too many germs, and then took everything out of her arms. She sighed at the act. He might be all broody, but he still took care of her in the smallest ways. And it wasn't because he didn't think she couldn't do it. No, it was because he *wanted* to do it. The difference was what made her love him even more.

She followed him in and opened her arms. Leif ran to her and hugged her hard. She stumbled back a bit, forgetting how big he was. After all, he was his father's son. He smelled of little boy and chocolate. It seemed Austin had let the kid raid her stash. That was okay since she knew her man only did when Leif had a good grade at school. She kissed his temple and squeezed him again.

"Hi, Sierra. How was work?" Oh, how the boy had changed since she'd first met him on that step in front of Montgomery Ink. He smiled more and looked as if he actually cared how her day was. She kissed the top of his head, and he wiggled away. A boy of ten wasn't too keen on affection, so she'd take what she could get.

"Work was good. Long."

Austin came to her side, cupped her face, and kissed her softly. "Sit down and let us take care of you. You don't look any better than you did this morning. What did the doctor say?"

She sighed, but because she was too tired to argue, she toed off her shoes and sat down on the couch. Leif pushed at her shoulder and she laid down. The boy then placed the throw over her, and she smiled.

"Thank you, honey."

He smiled then shrugged. Yep, still a boy.

"Just be better, okay?"

She nodded, and he went back to his homework at the coffee table. She watched him work on his math and sighed. He'd lost his birth mother so recently and yet had rebounded the way kids do. She didn't know how he'd been before the other woman's death, so she'd never be able to compare, but she liked to think Leif was on the right track.

"So?" Austin asked when he sat down on the other end of the couch. He put her feet on his lap and starting rubbing them.

Dear God she was in heaven. Seriously. Could she be any luckier?

"They didn't tell me much other than to get some rest, and they would call later with the results."

Austin frowned. "Results? I didn't know it took so long to tell you if you had a cold or the flu. Which, by the way, means you shouldn't have been at work, woman. You aren't going in tomorrow."

She raised a brow. "I felt perfectly fine today once I got going. I can't just call in sick. I own the place. Heel-loo...you kissed me." And she'd kissed Leif's head. Fuck. She was a bad mother. Maybe she should cover him in antibacterial soap or something. Was there a spray to keep kids healthy? Maybe a bubble?

Austin squeezed her foot, and she blinked back to attention. "First, hello, it's your lips. Of course I'm going to want to kiss you. I'm never *not* going to want to kiss you, so get that thought right out of your head. Second, honey, you can't work yourself to the bone. That's why you have the girls there. If you're not up to working, then don't go. It will just make recovery harder. You know that. When did the doctor say he'd call?"

"Tonight hopefully." She wasn't too worried about it

since that was what she was forcing herself to think. The fact that the doctor hadn't immediately known what was wrong with her had put an odd ache in her stomach. Hopefully, it was nothing and the man was just being thorough. After all, she had a weird medical history, so the man might not want to jump to conclusions. As long as he was speedy with the phone call, she wouldn't freak out.

Much.

The doorbell rang, and Sierra frowned. "Who could that be?" she asked.

Leif got up and ran to the door. "I've got it!"

Austin sighed and stood up after patting her leg. "Check the peephole, Leif. Don't open it unless it's family." He followed his son to the door, and Sierra closed her eyes, exhausted all of a sudden.

"What the fuck?"

At Austin's words, Sierra sat up, not so tired anymore, and got off the couch, her heart racing.

She froze when she got to the foyer. "Oh, Griffin, honey."

The man looked like he'd gone a few rounds with an MMA fighter. One eye was swollen shut, he had a cut on his lip, and his face held the signs of future bruising. He was holding his side and tried to smile.

"Hey, Sierra, darling. You think you can help me clean up?"

There was something in his eyes that worried her. He wasn't here to get cleaned up. He was here to tell the story of what had happened. She had a feeling they weren't going to like it.

"Leif, can you go to your room for a bit?" she asked, trying to keep her voice calm.

"Uncle Grif? What happened?" Leif asked, his voice low.

She put her hand on his shoulder and brought him closer. "We'll tell you once we figure it out, but why don't you go to your room? Okay?"

He met her gaze and nodded. He was a good kid, but he didn't like being left out. That much was clear.

"Come into the kitchen, honey," she said to Grif once Leif was in his room.

"Thought you'd never ask."

"Stop flirting with Sierra, and tell me who the fuck did this," Austin growled.

She shot him a look behind Griffin's back, but Austin didn't back down.

"It was Decker," Griffin said simply when he sat down on one of the stools.

Sierra froze. He couldn't have said Decker. Not the man who was Griffin's best friend. She'd thought they were closer than most of the Montgomery brothers in general. Austin had told her that brothers sometimes fought to relieve tension and steam, but she didn't think it was like this—not with the angry set to Griffin's shoulders and the bruises on his face.

Griffin didn't say anything as she looked over his face

and felt around for broken bones. She honestly had no idea what she was doing, and if it looked like he needed to go to the hospital, she'd freaking drive him there herself.

Men.

He didn't speak while she looked him over, and Austin loomed over her shoulder, waiting.

She went back to the bathroom for their first aid kit after giving Austin a look. Maybe Griffin didn't want to spill in front of Sierra. That was fine, but the man *would* tell them what happened.

When she got back to the room, Austin had his back to his brother, and she knew it was bad.

"Okay, stop with the macho bullshit, and tell me what happened."

Austin sighed and turned. "Apparently Decker and Miranda are...together."

She blinked and ignored the little dancer in her brain that was excited about one of her good friends finally getting what she wanted.

"And?"

Austin took a deep breath while Griffin sputtered. "And?" her soon to be brother-in-law gasped. "And? They fucking hid it!"

She crossed her arms over her chest, remembered the first aid kit, and then threw it at her fiancé. "Take care of your idiot brother, will you? And by the way, Griffin, listen to what you just said. They. You said they. Miranda and Decker. Together. *They* hid it. Maybe they hid it—and

217

it can't have been too long considering—because maybe they were worried about *some* people's reactions."

Griffin opened his mouth to speak, but she held up a hand. "It's been what, *maybe* a week that they've been together? Do they have to tell you everything they do?"

"He should have come to us, or at least Griffin, to tell us things were changing," Austin said softly. "It's a big change, Sierra."

She sighed. "Maybe they should have, maybe not. It's not up to us to decide. What *is* up to us to decide is not to get into a fucking fight over it." She gestured toward Griffin's bloody face. "Look at you. What did this accomplish, hmm? All it did was make you look like an idiot for hitting your best friend."

"He's sleeping with our sister, Sierra," Griffin said, his voice low.

"Yeah? So? You beat up all the men your sister sleeps with?"

Austin growled lowly. "First. She's innocent."

Sierra rolled her eyes, but she knew her man was only kidding himself with that statement.

"Second. We didn't get a chance to hurt the man who hurt her."

That time Sierra growled. "You've got to be freaking kidding me. You took out your anger on Decker? What the hell?"

Griffin shook his head then winced. She didn't feel any sympathy for him. "That wasn't it. Or at least not all of it. Shit. He hid it, Sierra. Why did he hide it? I was pissed because of that and because of the fact that, if he hid it, he's ashamed. And he shouldn't be ashamed of Miranda."

She closed her eyes and counted to ten. "You're going around in stupid circles that make no sense. You got into a fight because you *didn't* think. I hope you haven't ruined what you had with him. He's your best friend."

Griffin raised his chin, and she knew that nothing was going to be resolved right then.

"Okay, fine. Don't listen to me. But remember, they are consenting adults. Miranda has been through shit, and if Decker makes her happy, then good for her. Decker is family. Maybe not the same way Miranda is, but he's family. Remember the man you love and grew up with, and try to think about that. Trust the friend you love. Trust the sister you love, too. Okay?"

Her cellphone rang, and she sighed. This was as good a break time as any. "I need to answer that. Austin, take care of your brother's face. I don't want him bleeding in my kitchen anymore."

With that, she went to the foyer, grabbed her phone from her purse, and answered. Her doctor on the other end of the line sounded pleasant, not like she needed to freak out or anything, but her heart still raced.

"What is it?" she asked.

"Sit down, Sierra," her doctor said kindly.

She didn't want to sit down. She wanted to hear about

the test results. The results to the test she wasn't sure what it was for. However, she sat down on the couch, as ready as she was going to be.

"What is it? It's the flu, right? It has to be the flu." She didn't know why she was panicking so much about this.

"No, Sierra, it's not the flu. You're pregnant."

She blinked. That couldn't be right. She'd misheard. "I'm sorry. What?"

He let out a small chuckle, and she wanted to wring his neck. "You're pregnant, Sierra. Not that far along at all, but just enough that the test is positive."

"But..." Her head spun. "But I thought I couldn't. Or it would be hard. I mean, I was on birth control. I *am* on birth control. You know, just in case."

"And you know that birth control isn't foolproof. You're going to want to quit taking your pills and then come in so we can do a full exam and make sure everything is okay."

She clutched her phone. She'd lost a baby before and remembered the pain of finding out the life she hadn't thought she'd wanted had been lost forever. She wasn't ready for this. How could she be?

"I...I..."

"Breathe, Sierra. I'll have my office call you for an appointment. Hang up, and go get Austin. Tell him, if that's what you're ready for, and then we can talk options."

"Options?" she squeaked.

He sighed. "We'll discuss everything during your appointment."

They said their goodbyes, and she ended the call.

Pregnant.

They'd told her it was a small chance that she'd *ever* get pregnant if she'd tried, and yet here she was, knocked up and having to talk about *options*, whatever that meant.

"Sierra? Baby? What's wrong?"

Austin sat on the coffee table in front of her and cupped her face.

"I...I..."

He searched her face and sucked in a breath. "Whatever it is, we'll deal with it. Tell me, honey."

"I'm pregnant," she blurted out.

He froze and quit blinking. Right when she was about to open her mouth to ask if he was okay, a slow smile crawled over his face.

"Pregnant?" he asked, his voice breathy.

"Yes. I know it wasn't what we planned. Or rather, *when* we planned it, but yeah." Oh, God. What were they going to *do*?

He grinned then kissed her. Hard. "Jesus Christ. We're pregnant. Fuck. That's why you've been so sick. I should have known. Shea hadn't been as ill, but she was pretty weak when she was here with Shep and found out she was pregnant." He laughed. "How about that? You and Shea pregnant at the same time. The cousins, or second cousins or whatever, will be the same age."

221

Her mind whirled. "So you're happy?"

He looked at her like she was crazy. "Hell yeah, Sierra. We wanted this, remember?"

"But what if something goes wrong?" There. She'd said what had been worrying her.

His smile fell, but he still held her. "Then we'll deal with it. I'm with you and by your side, no matter what."

She launched herself at him and cried into his shoulder when he caught her. Damn, her emotions were all over the place.

"Shh, baby. We'll take care of this. Take care of you." He cursed. "I left Griffin in the kitchen, so he probably heard all of that. He won't tell the family since baby news is something we don't share without permission. But we won't be able to hold him back for long."

She pulled back and shook her head. "We need to talk to the doctor first. To make sure."

He searched her gaze and nodded. "Will do. Now I'm going to go finish cleaning up my idiot brother and send him on his way. You lie down and do nothing. You get me?"

She smiled softly. "I get you." She paused. "Are you okay with Decker and Miranda?"

He frowned for a moment, as if he'd forgotten what had happened five minutes prior in the kitchen, then shrugged. "It's not my business." At her surprised look, he rolled his eyes. "Okay, I'm trying to tell myself it isn't my business. We have other, more important things to worry about. They can deal with their own relationships—and is that weird to say—and we'll be here if they need us. How's that?"

She smiled and reached out to cup his face. "You're a good man, Austin Montgomery."

"I'm your man, Sierra soon-to-be Montgomery."

Yes, yes he was.

Thank God.

Chapter Fourteen

"He did what?" Miranda said slowly. She set the papers she was grading down on her kitchen table and frowned. She couldn't have heard right. There was no way that could have happened. No freaking way.

Maya crossed her arms over her chest and raised a brow. "Griffin hit Decker. Then Decker hit Griffin."

"You've got to be fucking kidding me." That didn't compute. They were best friends. The only reason they'd fight was...

She stood up. "You told Griffin?"

Maya had the grace to look ashamed. "No, I told Meghan and Mom. Come on, it's us girls, and it's a big deal, Miranda. Mom got really excited. Point for you two by the way. So Mom got excited, and when Griffin came over to help with Dad, she told him. She didn't know that Griffin would react like an asshole."

Miranda closed her eyes and counted to ten. Nope. Didn't work. "What the hell, Maya? Why couldn't you have waited? Why did you have to go and tell everyone?"

Maya tilted her head. "Why didn't you? And for what it's worth, Meghan and Mom weren't surprised. I wasn't either, and I know Jake won't be once he finds out. I *am* sorry the guys found out like that."

Miranda wasn't going to think about her mom's and Meghan's reactions. Not yet. She had bigger fish to fry.

"Tell me exactly what happened."

Maya sighed. "Apparently, Griffin freaked out when he found out. He went over to the job site and confronted Decker. According to Wes, Decker let Griffin get a punch or two in, and then Griffin said something about you, or something that sounded like it could have been derogatory about you, and Decker reacted."

Miranda paced her kitchen, her hands fisting. "So Wes knows. And if it was at the job site, Storm and the rest of the world know."

"Pretty much. For what it's worth, I'm sorry it happened like this. I was just so happy for you, I gossiped. I suck."

She picked up her phone to call...someone then thought better. "Yeah, you suck. You need to learn to not spread our family business within the family so fast. Okay?" Sure Maya wasn't the youngest of them, and for sure wasn't the least mature, but the other woman firmly believed that telling family members everything meant that they would always be there for each other. That worked only in a perfect world.

Clearly it didn't work for Griffin.

Or Decker for that matter.

"I'm sorry," Maya repeated, and Miranda nodded.

"I know, and I forgive you only because you're happy about me and Decker." She closed her eyes. She'd done her best not to think of her and Decker as a *her-and-Decker*, but it was getting harder and harder to keep on that track.

She loved him, true, and now she was falling in love with the man she had in her bed and her life. She had no idea what he felt and was doing her best not to worry about that. Instead, she focused on work, avoiding Jack, and enjoying herself with Decker while she had him.

Now her family knew, and things were falling apart.

"What are you going to do?" Maya asked.

That was the question, wasn't it?

"I'm going to go over to Decker's and see if he actually needs to go the emergency room. Knowing him and Grif, they both are probably broken and bleeding, and too macho and brainless to do something about it."

Maya came up and hugged her softly then trailed her fingers down Miranda's fading bruises. "My family keeps turning black and blue. I don't like it."

Miranda swallowed hard. "I don't like it either."

"Go fix him and then give him a piece of your mind.

Austin texted and said Grif was at their place, so that's something."

"How on earth do you keep all that information straight? And how do you get it so quickly?"

Maya smiled sadly. "I have skills. Someone needs to keep you all in line. I fucked up, and now you have to deal with consequences. I'm sorry."

"Stop apologizing. You might have told the family, but Griffin was the one who took it upon himself to hit someone so close to our family. Someone that *is* our family. That's on him." And Decker.

Damn it. She didn't want to deal with this, but she was at fault as well. She should have told...someone. It was a big deal even if she'd been trying to downplay it. Now she'd have to live with the consequences.

"You want me to lock up?" Maya asked.

Miranda rolled her eyes. "You can just leave, you know?"

"But you have better food."

Miranda kissed her sister's cheek then waved her off. "Fine, but stock up when you clean me out."

"Always do." Hence why she always had better food. It made no sense, but that was Maya.

That was family. She loved it even when it exhausted her. If only things weren't blown so out of proportion.

She pulled up to Decker's house and breathed a sigh of relief when she saw his truck and no one else. Maya said that Storm had sent Decker home, but there was always a possibility that Decker had gone somewhere else.

She got out and walked up to the door, knocking instead of going right in. They weren't at that stage in their relationship yet, and she needed to get her emotions under control anyway. Blowing up and yelling at him wouldn't solve anything.

Decker opened the door, and that last thought went out the window.

"You're fucking kidding me," she snapped then brushed past him.

"Come on in, Mir," he said dryly.

"Don't be a sarcastic ass, Deck. Look at your face." *Your beautiful, bearded face.*

"You liked my face last night."

She flipped him off then went into his kitchen for his first aid kit. The man kept it in his pantry so at least she wouldn't have to move far for when she needed ice. And from the look of Decker, she'd need lots of ice.

"Sit down on the damn stool, and let me clean you up."

Decker walked past her and raised a brow. "I take it you heard."

"Uh yeah. And thanks for calling me to tell me what happened." God, she was so fucking angry with him. With Griffin. With herself.

With everyone.

She slammed around the cabinets until she found what she wanted and pointed to the stool.

"I said sit."

"You're being pushy," he grumbled.

"Yeah? Well, you just had my brother's fist on your face." She looked down at his knuckles and cursed. "And from the look of those, Griffin probably looks pretty much the same."

Decker met her gaze, and she didn't like the pain she saw in them. Not the physical kind, but the kind she was afraid she wasn't enough to fix.

"I held back, Mir. He'll be fine."

She cursed again. "I don't understand men. And I said fucking sit!"

His brows rose at her tone, and then he sat down on the stool. "Mir."

"Deck."

"I'm sorry."

She sighed then wiped his face with a wet cloth. He'd already done it since he wasn't that bad off, but she needed to do it herself as well.

"You scared me." She lowered her head to his, and he put his hands on her hips.

"I'm sorry," he repeated.

"Don't be sorry. Just don't do it again. Okay? The two of you are some of my favorite people, and I don't like it when you fight." She pulled away and traced her finger over a cut on his brow. He hissed out a breath.

"I've never seen you look like this. It must have been a bad fight."

"It wasn't fun, if that's what you're thinking."

She traced another cut on his cheek and over the bruises on the side of his face. Griffin hadn't split Decker's lip, so she softly brushed her own over his.

"Don't do it again, Decker. Please."

He let out a breath. "I don't know if I can promise that, Mir. I'm not a good man."

She fisted her hands on his shoulders. "That's a cop-out, and you know it. You can use your words. Not your fists."

He closed his eyes, and she wanted to cry for him. God, she hated this, hated seeing him in pain that had to do with way more than one fight. She couldn't fix it, but she'd try to. It was all she could do.

"I would have stopped at the words, Mir. But then he said I was ashamed of you, and I lost it. I fucking lost it." He pulled back and looked at his hands as if he was surprised they were there.

"Griffin was wrong. You're not ashamed of me." She hoped that was the truth, but she didn't want to think about it if it wasn't.

Decker met her gaze, and the rawness in his eyes made her suck in a breath. "Never, Mir. I'm *never* ashamed of you. That's why I went ape-shit. You're mine for however long we're us, Miranda, and no matter what happens, I'm never going to be ashamed of what we have."

She swallowed hard at his words, ignoring the time limit he'd put on their relationship. After all, she'd pretty much done the same thing.

"How are your ribs?" she said instead of anything else that might have come out of her mouth. It was too important, so she didn't say it. "Do you need to go to the emergency room?"

Decker shook his head then cupped her face. "I'm fine, Mir. Nothing too damaging. Nothing other than my pride."

And his relationship with Griffin, but she wasn't sure they were talking about that.

She leaned into his palm and sighed. "I don't like you and Griffin fighting."

"I don't like it either," he said softly. "I should have told him." He said that last part so low she wasn't sure he was talking to her or himself.

"We *both* should have told him. We're adults. And though it would be nice to actually have privacy and just be the two of us, that's not reality. We're all so connected there's going to be hurt feelings and boundaries people think we shouldn't have crossed." She licked her lips and took the plunge. "I don't want to lose what I have with you right now because of what happened, Decker."

He leaned down and brushed a kiss over her lips. "I don't want to lose it either." He rested his forehead against hers. "It just fucking sucks, Mir. Grif's like my brother, and he looked at me like I'd defiled you or kidnapped you or some shit."

"You'll fix it. You both will." She prayed that was true. God, what was she doing to her family? All because she loved the wrong man? No, he couldn't be wrong.

He wasn't wrong.

Decker kissed her again, this time swiping his tongue along the seam of her mouth. She opened for him, closing her eyes on a moan. She let herself be drugged by his kiss, falling into him and letting him take control. He was just so good at it, so potent. While she loved making love with him, loved the feel of him over her, under her, deep inside her, she might have loved kissing him just as much.

His hands left her face and traveled down her body, cupping her butt. He pulled back and looked at her face.

"I fucking love kissing you."

She grinned. "I was thinking pretty much the same thing." She traced his lips with her fingers, and he nibbled on the tips. "I'm glad your lips aren't cut. That would make it hard for you to do this."

He bit down on her finger with a little more pressure, and she gasped. "Something's hard, and it's not this."

She rolled her eyes. "Oh look, a penis joke. I'm so surprised."

He stood quickly and lifted her off her feet, his hands under her bottom. She let out a squeak then wrapped her legs around his waist.

"I'll show you not to sass me, woman."

"You're hurt. Put me down before you do more damage to yourself." She wiggled in his hold, and he squeezed her ass.

"Orders too? I think you deserve a punishment, baby."

Her mouth went dry. "Uh...what?"

He set her on the kitchen table and put his hands on either side of her. "You said you wanted to feel what it would be like if I made your ass red. You still in, Mir?"

She swallowed hard and nodded. She wanted to try everything with him. Everything.

He put a finger under her chin and raised her head. "Words, Mir. You have to say it out loud."

"I want you, Decker. I want it all." She cursed inwardly at her slip of the tongue. Something came and went out of his eyes, and she pushed it away. "I mean I want you to spank me."

There.

Fixed.

Hopefully.

He kissed her again, and she moaned into him, taking him for all he was worth. And he was worth a hell of a lot. She wrapped her arms around his neck and pulled him closer, wanting more of him. His hands remained on the table, but she could feel the heat of him, the need of him.

When he pulled back, she had to gulp in deep breaths. He moved her from the table and stood in front of her, arms crossed over his chest so his forearms bulged in that damn sexy way.

"Strip."

"You don't want to do it for me?" she asked.

He narrowed his eyes. "Well, we were up to five swats. You just made it ten. You want more, little girl?"

Probably not for her first try, so she shook her head then remembered his rule. "No. Ten is good."

His lips twitched. Yeah, he'd caught her not answering correctly, but hopefully he'd let her get away with it this once.

She quickly took off her clothes, leaving them on the floor instead of folding them because that would take too long. Was there something wrong with her that she loved the fact that she was there naked while he was completely dressed? Maybe it was because she knew he'd take care of her...then get naked right alongside her.

"Turn around, bend over, breasts on the table."

She sucked in a shaky breath then did what he wanted. Her already hard nipples stiffened even more, and she winced when they touched the table. It wasn't too cold, but it didn't feel all that great.

She felt him come up from behind her and stand so close she could feel the heat of him, but not his body. It took all within her not to press back to get closer.

His hand covered one cheek, and she let out a moan. God, he was so...*hers*.

He moved his hand back, and then she yelped when he connected. The sting shot right through her, but then he rubbed the spot he'd hit, and she whimpered. He slapped her ass four more times in quick succession, but never in the same spot on one cheek. He soothed the sting again, and she sucked in a breath. Her pussy ached, and she knew she was wet, ready for him.

He spanked the other side, and she let out a moan.

"That's a good girl. Be as loud as you want, Mir. Show me what you want."

She moaned louder when he spanked her again. Three more to go, but she wasn't sure she'd make it. Her knees shook, and she moved her arms so she gripped the table.

He leaned over her so his mouth was right by her ear. "Your ass is so fucking pink right now. About as pink as your cunt. You know how much I love eating that juicy cunt of yours, and right now, baby, you're sopping. I'm going to lick up each drop and fuck you with my tongue so you'll come on my face. Then I'm going to fuck that pretty mouth of yours before I sink my dick into your sweet pussy. How does that sound, baby?"

Her clit throbbed at his words, and she wiggled against him, needing the friction.

"I want it all. Please. Make me come, Decker. I don't think I can take much more."

He bit her shoulder then kissed her. She ached for him, craved him. "You'll take all of it, Miranda. All of it."

When he moved back, she whimpered, wanting more. Damn him, she wanted all of it. He spanked her again, and she screamed. God, it hurt, but the kind of hurt that made her want to come or beg for more. Maybe both. He spanked her again and then again, and then she was free.

Her body shook, and she opened her mouth to beg for Decker to do something, but then his mouth was on her, and she was screaming for a different reason. He feasted on her pussy like she was the most decadent dessert ever.

He sucked on her clit, his wide tongue lapping her up. She squirmed, wanting more.

"Oh my God, Decker. Please. I'm going to come."

His hands spread her cheeks, and she blushed. God, he was so...dirty. She loved it.

He speared her with his tongue then sucked on her some more. Her body warmed, and her back arched. When she breathed out his name, she came, pressing her ass against his face.

Before she could finish coming down from her high, he had her rising again. This time, he was using his fingers to find her G-spot and rubbed on that bundle of nerves until she came again.

Panting, she tried to speak, but before she could, he pulled her down from the table and into his arms. He crushed his mouth to hers, and she fell once more. She could taste herself on him and wanted to reciprocate.

She pulled away then went to her knees. He cupped her face, and she looked up at him. "Shy?" she teased since he was still dressed.

He rolled his eyes then stripped off his shirt. Damn, the man was built. And she'd lick every inch of him later.

Right now, she had a certain body part she wanted to see. She helped him undo his pants and then gripped his length when he was free.

Decker sucked in a breath then ran a hand through her hair. "Do I need to take the piercing out?" he asked, his voice a growl.

She shook her head then licked the tip of his dick right under the piercing. "We've practiced a few times without it in, and if you're okay if I don't deepthroat this time, we should be okay."

He pushed her hair from her face then gripped it in his fist. "Just be gentle," he said on a laugh.

She rolled her eyes then licked her way down his cock to his neatly trimmed hair. She worked her way back up then sucked on the tip, rolling her tongue around the metal ball. Decker groaned, and his hand in her hair tightened. She swallowed him to the back of her throat, swallowed, and relished the way his body shuddered. Then, carefully, she pulled back. Usually, she'd go crazy and let him fuck her mouth, but she didn't want to break a tooth.

She repeated the motions, loving his taste and the way he fought for control, until Decker pulled away. He had her by the armpits and on the table before she could blink.

"Decker..." she breathed then closed her eyes on a moan as he sucked a nipple into his mouth.

"You need to pierce these," he said low, pinching both her nipples hard between his fingers. "They'd look fucking hot with little hoops, and they'd be hidden at work.

She shivered. "I will if you will."

He grinned. "Done."

Oh shit. Well, it looked like she was getting her nipples pierced. If it put that look on Decker's face more often, then yay for her.

"Feet up on the table and spread yourself so I can see that greedy little pussy of yours."

She did as she was told, feeling open and vulnerable. Decker groaned then leaned down to get a condom from his jeans. He carefully rolled it over his cock then positioned himself at her entrance.

"You think you can be a good girl and hold yourself open for me while I fuck you, baby?"

She nodded. "I think."

He grinned. "We'll see."

Oh God. She couldn't wait.

Decker's eyes were on hers as he gripped his cock at the base then slid into her one inch at a time.

Her mouth dropped open as he stretched her. His piercing rubbed along the side of her inner walls as he pushed deep. Seriously, anyone who'd never made love with a man with a cock piercing was for sure missing out.

Not that she'd share Decker with anyone. Nope, the man was all hers. For however long he wanted her.

She sucked in a breath at that thought, and then he slammed home. Stars burst behind her eyes, and she shook, tears forming. God, she was so *full*. He gripped her hips and stared into her eyes.

"You want to wrap your legs around me? Or do you want me to go this deep with your legs spread?"

She licked her lips, willing herself to speak. How could she think when he was so deep within her, so *part* of her?

"Both. Whatever. I'll start here then wrap when I can't hold back anymore."

He grinned and nodded. "Right answer, Mir. Right fucking answer." He pulled out, and she moaned, her pussy gripping him. "Jesus, you're so tight. I love making love to you."

Love.

He'd said it again. Tears formed once more, and she blinked them away. Not here. Not now.

Maybe not ever.

He pumped his hips, fucking her hard, and she lost her train of thought. Good. He had one hand on her hip, the other rolling and pinching her nipples. He never stopped his grueling pace, even as he leaned over and captured her lips in a fierce kiss.

She loved him so much, and yet she'd never tell him.

She couldn't.

She pushed those thoughts away and wrapped her legs around him, wanting to be skin-to-skin, heart-to-heart. She bit down on his shoulder, and he growled, picking up speed. The orgasm hit her hard, suddenly. She bowed her back, throwing her head back. Decker came with her, gripping her hips so hard she knew he'd leave bruises. Bruises she'd cherish and never want to fade.

He'd already marked her heart. Now he'd marked her body in the ways she craved.

When she felt his cock stop throbbing within her, he stood there, naked in his kitchen, with her naked on his table. His forehead pressed against hers, and she closed her eyes, lest he see the true depth of her feelings.

It was too fast, too soon for her to reveal what she'd known for far too long. She knew that in her mind, but it didn't matter in her heart.

She had to keep her eyes closed, or she'd see the cuts and bruises on his face, on his side from where he'd fought with Griffin. So much rode on the connection they shared and how they dealt with it. One wrong step and she could shatter not only her heart but the life of the man she loved and had fought so hard to have.

It all had to be worth it in the end.

Because if it wasn't, she'd lose herself forever.

Chapter Fifteen

Decker took a deep breath then lifted the large hunk of wood onto his workbench. His muscles strained, and he knew he should have gotten help from one of the guys, but he hadn't wanted to bother them.

He hadn't wanted to bother them with a lot of things.

He hadn't spoken to any of the Montgomerys, other than Miranda, that morning since the day before when the news broke. He wasn't sure which side anyone had landed on, and it killed him that there were sides to begin with.

His fault, he reminded himself.

Now he was alone in his workspace on a Thursday night because he hadn't had the gumption to find out if he'd ruined it all and he'd lost everything. He looked down at the wood on his bench and cursed.

He might be doing this all for nothing. Griffin had wanted bookshelves, so Decker was making them. The man had also asked for them before he'd found out about everything with Miranda. So now it could all be a waste. A waste that would kick him in the ass if he couldn't fix it.

His face ached from his friend's fists, and his side hurt like a mother, but they were small wounds in comparison to the slash across his heart. He'd never thought Grif would react that way.

Yeah, he knew it would be bad, but the betrayal on the other man's face was almost too much to bear.

He sighed and looked down at his knuckles. Miranda had tended his wounds, kissed them to make them feel better, and cared for him. His dick twitched at the memory of his hands on her and her mouth on him. He'd pushed her the night before in his kitchen, and then later in his bed, but she'd been right there, taking it all and begging for more.

He never thought she'd be able to do that, take all of him, be with him in a way that soothed him and touched all the bases. He'd known he wanted her and wanted her in his life. He just hadn't realized how much until she was there.

And things were going to go to shit once she figured out the truth.

He cursed then started working on the shelves, the loud noises and music pounding in his ears doing nothing to drown out his thoughts.

On the one hand, he wanted Miranda. Wanted her until she decided she couldn't take him anymore. On the other, he was just delaying the inevitable. He let out a sigh. Fuck, when did he turn into a whiney bitch?

He cursed again then started back on the shelves. He'd do the cutting with the saw, but he'd do the intricate carving into the wood with a hammer, chisels, and his hands. They were just shelves, and he might not have taken such care making them look unique if it hadn't been for his best friend. He'd have made them look distinctive just because it was Griffin, but the memory of betrayal on his friend's face was so vivid, that Decker was trying to work even harder.

A couple of shelves wouldn't fuse their relationship back together, but maybe they'd pave the way to a point where Griffin didn't hate him.

Fuck. He should have told everyone about him and Miranda when he'd had the chance. The secrecy—if only for a week—had been the final straw. They were always going to think that he wasn't good enough for their little girl, but the fact that he'd hidden it just made it worse. She'd told him that her mother was thrilled, but he wasn't sure how he felt about that.

Thank God Miranda was with him though. She'd soothed his wounds and held him when he'd wanted to flee. She didn't take shit from anyone, and that was something he could admire.

He turned off the saw to hear the phone ringing. When he looked at the read-out, he sighed.

"Hey, Austin," he said as casually as he could.

"Hey."

The silence between them wasn't as comfortable as it used to be, and the loss ached more than he'd thought it would.

"I take it you've heard," he said at last then winced. Smooth.

Austin let out a breath, and Decker sat down on one of the stools. "Yeah. Yeah I did. You okay?"

Surprised, Decker blinked. "What?"

"You okay? I saw Griffin since he came over here to get cleaned up." He paused. "No, he came over to tell me what happened, and then we cleaned him up, but we reached the same outcome. He looked like shit, man. How are your hands?"

Decker swallowed hard, shame pouring through him. He could taste the bile on his tongue, and he shuddered. He'd beat up his best friend and then his best friend's brother asked about his goddamn hands. Decker looked down at his bruised and scraped knuckles and ran his tongue over his teeth.

"They'll be fine. I'll be fine. Miranda took care of me." He could have bitten off his fucking tongue. That last part just slipped out, and now he was stuck, her name out there on the wind.

Austin let out a rough laugh, only there was no humor in it. "Shit, Deck. I wish you would have told us, but I can't be mad. Not when Sierra ripped Griffin and me— mostly Grif—a new one."

Decker frowned. "What do you mean?"

"You two have been together what, a week? A couple days?"

"Pretty much, but we still should have told you."

"Yeah, maybe. Maybe you should have asked permission or some shit, but even saying that makes me an asshole. Miranda, despite the fact that I try to forget it, is a grown woman. She can make her own decisions. The family and I have no right to put you through hoops." He paused. "Well, maybe some hoops, we're her older brothers and sisters, after all. But it's not like you're a stranger, Deck."

"Yeah? And that just makes it worse in Griffin's eyes."

"Griffin was blindsided and acted like an asshole. I know he's been having trouble with his book, and since you two are so close, he felt the sting on both fronts—not just you, but Miranda too. So yeah, he's a fucking idiot, but he's just the Montgomery who acted. The two of you will fix this. You know it."

"Do I? Damn it, Austin. I fucked up. I'm trash, and I'm dating your sister. Don't you get that? Grif had all the right in the world to beat the shit out of me. What he didn't have the right to do was belittle Miranda in the process."

"You know he didn't mean it that way."

"Maybe. But he said it and I reacted. I just did. You get that? I reacted, and I bloodied my best friend's face. At work. At *your* family's job site. Storm told me to take off yesterday, so I'm not going in today. I have vacation days lined up, so until I can figure out what the fuck to do, I'm taking them. Storm and Wes will deal. They're good without me."

The last words ripped from him, and he let out a breath. Maybe everyone would be better off without him there. He could go to a satellite job site out of state. Or he could find another job altogether. It would make it all go away if he was the one to leave.

But then he'd be leaving Miranda, and he was too selfish for that. He wanted her, loved her if he was honest with himself, and now he'd deal with the consequences.

It didn't make it any easier to live with though.

"We're not good without you, Decker. Don't you get that? You're family, too. It just surprised us. Though, according to Sierra, it shouldn't have. I don't understand how she can know things before they happen. It must be some weird woman superpower."

Decker grinned despite himself. "I'm telling Sierra you called her weird."

"Shut up, ass."

"Love you, too."

Austin sighed. "You do. We all do, Deck. Just don't hurt her, okay? She's special to all of us, and if you make her happy? Well, then you're the best thing that ever happened to her. And if she makes you happy? Then fuck yeah. Perfection."

Decked closed his eyes and pinched the bridge of his

nose. "It's been way less than a month. Stop getting ideas. Just let me breathe."

"You're in deep, Deck, and you know it. But I kind of like the idea I think. So just try not to fuck up, and we're good."

Easier said than done.

"And since you're going to brood on that one for awhile, I'll let you go. Just give Grif some time. He's an idiot, but he's our idiot. Yours too. And come to the next family dinner. That will help things get less awkward."

"By getting the horrendously awkward feelings out of the way in one go?"

"Pretty much." Austin paused. "Speaking of awkward family dinners, have you heard from Alex?"

Decker frowned. "No. Not since he told us about Jessica walking out. Things are bad, aren't they?"

"Things are blowing up left and right in this family, and I don't think I'm strong enough to keep everything together."

It was one of the most honest and open things Austin had ever said to him, and Decker saw the open plea in it.

"I'll try not to help burn it to the ground."

"And while you're doing that, if you could help with fighting the other fires, that would be great too."

"At some point, you need to let people live their own lives."

"I am, but I also need to be here if they can't do it or figure out they're not alone."

Yeah, that wasn't too subtle of Austin, but Decker let that go. When things went to shit, he wouldn't be going to the Montgomerys for help. If, and when, Miranda left him because she finally saw the truth of his character and past, then he'd lose the family he'd made forever.

Miranda was worth that though.

Worth that and more.

"Thanks for calling," he said after a moment. There really wasn't much more to say until they all figured it out.

"Be well, Deck. Take care of yourself, and make sure my baby sister is happy. You get me?"

Decker smiled. "I get you."

They said their goodbyes, and he ended the call. He didn't feel better than he had before, but he sure as hell didn't feel worse. Austin was like that. The other man might not be fully on board, but he did his best to make sure his family and friends were taken care of.

And Decker would do everything he could to make sure he never hurt Miranda.

He went back to work, putting his all into his project. He liked working with his hands. It was also comforting to know that allowing himself to channel his frustration in such a way could result in something beautiful and useful for someone else.

When the doorbell rang, he must not have heard it at first, but when his playlist changed songs, the sound of someone pressing the damn buzzer over and over hit his ears. Gunner barked in time with the doorbell, and Decker frowned.

He wiped his hands down and made his way to the front door. It better be a fucking emergency if they were going to hit the damn bell over and over again. Anyone who knew him would just call, and he would have seen his phone light up to let him know they were outside while he was working

He opened the door without looking through the peephole then tried to slam the fucking door closed.

"Boy, don't you fucking do that," Frank Kendrick slurred as he put his hand on the door, to keep it from slamming. Decker's father also put his foot in the doorway so it couldn't be closed.

"Get the fuck off my property," Decker said, his voice low, cold. He wouldn't yell. That would only egg the man on more. If he was calm and collected, he had a better shot at winning this fight. Decker might be bigger, but Frank would cause a scene. A scene that often involved cops and lies.

"You think you're all high and mighty because you're working for the Montgomerys? You're fucking trash, you little piece of shit. You're lucky they don't see who you are, see the truth. Because as soon as they do, you're fucked. Maybe they just feel sorry for you. That's why they let you stay there."

The words hit him, and Decker held back a wince. He kept his face like stone, but it was fucking hard.

"Just leave, Frank. I'm not in the mood to deal with your bullshit." He looked into his father's glassy eyes and held back a curse. He didn't want to think about what his mother looked like right now. If Frank was here and already on a tear, things were bad at home. He'd call the cops, but what would happen?

He held back a sigh. He'd call anyway. It didn't matter if she pushed them away. He'd never stop trying to protect his mother from the man in front of him.

"Fuck you. You should have come over when your momma asked." Frank gave him that sly smile of his, and Decker's stomach revolted. He barely held back the bile in his throat. Holy shit, he couldn't stand Frank, couldn't stand the memories that came from the large fists that held his door open. If Decker looked too hard, he'd see his own fists there. He would see the resemblance that made him want to run from Miranda and everything she represented to him.

If Frank didn't leave soon, Decker wasn't sure he could take it anymore.

"What did you do to her?" he asked before he could stop himself.

A pleased looked came into Frank's eyes, and Decker held back a curse. "She's where she should be, you little fucker. Home. On her knees." The man swayed on his feet. "Next time she calls, you come over for dinner. We're a fucking family, boy. Those Montgomerys aren't your blood. I am. Remember that. Remember the blood that runs through your veins. You're not some high-class asshole who thinks he's better than everyone else. You're nothing."

No matter how drunk Frank got, he was always able to give speeches that kicked Decker at the knees. Maybe one day he wouldn't let it hurt him, but Frank's words sounded just like the refrain going on in a loop in his own head. That didn't help matters. All he wanted to do was get Frank out of there and get drunk.

Drunk like his old man.

See? Nothing. He was *nothing*.

Decker was done with this. He pushed the door closed with all his strength, ignoring Frank's cursing. If one of his neighbors called the cops, it'd be on Frank, not Decker. And honestly, it wasn't a new thing to have the cops called where Frank lived. It just hadn't happened at Decker's own place before.

Frank cursed and yelled a few more times before stalking off. Decker hadn't seen a car in his driveway or out on the street, so the old man must have walked from one of the local bars. At least he hoped to God that was the case.

He went to his phone and called the cops so he could explain about his mother. The guys there knew the house and knew, too, that nothing good ever came from their interference, but hopefully they'd help.

After he hung up, he felt drained and not in the mood to deal with people. What he really wanted was a fucking drink to forget everything. He wouldn't end up as drunk as the old man—at least he hoped not—but he couldn't stay at home and drink alone. Instead, he headed on foot to another bar that he knew his father didn't go to because the old man had been kicked out and banned years before.

He set his phone to silent just in case the cops called back with news, but he didn't hold out much hope. He didn't want to talk to anyone else. Most of all, he couldn't face Miranda in his condition. He was looking piss-poor and feeling like shit—she didn't need to see him like this.

Yeah, just another notch on the long list of reasons why Miranda should just leave him and call it over.

If he lied to himself, he could call what they were doing just sex and be over it, but he couldn't. They had a connection that had nothing to do with sweaty bodies and the way they fit together. No, it was all about the way she warmed him from the inside out. She made him want to try to be a better person, yet he knew that couldn't happen.

He sat down at the bar, held up two fingers, and sighed when the bartender slid two shots of bourbon in front of him. He didn't care what he got, as long as he got something to burn the ache away. It took another full minute before he realized who sat next to him.

"You look like shit, bro," Alex slurred, his eyes way past glassy. He didn't know how long the other man had been there, drinking alone, but Decker wasn't in any place to judge.

"You look just the same," Decker said then downed his

shots. The fiery burn warmed him for only a moment before the coldness seeped in again.

"Want to talk about it?" Alex asked, his eyes on his drink and not Decker.

"Not particularly," he said honestly then ordered a beer. He'd pound those rather than the hard stuff so he could maybe wake up the next morning.

"Good, because I didn't particularly want to hear it." Alex held up his drink in a toast. "To not giving a fuck."

The other man drank his before Decker could hold his drink up with him. Shit, things were bad. Things had *always* been bad and just getting worse. He wasn't sure how to fix it or even if it was his place to fix to begin with.

All Decker knew was that the walls were closing in, and he wasn't sure he could find a way out. Tomorrow would come, and he'd have to deal with it all, but right then, he'd just drink until the pain went away.

If it ever did.

Chapter Sixteen

Work was starting to suck.

Miranda pinched the bridge of her nose and tried to remember why she liked her job. She didn't like it because of the people she worked with. She liked it because she loved seeing students' faces when they *got* it. When they figured out how to solve for x, find that elusive volume of an oddly shaped image, or someone made the equation equal on both sides. When they got *that*, her job was worth it.

What wasn't worth it was working late on a Friday evening when the students were gone and the asshole in her life was there as well.

The police hadn't done a fucking thing to protect her.

Not one thing.

They'd taken her statement then took his.

It turned out to be a case of he said versus she said.

Seriously. Her face had looked like someone had bashed it into a wall because, hey, look, that's what Jack had done, but there had been no physical evidence. At least nothing the police had looked into. Jack had gotten a warning, and his lawyer and money had gotten him freedom.

Meanwhile, Miranda had to work with him every day. He didn't come into the teacher's lounge anymore, thank God. No, instead he ate at his desk or somewhere else so she didn't have to see him. She was grateful because the more she had to see him, the more likely she wouldn't be able to hold her brothers back from beating the shit out of him.

Brothers *and* sisters, as she thought of Maya and Meghan.

It annoyed her to no end that she was stuck in this position. On the one hand, she could blame herself since she was the one who had gone on a date with a co-worker, but she wouldn't. It wasn't her fault that Jack had hit her. It wasn't her fault that Jack now lived free while she had to check the hallways before leaving her classroom.

No, the responsibility lay on Jack's shoulders.

That didn't make it any easier to stomach though.

With a sigh, she went through her papers again. She needed to finish the evaluations and have them on the principal's desk before she left. Her boss would be leaving the school in less than an hour, so Miranda had to hurry up. Thankfully she was almost done, but this was not how she'd envisioned spending her Friday evening.

Actually, she didn't know *how* she'd be spending the rest of her evening. She hadn't heard from Decker since she'd left him the day before after sleeping over. She'd done her best to soothe his wounds—and some of her own —and then had to go to work. She'd called him to see if he wanted to get dinner, but he hadn't answered. She left a message and hadn't called or texted again. If he wanted to talk to her, he'd have to make the next move.

She rubbed a hand over her stomach. That didn't sound good. The idea of him not wanting to talk to her at all after what happened with her family made her eyes sting, but she didn't cry. It was one freaking day. He was allowed to need space. She wasn't a clingy girlfriend, but after what she thought had been a freaking emotional day and time on his kitchen table, she thought he would be okay to talk.

Apparently she was wrong.

She wouldn't freak out, but the common courtesy of actually calling back would have been nice.

She sighed then went back to her work. When she was done, she'd either stop by his place or just head to hers. She wasn't in the mood to deal with a blow-up right then.

It took another thirty minutes, but she finished then headed over to the principal's office with her files and her bag. She'd head directly to her car and hopefully over to Decker's from there.

The principal was on the phone, so she set the forms on his desk, got a nod in recognition, and then headed back out. With a sigh, she figured she'd just go home and maybe call Maya or something.

It had been a tough week, and she wasn't in the mood to deal with drama. She could do that in the morning. Maybe he'd even call before then.

"You stupid bitch."

Miranda froze, ice creeping up her spine. Damn it. She'd been so focused on Decker and getting out of there that she hadn't checked the hallway to make sure she was alone...or at least that *he* wasn't around.

"You shouldn't be near me, Jack," she said softly. She turned to him to see the blond man glaring, his shoulders hunched.

"Why? What happened to you, hmm? Nothing. Instead, I have to deal with the cops hounding me."

Was he serious? The cops had done *nothing* because the asshole had talked his way out of it.

"Go away, Jack." She swallowed hard, the bitter, metallic taste of fear coating her tongue.

He stalked toward her, but she raised her chin. She'd run if she had to and probably should, but she wouldn't be afraid at her work all the time. She could protect herself, and *would*, if necessary.

"Why? It's my place of business as well. You're the one running around like a timid mouse with her tail between her legs."

"I'm done with this, Jack. You hit me. Threw me against a wall and threatened more. You might think you've gotten away with it because you're good with cops or whatever, but I'll never forget. My family will never forget."

"You're ruining *everything*," he spat.

She had no idea what he was talking about, but it was clear he was mentally unstable. She needed to get out of there as quickly as she could. She turned to run, but he gripped her arm.

"Let me go, Jack," she said as calmly as she could.

"It's always a hysterical woman ruining *everything*."

"Jack," she whispered, her voice not as calm as before. She didn't know why he was doing this, but she knew she was only a small part of the larger problem.

"Is there something wrong here?"

Jack immediately let her go, and Miranda sighed then blinked at the familiar voice.

"Luc?"

The man who had once been a close friend to the family—more importantly Meghan's good friend—frowned toward her. His dark coffee skin pinched at the corner of his mouth when he looked toward Jack. His honey-colored eyes made him look like he was ready to commit murder. She didn't know why he was here, but she was so freaking happy he was.

"Jack was just leaving," Miranda clipped.

Jack snarled but gave a tight nod. "Miranda and I were just having a discussion."

Luc raised a dark brow. "Really? Because from where I'm standing, it looked like you were forcing her to do something she didn't want to do. You want me to call the police, Miranda?"

For a moment, she thought she should but then remembered the look on the older cop's face. Jack hadn't done anything wrong this time, had he? He'd scared her, but that had mostly been because of what had happened during their last encounter. Though they'd had a witness this time in Luc, she wasn't going to press her luck with Jack.

She shook her head. "No, I just want to go home."

Luc searched her face then gave her a nod. "You better get out of here before I change my mind."

Jack sneered but stomped away toward the front of the building. Immediately, Miranda's body started shaking. Luc's arm came around her shoulder, and she settled into him. She hadn't seen him in years, and yet she felt comfortable with him, like another brother in her long line of brothers. He led her to the outside to one of the benches, and she let out a sigh.

"So, what are you doing here?" she asked, her body finally starting to settle.

Luc squeezed her once then moved to give them space. "I'm working on some of the electrical work. It's my first job since coming back to Denver."

Luc was an electrician, and for a while, had even worked with Montgomery Inc. and her family. He'd moved away suddenly one year, and she'd never gotten the full story. Not that it was any of her business.

She turned to him, a true smile on her face. "You're moving back?"

He nodded, though he wasn't smiling. "Already moved back. Now I'm just looking for a job that's not day-to-day."

She shook her head. "Talk to Wes and Storm. You know they'd hire you on in a minute."

He shrugged. "We'll see. I kind of left suddenly before."

She wasn't going to ask about why since, again, it wasn't her business, plus she had problems of her own. "Talk to them. The worst they can do is say no."

He gave her a small smile, and his eyes lit. The man was damn handsome, that was for sure. "I suppose." He looked around the parking lot and frowned again. "I don't like the way that man was touching you."

"It's a long story, but I'm moving on." She had to, or she'd be afraid for the rest of her life.

"I'll be around for another week or so getting things back up to code, so I'll keep an eye out."

That time she did roll her eyes. "You're like another brother, you know that? I have enough of them already."

He met her eyes then shrugged. "You're Meghan's little sister. I'm not going to let someone bully you."

She smiled then shook her head. "All of you are so

protective, and I like it, even though sometimes it grates on me." She stood up and grabbed her bag. "Thanks again for being there. I was going to run, but you being there helped. I'm headed out now, but thank you."

He stood with her and walked her to her car. "I'd say any time, but I don't want it to happen again. Be safe, and see you around."

She hugged him again, and he hugged back hard. "Thank you," she whispered then got into her car. It was nice to see a familiar face—even nicer when that face was there when she hadn't known she needed him.

Instead of heading home, she drove to Decker's house. As much as she wanted to give him space and deal with things on her own, she couldn't. No, she needed to see him. Needed to know that she wasn't alone. God, she sounded needy, but Jack had scared her more than she wanted to admit. She might want to act tough, but she sure didn't feel like it right then.

She pulled into his place and saw his truck. He was home at least. That was something. When she got out, she took a deep breath then made her way to the front door.

Decker opened it without her knocking. Apparently, he had seen her pull up. He pulled Gunner away to stop him sniffing at her, and she reached down to pat the dog's head.

"What's wrong?" he asked, his voice low. His eyes looked dark and his face pale. In fact, it looked like he'd been sleeping off a bender.

What the hell?

She shook her head then sucked in a watery breath.

He held open his arms, and she sank into him. She inhaled his scent, letting it settle her. He closed the door behind her then lifted her into his arms. She sighed at the movement then nuzzled her face into his neck, inhaling again. He'd recently showered so the smell of soap and man mixed into a heady combination.

"What happened?" he asked once he sat down on the couch with her on his lap. Gunner sniffed at them then sat at their feet.

She told him about Jack and then Luc coming in, and all the while, his arms around her tightened. She rubbed his shoulder, trying to soothe him, though it probably should have been the other way around. That wasn't fair though, and she knew it. She was just in a mood with him since he hadn't called, and frankly, wasn't much better off herself.

"Jesus Christ," he muttered when she finished. "Thank God Luc was there, baby." He kissed her temple and rubbed her thigh, his large hand possessive yet protective.

"I know," she said honestly. "I'm not going to lie and say it didn't scare me, because it did. But I was ready to run. I didn't right away because I thought I could face him, but that was stupid."

Decker let out a sigh. "Yeah, it might have been. I know we've been practicing with your self-defense moves

—and we'll be working harder on those in the future—but running is always the best defense if you can do it. You don't know if he has a weapon or not. Yeah, he's in school with you, but that didn't stop him from coming at you. I hate the fact that you have to deal with him at all."

She sighed then leaned into him harder. "The only way he'd go away is if he does it on his own or if something worse happens. I'd rather the latter not happen at all."

Decker's arms tightened, and she sucked in a breath before he loosened them. "I'll fucking kill him if he touches you again, Mir."

She turned and cupped his face. "I don't want you behind bars, so don't promise things like that. Okay?" She met his gaze and saw the pain in there warring with worry. She didn't know what was going on in his mind and felt a stab of pain that he didn't trust her to share. They might not have been together long, but they had been friends for years. She wished he'd share what was on his mind, but she wasn't sure he'd do it. And now that he was also working with her problems, right then wasn't the time to ask him to share everything.

"I missed you today," she said before she could stop herself.

He met her gaze and nodded. "I missed you too."

Relief slid through her, and then she cursed herself. Why did she care so much about what he thought? How he felt? She'd been perfectly fine throughout the day and had even planned on letting him be. But then Jack had seen her in the hallway, and she'd needed reassurance. After tonight, she'd pull back and remember that she was okay alone.

But she didn't *want* to be alone, and she had to be okay with that fact.

He still looked like something was off, and she didn't know how to fix it. "What's wrong, Decker?"

"Nothing," he said quickly. Too quickly.

"Just tell me. You don't have to keep things to yourself. I hope you get that."

He searched her face then let out a breath. "I'm a little off center since yesterday, and I need to find my bearings. It's nothing you've done, so don't think it's about you. It's about me. Okay? Forgive me?"

She shook her head. "There's nothing to forgive. Just know that I'm here if you need me. We're together, right? That means we can talk about things."

The corner of his mouth lifted. "That's right."

She ran her fingers through his beard and sighed. "I don't want to think about everything that hurts anymore." When she brushed her lips on his, his fingers tightened on her thigh.

"Yeah? What do you want to think about?" he asked, his voice rough.

"Make me forget? Just for the night?"

He searched her face and nodded. "Anything you want, Mir. Anything."

She swallowed hard, ignoring that ache in her heart.

This was just temporary. They hadn't talked of a future, and it was too soon to do so, but Decker had been very careful to scare her at first. He'd tried to show her the man he was, or at least the man he thought he was, and her trying to change him wouldn't work.

She didn't want to change him. She just wanted him.

"Stand up and go around to the back of the couch," Decker ordered. "Put your hands on the edge and stick your ass out."

She shivered then stood up. When she got into position, she licked her lips, wondering what he was up to.

She heard whispers and then claws on wood as Gunner walked to the back of the house.

Decker came from behind and slid his hands down her sides. When he gripped her hips and pressed the long, rigid length of his denim-clad cock against her butt, she sucked in a breath. She still wore her dress from work, and since it came to her knees, she couldn't really spread her legs the way she wanted. He tugged at the light sweater she'd worn over her dress, and she let him strip it off of her slowly. That left her in her dress, stockings, and her underwear. If he wasn't careful, she'd strip out of everything so she could feel his heat against her skin.

"What do you want today, Mir? You want my cock in your pussy? In your mouth? You want me to make your ass red? I could tie you to the bed and fuck you hard while you're begging for more. I have so many fucking ideas when it comes to you. Want me to go on?"

She wiggled against him. So many possibilities. "You decide. I like it when you decide."

He reached around and cupped her breast, bringing her back to his chest. He took her face with his other hand and brought her lips to his.

"That's what I like to hear, baby," he said when he pulled back. He bit her lower lip and tugged slightly. Her breath quickened, and she rubbed her thighs together.

God, this man was too much.

"I thought I wanted you over the couch, but I think I want you in bed for now. That way I can see your breasts and that pink pussy of yours when I get you naked. You want me to fuck you in my bed, Mir?"

She nodded.

"Words, Mir." He pinched her nipple through her dress, and she gasped.

"Yes. Fuck me in my bed."

"That's my girl." He smiled, and she fell that much more in love with him.

She wouldn't think about that now. Her heart wanted him, and that was all that mattered.

He led them to his bedroom then stopped in front of the guest room. His mouth crushed against hers, and she moaned into him. His fingers dug into her butt, and she rocked against him.

"Can't. Wait."

He lifted her up, slamming her back against the closed door. Her legs wrapped around him, and he thrust against her, his cock hitting just the right spot over her panties. He ripped his mouth from hers, his chest heaving.

"You're so fucking beautiful, Mir."

"Fuck me," she gasped, digging her heels into his lower back.

His hand went up her leg and froze. "Jesus Christ. Are you wearing stockings?"

She wiggled so the tip of his cock pressed against her clit. "Yeah. Not the ones with the garters, but thigh-highs."

"Fuck. You're keeping these on all night, baby."

"Just get in me, and we can talk about my wardrobe later."

He grunted then rucked her dress up over her waist. "Dirty, dirty little girl. I'm going to have fun finding out how dirty you are." He shoved her panties out of the way then speared her with two fingers. She gasped, her body clenching around him. "You're so fucking wet, Mir. I didn't even touch you, and you are soaked."

With one hand under her butt to keep her steady, he removed his fingers then traced them over her lips. She licked her lips and the tip of one finger.

"That's it, baby. Taste yourself. You like that?"

She nodded, wanting him to taste her as well. She pushed at his hand, moving it toward his mouth, and he smiled.

"You're a little minx. I love it."

She ignored the word love then almost came at the sight of him licking her cream off his fingers.

"So fucking sweet," he said then crushed his mouth to hers again. The taste of her on his tongue was even better than before.

"Inside me. Please," she gasped.

He pulled away, keeping one hand on her butt. He nodded then reached down to undo his pants. When she reached down to help, he shook his head.

"Hold my shoulders, baby. This is going to be a rough ride."

With that, he shoved her panties out of the way again then impaled her with one stroke.

They both froze, her body clenching around his cock in little spasms.

"Fuck, you just came with that, baby." He kissed her again. "So. Fucking. Hot." With each word, he pumped into her, bringing her close to the edge again.

He met her gaze, and she swallowed hard. He thrust in and out of her, slamming her against the door with each move. She held on, rocking her hips to meet him. With their clothes still on, she'd never felt so sexy, so *wanted*.

He reached between them and rubbed along her clit, flicking it with his fingernail. She gasped, her body bowing until she came in a rush. He followed right after, shouting her name as he filled her.

Filled her.

Fuck. No condom.

She could feel every inch of him, every spurt deep

within her body. His piercing rubbed all the right places, and she shuddered. He met her gaze, his eyes wide.

"Oh God, I'm so sorry, baby. I didn't mean to forget the condom. Shit. Shit."

She shook her head then cupped his face, kissing him softly. "I'm on birth control. I'm safe."

He shuddered out a breath. "I'm safe too. I have papers and everything, but fuck. I'm sorry, Mir. I should have thought."

She kissed him again. "It's okay. We're good. And I liked feeling you bare inside me."

He grinned then, slowly. "Yeah? Well, I liked being able to feel every inch of you around my dick. You want to stop using condoms altogether?"

She nodded, well aware his still-hard cock was pressed deep inside her. "But you get to sleep on the wet spot."

He threw his head back and laughed. "God, you're amazing. I—" He froze. "I'm glad you're here."

She swallowed hard. He hadn't said what she thought the words were going to be, and she knew it would have only been in the heat of the moment anyway.

It didn't matter what he felt, but she loved him enough for the both of them.

She just prayed it didn't break her in the process.

Chapter Seventeen

He hadn't felt this nervous in...well, ever. Decker took a deep breath then knocked on the door. Hiding for over a week hadn't helped him, and if he didn't face the consequences, he'd just keep fucking things up.

Miranda had pushed him into this, but he was the one taking the steps.

When Grif opened the door, Decker braced himself for a punch.

Only it didn't come.

"Hey," his best friend said.

"Hey." He stuffed his hands in his pockets and rolled back on his heels. It had never been this awkward between them, not in the twenty plus years they'd been friends.

Decker had done that though, so he'd best remember it.

"Shit, man, just come in. Us standing out here and staring at each other isn't helping things."

Well, he guessed that was better than nothing.

Grif stood back and let Decker in. Griffin had a fantastic house that had so much potential. Too bad the other man was the least crafty of the Montgomerys and worked in a whirlwind of clutter while he was on deadline.

"Ignore the mess," Griffin said as he walked into the room behind him.

"I always do," Decker quipped then held back a wince. He was here to apologize, not antagonize the man.

Griffin let out a chuckle. "True. Guess I really need those bookshelves you're making me."

Decker lowered his head and closed his eyes. If only it were that easy, but if Griffin didn't want to talk about the hard stuff yet, then he'd roll with it.

"I'm almost done with them," he said.

Griffin turned to him, his eyes thoughtful. "Really? You kept working on them?"

Ah, so apparently, they *were* going to talk about the hard stuff. Good. Get it out there. "Yeah. I wasn't going to quit." He met Griffin's gaze. "I'm still not quitting."

Grif let out a breath. "Fuck. This isn't easy."

Decker didn't say anything. Grif had to make the next move since Decker was the one who'd come to his place.

"I shouldn't have hit you. For that I'm sorry."

Decker shook his head. "You're wrong about that. I

deserved the punch, Grif. I hid my relationship with Miranda, and you were blindsided. I took the fist to the face because it was necessary."

Grif sighed. "Maybe you're right, but I shouldn't have said anything about Miranda. God, I was just so surprised and angry, and maybe even a little hurt, that I said things that were wrong and that I didn't mean. For that, I am truly sorry."

Decker nodded, a weight lifting off his chest. "I don't want to hurt her, Grif."

"I know that. I should have known that before too. Apparently some of the family saw the way you two were around each other when I didn't. Maybe if I'd seen that, I wouldn't have been such an asshole."

"I'd say you're always an asshole, like I usually do, but we're just now getting along."

Grif snorted then flipped him off. "Asshole," he said but didn't put any feeling behind it. "I don't know what's coming next, or how we're all going to handle it, but as long as Miranda is happy, I am. I shouldn't have made it all about me, and for that, I'm truly sorry."

"I...I don't know what we're doing next or how everything is going to end up, but..."

"But..." Grif echoed. "Yeah, it's that, but that's scary as hell. I don't want to lose you if things go to shit, Deck. So don't let things go to shit. Okay?"

"I'll try my best."

Grif let out a breath then clapped his hands once. "Okay then. You want to see where I want the shelves?"

Decker knew since he'd already cut down the wood, but he let Grif ease back into the friendship they used to have, or rather, the kind they'd have now that things were different. The fact that Griffin forgave him even after their fight gave Decker hope. The others in the family hadn't come out and said they were happy to his face, but nothing had been like it was with Griffin.

Maybe, as long as his legacy from his father didn't fuck it up, he had a shot at making things work.

Scary thing about hope—things usually crashed down once he let himself go there.

AFTER HE LEFT GRIFFIN'S, HE HEADED TO HIS PLACE to meet Miranda. She had the day off since it was the weekend, but she needed to grade papers. Apparently, his presence took her focus from red pens and math assignments, so she worked at her apartment. She was supposed to meet him at his place soon so they could work out and he could see how her defense lessons were coming along. Today, they might actually do some real boxing.

If the law wouldn't protect her, then he'd show her how to protect herself. He got a kick out of watching her punch the bag with all her strength, each time gaining accuracy and precision. She wouldn't be helpless again if he could help it.

He got to his place and changed into his workout gear. He was just pulling out two bottles of water from the refrigerator when he heard the knock at the door. He'd see about getting her a key so she wouldn't have to keep knocking. They'd been friends for long enough it shouldn't have been a problem, and considering the fact that he'd been balls-deep in her that morning without a condom, a key to his place wasn't out of the question.

See? He was growing.

Learning to trust.

He could do this.

He opened the door and couldn't hold back the grin at her workout gear. It was still relatively warm outside, so she'd worn tight, short-shorts and a tank over a sports bra. If he wasn't careful, he'd strip her down for a hard fuck on the floor before they even made it to his basement.

He swallowed hard and let her in, trying to hide the rod in his pants. She wrapped her arms around his neck and brought his lips in for a kiss.

"Mmm, tasty," she murmured. She pressed her body against his, so there would be no hiding his hard-on.

"You're in a mood," he teased as he took her hand. He led her to the basement since if he didn't do that he'd fuck her up against the wall. Her safety was more important than his dick.

"So?" She pinched his ass, and he jumped.

"Jesus, woman. Let me show you how to box and see your moves, then I'll see *all* your moves."

"Promises, promises."

He pinched her ass back then nudged her toward the punching bag. "You all stretched out like I asked?" He'd asked her to stretch at home since the last time she'd done that in front of him, he'd ended up taking her from behind, and they'd forgotten the rest of the lesson.

She lifted a brow, her cheeks blushing. Yep, she remembered the last time as well. "Yep, all stretched out."

"Good," he grunted and got out the tape. "I'm going to tape your hands to protect them, but we aren't doing much today. Got it? I don't want you to hurt yourself."

She nodded and held her hands out. He carefully taped them then kissed each palm before letting her go. She let out a sigh that went straight to his balls, but he stood up and went behind the bag anyway.

"Now, get in the proper stance. No, your arms need to be lower, remember?"

"Got it." Her eyes were on the target and not on him. Good.

"I want you to do a soft jab. Nothing too hard. Remember where your thumb is. I don't want you to break it."

She nodded then did as he asked. He grinned in approval then went about the rest of the lesson, doing his best to show her how to protect herself while secretly hoping she'd never have to use her new techniques.

"You have good form," he said after she did another punch.

She smiled up at him, and he was lost.

Damn it, he loved her.

Loved the way she put all of herself into everything she did. Loved the way she looked without makeup, with makeup, and just in general. Right now, she had that glow that came with working out but not getting too sweaty. She also had a high ponytail that bounced whenever she moved.

He wanted to wrap it around his fist when he fucked her. Wanted to feel her clench around him when he came hard.

But what he wanted most was for her to stay...to stay with him, in his house, in his bed, in his life.

That scared him more than anything.

"I try," she replied, and he blinked to get out of his head.

Dreams like those were dangerous, and it would be best to remember that.

"Want to do a few more rounds?"

She wiped her forehead with her arm and nodded. "I do, but do you want to spar? That's the right word, right?"

He snorted. "Yeah, that's the right word, but you're not ready to spar with me."

She rolled her eyes. "I don't mean a full-on battle or match, Deck. I *know* I'm a beginner, but I figured it would be fun to hit your hands or something. See what happens when you block me."

He nodded. "That's a better idea."

She grinned, and he had a feeling he might like the next words out of her mouth. "And when you pin me to the ground, I'll let you cop a feel."

Yep. He liked it. A lot.

He reached out and cupped her breast, running his thumb over her nipple. She sucked in a breath, and he grinned when her nipple hardened against his hand.

"I can cop a feel without having you punch me, Mir."

She gripped his hand and pressed him closer. He groaned then gripped her hip with his other hand. When he brought her to his chest, he pressed his mouth to hers, craving her taste. She rocked against him, straddling his thigh so he could feel her heat.

When he pulled back, he had to swallow hard so he didn't throw her down to the mat and fill her right there. He tugged on her ponytail, and she gasped.

"I thought you wanted to spar." He bit down on her bottom lip. He reached around to pat her ass in those short shorts then gripped one butt cheek. She rose up on her tiptoes, aiding him. Since he could, he traced a finger along the crack of her ass then down to her heat. She spread her legs more, and he grinned. He tugged her shorts to the side slightly and skimmed her labia. She shuddered, and he grinned before biting down on her earlobe.

"You're wet for me," he whispered.

"I'm always wet around you. It's beginning to become a problem."

He grinned then pulled back, dropping both hands to her hips. She whimpered, but he knew if he drew them both out, it would be better. Hard and fast worked, and they'd get to that eventually, but right now, a tantalizing tease was what they needed.

"Show me your stance."

She blinked up at him and frowned. "What?"

"Show me what you've got." He grinned at her raised brow. "I know what's under your clothes, Mir. I want to see how hard you hit." And he wanted to see under her clothes, but that would come later.

She grinned then. "You'll be sorry you asked."

He chuckled and pushed at her hips until she stepped back. "I'll enjoy every bit of it. Now get in your stance. I just want you to hit my palms. Not as hard as you're going to hit in a normal situation. I just want to get a feel for you." She licked her lips, and he held back a groan. "You know what I mean."

"Yeah, and I'm a little sad you don't want to feel me up the other way."

"Later, Mir. I promise I'll feel up every inch of you and even let you suck my dick."

She threw her head back and laughed, and he smiled. "You're a dork, but sure. You show me how to hit correctly, and I'll suck your dick. I like tasting you anyway."

He groaned out loud this time and adjusted himself in his shorts. "You're bad for my concentration, but I'll persevere. Anything to get that pretty mouth on my cock." She licked her lips once again, but he did his best to ignore it. "Now show me how good you are."

She put her feet in position then raised her fists to the correct height. He nodded then held up his palms. She crossed her body and hit his left palm with her right fist, and he grinned.

"Nice form. Again."

He let her get in two more crosses and then started her on jabs. She had great form, and though she wasn't putting all her weight behind it, she wasn't flinching when she hit skin. That was half the battle. It helped that he wasn't attacking her back. They'd practice that later.

When it looked like her arms were getting tired, he lifted his chin. "Okay, we can stop now. I like the way you look when you're punching back."

She rolled her eyes then shook out her arms. An odd light passed over her eyes, and he cursed himself. There was a reason they were practicing like this, and the fact that she even had to fight back at all made him want to kick someone's ass.

He pulled her close and hugged her to his body. When he rested his cheek on the top of her head, they both let out a sigh.

"I won't be a victim," she whispered.

"You aren't, baby. You never were. You fought back that night, too. You remember? You got yourself to safe places both times. This is all on Jack, and we're going to pray you never have to use any of what I'm teaching you down here."

She moved her arms then gripped his ass. "Well, I could always use the one-on-one time. You know what I mean? What if I had bad form? What would you do to punish me?"

He let out a little growl then backed away just enough so he could see the length of her. Apparently, they were done talking about Jack, and that was fine with him. He'd rather see how sweaty they could get when they arched against one another rather than punching a bag.

"On your knees," he growled.

Her eyes widened, but she went to her knees. He had the mats down so she wasn't kneeling on concrete, but he'd move her to the other padded area if she needed it. It didn't matter. As long as he had her lips wrapped around him, he'd be a happy man.

Her hands tugged at his shorts, but he pulled at her ponytail, forcing her gaze to his.

"The piercing is still in, but I want you to deepthroat. We'll be careful, but if you want, I can take it out. It's up to you."

She licked her lips then slowly pulled his shorts down to uncover his erection. "I want all of you, and then I want you and your piercing in me. It hits my G-spot perfectly, and I'm greedy."

He grinned then gripped the base of his cock. "I'm in

control here, Mir. I'll let you suck me, let you cup my balls, but I direct."

She sucked in a breath. "Like I'd have it any other way."

Fucking perfect. She was fucking perfect for him.

"Open your mouth."

She did so immediately, her tongue flat and ready for him.

He tapped her lower lip with his cock, careful not to hit her teeth with the piercing. If he took it out, he could be rougher when he was at the front of her mouth, but it was okay; he just liked the feel of her on him.

His hand cupped her jaw and opened her mouth wider. With care, he slid the tip of his dick in and out of her mouth, loving the way her pupils dilated on each stroke. With each pass, he went a little deeper, stayed a little longer. When he reached the back of her throat, she sucked in a breath, and he pulled out, not wanting her to gag. She hadn't yet when they'd been practicing her going deep, but he didn't want to hurt her.

"Cup my balls. Play with them."

He continued to slide in and out of her mouth, loving the way her tongue tapped his length on the way out. Her hands went to his balls, rolling them in her palms. When her fingernails scraped them, he pulled on her ponytail, fighting for control.

"Fuck, that feels good, baby."

She gasped when he pulled out, his dick wet from her mouth. "Let me finish."

"You want me to come down your throat? You sure you want me to do that rather than in your pussy?"

She grinned then squeezed his balls. His eyes crossed, and he gritted his teeth. "You have great recovery time, Decker. By the time you finish licking my pussy, you'll be ready to fuck me."

He cupped her face and tapped her cheek with his dick. "You're a dirty girl, Miranda Montgomery."

"Only for you."

Hell yeah, only for him.

"Get ready." He slid down her throat then fucked her mouth, careful not to pull back too hard and hit her teeth with his piercing.

When she squeezed his balls again, he shouted her name. He held her head still by keeping his hand in her hair then came down her throat. When he pulled back, she licked up and down his length, getting every last drip.

"Fuck, I love it when you clean my cock."

She grinned. "You better clean my pussy then."

"Shit, you and that mouth are going to get you in trouble."

"I like being in trouble if you're the one handing out punishments."

He chuckled then pulled her up so she was standing and crushed his mouth to hers.

The salty taste on her tongue only turned him on more. He gripped her ass and rocked her body against his.

"Take off that sports bra and show me those pretty pink nipples."

She took it off quickly—much faster than he thought possible, considering how tight it was, but, hey, they were ready. Instead of waiting for him to play with her breasts, she cupped herself and moaned.

"Holy fuck, you're so fucking hot, Mir. Tug at your nipples. Yeah, just like that. Roll them between your fingers."

He quickly divested himself of his clothes and toed off his shoes and socks. He licked his lips then pulled on her shorts, stripping them off her legs. She still wore her shoes, but it would take too long for him to deal with them. Instead, he knelt between her thighs and latched onto her clit.

"Decker!"

She put one leg on his shoulder, his tongue laving at her clit and her opening. He pulled back when she tilted. He looked up her body and into her eyes, loving the ecstasy on her face.

"Hold my other shoulder with one hand. Then I want you to keep playing with your nipples while I make you come on my face."

She nodded then went back to pinching and pulling. Oh yeah, she knew what she liked.

His hands were on her ass, spreading her so he could

get at that little rosette. With his eyes on hers, he took some of her juices and slid them back. Her eyes widened, and he grinned.

"Just a little right now, Mir."

"Is that the same as saying just the tip?"

He gave a rough chuckle then rubbed his beard on the inner silk of her thighs. "That's exactly what I'm saying. We'll try just the tip another night. Right now, I'm going to play with this little virgin hole of yours while I lick you up."

She nodded, and he knew he was lost.

He gently rubbed her before breaching her entrance with his index finger. She sucked in a breath, but he wasn't planning on going any farther. He just wanted her to know what it felt like. Patience would reap rewards for both of them.

He went back to her pussy, licking and sucking on her clit. When he hummed against her, her body tensed then shook. He kept lapping during her orgasm, loving the blush on her skin.

While she was still shaking, he pulled away and tugged her down so she was below him on the mat. He entered her in a single stroke, leaving them both breathless.

"Jesus, I forget how big you are."

He laughed then kissed her, thrusting in and out of her in a short, teasing rhythm. "So. Fucking. Perfect."

Her eyes widened, and he kissed her again, trying to make sure she knew he wanted her, wanted all of her.

When her shoes dug into his back, he moved to one forearm and lifted her ass with his free hand, all the while maintaining his rhythm.

"Play with your breasts, baby. I love when you do that."

She gave him a small nod, and her mouth parted, then she rolled her nipples between her fingers. He thrust again, harder and harder until she let out a little squeal, and her body bowed as she came. He couldn't hold on anymore, and he followed her, pumping hard one last time so he was deep within her to the root, filling her up and knowing that this was as close as he'd ever been to another person, as close as he would ever be.

Their chests heaved together, and her hands lazily went up and down his back.

"I'm still wearing my shoes."

He laughed then. "Well, it was a workout look for sure."

She rolled her eyes. "The next time you fuck me while I'm wearing shoes, it has to be the heels. Okay?"

He kissed her. "Deal."

As that image filled his mind, he thrust inside her, once again hard. Her eyes widened, and then she grinned.

"Oh yes, I *so* like working out with you."

"Anytime, Mir, anytime."

Chapter Eighteen

The suitcases on the floor didn't make sense. Meghan blinked once. Twice. Why were there three suitcases on the floor? She wasn't aware of Richard having a business meeting out of town. They weren't going on a vacation together; they hadn't been on one since their honeymoon.

It wouldn't be the first time he'd forgotten to mention that he was leaving, but then he usually told her to pack for him because he was so busy. He'd always said that, since she didn't have a job and only had to deal with the kids, she had more time to help him with things like that.

She'd always done so because it was easier than fighting.

So why were his suitcases on the floor?

In the back of her mind she knew what was going on,

knew that her world was coming to an end, but she didn't want to face that.

If she allowed her mind to form the thought, then it was really happening.

She swallowed hard and ran her hands over her slacks. She'd much prefer to be in jeans or a sundress, but she'd wanted to dress up for Richard since it was their anniversary.

Oh, that had to be it. Maybe he was surprising her with a trip to celebrate their eight years of marriage.

Even as she thought it, she knew it wasn't so, but she licked her lips and prayed she was wrong.

The sound of stomping feet, little girl screams, little boy giggles, and claws on hardwood reached her ears, and she paled. No, they couldn't see this. She didn't know what *this* was, but her babies couldn't be here for it. Her mother's instinct told her as much. She turned toward the sound, holding out her arms.

Sasha ran right to her with Cliff on her tail. Her baby girl wasn't crying, so they must have been playing a game. Their lab mix, Boomer, shuffled after them, taking his babysitting duties seriously. That dog loved her kids more than she'd ever thought possible. She was lucky Richard had let her keep him.

"Mommy! You're it! Tag!" Sasha giggled, and tears pricked Meghan's eyes. She ran her hand over her daughter's baby-soft hair and sighed.

She had to get the children in the backyard, or at least out of the living room.

"Dork, *I'm* it and chasing you," Cliff said, his smug smile flaring under bright eyes. He reached out and patted Sasha's cheek with such a soft caress Meghan had to blink away the tears. "Tag. You're it."

Sasha giggled again. "Okay. Mommy. You're it now."

Meghan nodded then pasted a smile on her face. "I'm it? Well, it looks like you're going to have to run away so I can chase you. Why don't the three of you go out in the backyard so we can play?"

She tried to keep her voice calm, but Cliff's all-too-intelligent eyes saw too much. He always saw too much.

The front door opened behind her, and she raised her chin. Too late. Always too late.

"Good. You're here. We can dispense with the formalities then."

Her husband's clipped tone grated on her nerves, but she did her best to ignore it. She turned on her heel, putting her hands on her children so the two of them were behind her.

"Richard," she said, her voice calm. "What are the bags for?"

Richard gave her one of his patented pitying looks, and something inside of her shriveled.

"You're really not that stupid, are you?" He shook his head. "Of course you are. You just can't take a hint. I have to spell everything out for you. Without me to tell you what to do, well, you'll fail, but I'm done." He met her eyes and smiled.

Actually smiled.

"I'm leaving you. I have a place set up for my things. My lawyer will call you to handle the proceedings. Don't worry, Meghan, I won't leave you with nothing. You gave me nothing but cheap bitchiness and bad sex for eight years, but I will pay you for it like the whore you are."

She sucked in a breath. Her children cried behind her.

"Get out," she said softly.

Richard chuckled. "What's that?"

"Get. Out." She grabbed two of the bags and shucked them at him. "Get out. You can leave. Just go and never talk to me like that in front of my children."

Cliff shuffled a bag behind her, setting it next to the other two. Her heart broke then. Shattered into a thousand pieces, but she wouldn't break fully. She wouldn't cry.

"Cliff, take Sasha and Boomer upstairs."

"Mommy!" Sasha wailed, but Cliff did as he was told.

Her brave, brave boy.

"They are *our* children, Meghan. Remember that." He took his bags and set them on the porch. "My lawyer will be contacting you. Don't break down and act like an idiot, Meghan. It's unbecoming."

With that, he closed the door quietly, but in her heart, it slammed. The echo bounced around until it became nothing.

Nothing.

She shook her head. She couldn't afford to break down, not yet. Instead, she called her mother, explained in soft words that Richard had left her.

No, she didn't want anyone to come over.

Tonight she just needed her babies.

Tomorrow she would deal with the details. It was, after all, what she was good at.

Tonight she would make sure her babies knew she loved them.

She fed them dinner—pizza since she didn't have the desire or energy to cook—gave them their baths and answered their questions as best she could, and held them until it was time for bed. They didn't talk of anything important, but she assured them she would be there no matter what.

She supposed that was the most important thing of all.

The children had heard Richard's words, had known he was gone. He hadn't been there in truth for years anyway.

When she went upstairs, she found their respective rooms empty, but the guest bed was filled with little children and a dog.

"We want to sleep in here. With you." Cliff's lower lip trembled, and she nodded. She hadn't wanted to sleep in her own bed anyway, and the children seemed to know that.

She tucked the kids in on either side of her and let Boomer lay on her feet. After reading and whispering nothings, the kids fell asleep. She couldn't, however. She wasn't sure she would be able to sleep again.

Instead, she quietly got out of bed and made her way to her bathroom. She ignored the large bed and the half-empty closet. Those would be things she'd deal with in the morning and the coming days.

She turned on the hot water and filled the bathtub, adding lavender oil and bubble bath to the tub so she could scent something other than betrayal.

When it filled, she sank into the tub, ignoring the blistering heat. She could barely feel it anyway. With the door closed and the steam filling the room around her, she let herself go. Her body shook with uncontrollable sobs as she wept.

She wept for what was lost.

What she'd never have again.

What she'd done wrong.

Happy Anniversary.

Chapter Nineteen

L uc Dodd turned off his truck and tapped his fingers on the steering wheel. He didn't know why he was so nervous about going in there and talking to people he'd known for years, or rather, people he'd known years ago. He'd moved back to Denver only a couple weeks ago, and in the time it had taken to set up his place and start looking for jobs, he knew he'd have to buck up and do what was right, not what was easy.

Oh, who was he kidding? Nothing about this was easy.

He'd left Denver for his own reasons, and the Montgomerys had been curious, but they were nice about him leaving them without an electrician. He was sure that they'd hired a new one or even a new set in the years he'd been gone. He just hoped there was room for him. There were only so many freelance jobs out there for a guy with his Master Electrician certification, but no business. He hadn't wanted to own his own business. That wasn't who he was. He also didn't want to work for the city for lousy pay and even lousier hours.

He could find another private company, but that's not what he was going to do. It felt wrong not to try and go back to work for the company that had fostered his career in his early days. He'd known them since he was in high school, coming around to study with the eldest Montgomery girl, Meghan. The Montgomerys had opened their doors and their arms, never concerned that their daughter was hanging out with a kid over a foot taller than her and way bigger. She'd been one of his best friends, although it had taken a while for him to learn that he wanted something more.

He'd been too late for that, and well...the rest was history.

He made sure he hadn't creased his resume then headed toward the front office of Montgomery Inc.

Wes stood at a desk in the front area, a frown on his face. "Storm? You know where Tabby put that invoice? Shit. She's going to kill me for fucking up her desk."

"Yes. Yes she will. Maybe you should just check your email. You know she probably sent it to you." Storm's voice came from the back, and Luc could hear the smile in it.

Wes ran a hand over his neat hair. "Shit. I'm not normally this disorganized, but she leaves for vacation, and I lose it." He looked up and froze, the tip of his ears blushing. Then he blinked, his mouth broadening into a wide smile.

"Jesus Christ. Luc?" He came around the desk and patted Luc on the back in a half hug.

Luc relaxed marginally at the welcome. "Some things never change around here," he teased.

Wes rolled his eyes. "Tabby runs our lives, and apparently I'm not as good as I thought I was."

"Someone mark this day on the calendar. Wes admitted to not being good at something," Storm said as he came out of the back room.

"Suck me."

"Uh, no," Storm said then hugged Luc. "Dude, I didn't know you were back in town. What brings you here?"

Luc shuffled his feet and sighed. "I'm here for a job actually."

Storm's eyes widened, and Wes smiled.

"Seriously?" Wes asked. "Hell yeah. Is that your resume?" Wes plucked it out of Luc's hands and starting studying it.

Storm gave Luc a look that saw too deep. "You're back for good? I mean in Denver. You're not planning on moving out again?"

Luc shook his head. "I'm home. I'm through running." He hadn't meant to say that last part, and Storm seemed clued in. Well hell.

"You've been around," Wes said then whistled. "I see

you're up to date on all your certifications for Denver and Colorado, so that's great. When can you start?"

Luc blinked. "Just like that?"

"Just like that," Storm said then grinned. Luc relaxed again. "You were one of us before, and now you're back. Why wouldn't we take you?"

Luc ran a hand over his face. "I've been so fucking nervous coming back."

Wes shrugged. "Don't be. We all need to do things on our own every once in awhile. You just did it for what, five years?"

"Eight," Luc corrected.

Storm narrowed his eyes and nodded. "You'll be happy to see Meghan then, I guess."

Damn, the man saw too much.

Wes let out a curse. "She'll be happy to see you with what's going on."

Luc turned sharply to the other twin. "What? What's wrong with Meghan?"

"That fucking bastard left her last night." Wes growled. "That little prick already had his lawyer call her, but we're going to handle it like a family. I have a friend who is a fucking shark of a divorce lawyer, so he's going to help Meghan. And well, Alex, too, if he'll let me."

Luc let out a curse. "Alex too?" Jesus, what was going on with the Montgomerys?

"I'll fill you in later if you want to talk over a beer," Wes said.

Luc wanted to, but something else was clawing at him. "I'm going to pass on that tonight, but maybe tomorrow? I have things to do."

Wes nodded. "Sounds good. Oh, and can you start tomorrow, too?" He grinned and Luc rolled his eyes.

"Yes, I'll be here so you can tell me what I need to do."

"Good, see you then. And, man, it's good to see you."

He said his goodbyes, aware that Storm was staring at him, and then, before he thought too hard, he found his way to Meghan's. He knew her address by heart since she sent Christmas and birthday cards every year, but he'd never been to this place. He hadn't had the courage, even after all these years.

He pulled into her driveway and cursed himself. What the fuck was he doing there? She didn't need him. She'd proved that years ago. But that was then, and now he was back and working for her family. He had to let her know he was here. At least as here as he could be.

He got out of his truck and made his way to the door, praying he was doing the right thing. He knocked then sucked in a breath when the door opened.

Jesus Christ, she'd gotten even more beautiful.

Her long brown hair flowed in waves down past her shoulders. Though her face was pale, the softness radiated from her pores. She had on an old shirt and jeans with a hole at the knee.

He'd never seen anything sexier.

"Luc?" she said on a breath. Her eyes filled, and he cursed.

"Oh shit, Meghan. I didn't mean to make you cry. I can leave." He took a step back, but she reached out and gripped his arm.

"No, don't go. Just...*Luc*. You're here."

"I...uh...stopped by Montgomery Inc. for a job, and well, they hired me. So I'm back."

"You're back," she said softly, tears sliding down her cheeks.

Unable to help himself, he brushed one away with his thumb. "Don't cry, Meg."

"Mom took the kids so I could be alone. I don't think I should be alone."

He cupped her face and nodded. "Want to make me some coffee and you can tell me about those babies of yours?"

She gave him a wobbly smile and nodded, taking a step back so he could walk in.

He knew it was a mistake to get close again, and the hauntingly beautiful pain that scattered in his bones reminded him of what he'd lost before.

He wasn't going to leave though. He was back in Denver, back with the Montgomerys. He just needed to know where he fit.

And with the crying beauty by his side, he knew that would be easier said than done.

Chapter Twenty

The pain was like nothing else, but she gritted her teeth and breathed through it. Miranda had done this before, after all, so it shouldn't have been such a big deal. She would not make a fool of herself in front of her family.

"How you holding up there, Miranda?" Austin asked, his voice soft, caring.

Damn the man and his tattoo gun.

Instead of cursing him, she looked over her shoulder and gave him a bright smile. Probably too bright from the way he grimaced, but whatever.

"Is Austin hurting you?" Maya asked as she looked over from her station. "If you'd have let me do it, I wouldn't have hurt you. That big lug is a sadist."

This time, Miranda's smile was real. "You did my other tattoo, you weirdo. And it hurt just as much as this one. I'm just not into needles." She would have said pain in general, but the memories of Decker's spankings were too new.

"From that blush on your face, I *really* don't want to know what you're thinking about," Maya teased.

Austin groaned and cursed. "For the love of God, please stop. I do *not* need to know. Now, Miranda, you ready for me to finish up here? This stack of school books is going to look awesome since it's going to be toppling over your Montgomery brand."

She nodded. "I'm glad that you're working it all into one piece. And once I figure out what nerdy math ink I want, we can add that to the other side."

Austin chuckled. "You're such a geek, but we love you."

Miranda smiled then held back a wince as he went back to work. While she loved the look of ink, she wasn't as into the process as her siblings. There wasn't anything wrong with that, but at some point, she might have to take a break. Talk about being a wimp.

Austin and Maya shot back barbs to one another while Callie, the newest member of the team, added a few of her own. The shop really was a family of its own and added on to the other Montgomerys, Miranda counted herself lucky.

When her dad came into the shop, she blinked back tears. They'd told her he was on his way to finishing up his treatments, and the outlook was good, but that didn't mean it was easy. From his build, it looked liked he'd lost a good twenty pounds or more. He looked frail, yet there was that inner strength she knew he possessed—the same kind that he'd passed on to each of his children.

Since she was in the chair and couldn't move, he came to her, a bright smile on his face.

"You look like you're having a fun time," he said, his voice that deep baritone that had soothed her hurts when she was a young girl. He ran a hand through her hair, and she smiled again.

"I am." She winced as Austin dug into the shading.

"Liar," her dad whispered, and she had to hold back a laugh.

"Don't make her move, Dad, or I'll have to work longer."

Miranda froze, and both men laughed. "You two are mean."

"Nah, we just love you." Her dad patted her cheek.

"What are you doing here? Not that I don't love seeing you, I just didn't know you'd be dropping by."

Harry shrugged. "I was bored at home, and I wanted to give your mom time that had nothing to do with caring for me." He grinned, but Miranda saw the sadness in his eyes. Her mom and dad were tough as nails, but sickness hurt even the strongest people.

It didn't look like he wanted to talk about treatment or himself, so she let that slide. They'd talk about it later at his house.

"So, what is Mom doing?"

Harry grinned then. "She's getting a massage with Sierra. Those two ladies need it." Something in the way he winked at Austin had her leaning forward. Thankfully, Austin had been adjusting the needle at the time.

"Wait. What's going on?" She looked over her shoulder at a blushing Austin. Something clicked, and she squealed. "Sierra's pregnant, isn't she?"

"Oh my God! You've been hiding another baby?" Maya came running to Austin's cubicle, and Harry started laughing.

"Sorry, son," he said, not sounding sorry at all.

Austin sighed then put the tattoo gun down. "You all are going to get me in trouble. She wanted to be here when you guys found out."

Miranda bounced in her seat then scrambled so she could hug him. "I'm so freaking happy for you, and I'll promise I'll be this excited when I see Sierra, too."

Austin pulled back and pinched the bridge of his nose. "I swear to God, Maya Montgomery, if you tell *anyone* about this, I will beat you. Got me?"

Maya rolled her eyes but looked a little sad as she did it. "I'm sorry. I'm a gossip. I will work on being better. And my first goal is to keep this a secret until you guys tell the rest of us. Which will be when, tonight?"

Miranda snorted at the hope in her sister's eyes. "Yeah, sorry. It'll have to be soon because I don't think I can keep this from Decker."

Austin leveled a look at her. "It's still weird to hear you saying things like that about him."

She shrugged. "Get over it because I don't see things changing any time soon."

It was a bold thing to say, and she immediately regretted it. But honestly, she was *happy* with him. He was starting to talk about things a month or two in advance, which always was a good thing. He'd finally told her about his dad showing up at his place and why he'd been so remote that day. It killed her that she couldn't do anything about it, but the fact that he was talking about it with her was a good step in the right direction.

Her dad rubbed her shoulder. "I'm happy for you. Happy for all my kids." An odd light flickered in his eyes. "It's nice to see everything we went through when we were raising the eight—no, nine—of you was all worthwhile."

She swallowed hard and refused to meet Maya's or Austin's gazes. No doubt once she did, she'd break down, and today was a day for happiness and ink, not regrets.

"Okay, Austin, let's finish up my tattoo, or I'm going to run away and not let you near me with a needle again."

Austin let out a soft laugh. "Sure, hon, but remember, Maya gets the right side and then I get to do another one on you so we're even. So get thinking."

She winced. Their competitive edge was going to hurt, but at least she'd have amazing ink in the process.

By the time they were finished and she had a shake

over at Taboo with her dad, it was getting late, and she had to get home and get some grading done. She and Decker didn't have plans that night, and she was fine with getting caught up with work so it wouldn't be hanging over her head when she was with him.

The fact that he'd given her a key that morning had put a rosy haze on everything she was doing, and she couldn't help but do a little mental cheer at what was happening. The man she loved, the man she'd *always* loved, wasn't running away. He actually seemed *happy* to be with her and made her feel like she was beautiful, like she was treasured.

She couldn't ask for anything more.

At least not right then.

She pulled into her parking lot and winced as she pulled on the tape covering her back. Austin said she hadn't bled too much, thankfully, but she was still leaking plasma into the covering he'd taped to her. Not fun, but with two tattoo artists in the family, she at least knew about the importance of aftercare.

When she got out of her car, she inhaled the crisp scents of the mountain air mixing with that of the trees. It would be fall soon, and she couldn't wait. She loved the temperature change that would eventually lead to snow. Well, knowing the way Denver weather worked, that could happen within the next few days in September since one never knew what was happening next.

She took another step toward her home, and the hair

on the back of her neck prickled. She turned, only to see the front of a car coming right at her.

Before she had the chance to scream or duck, the car hit her.

She couldn't feel the pain, couldn't feel the impact.

No, instead all she felt was the air getting knocked out of her and then her body slowly rising in the air. She felt the glass of the windshield break below her body before she rolled to the ground.

She blinked twice, and then the pain hit her like an aftershock. A thousand knives stabbed at her body, fileting her skin, igniting her flesh on fire. Her bones ached as if someone had shattered them to pieces.

Her head whirled, her body fighting off nausea.

She tried to scream, but all that came out was a bloody cough before she saw only darkness.

She blinked her eyes open. A man stood by her head, his dress shoes shiny under the lights.

The punch to her face knocked her out again.

"Multiple breaks, contusions, and possible internal injuries."

Miranda tried to moan when she woke, but nothing came out.

"Miss? Miss? She's coming to. Miss? Can you tell us who we can call?"

"Decker," she whispered.

The person, maybe a nurse, she couldn't tell—it hurt too much to think—nodded then went off to do something.

Miranda couldn't think. They moved her, prodded her, but she couldn't feel them. She could feel only the pain. Why did it hurt so much? Why couldn't she just go to sleep? It would be better if she could just sleep.

"Found her ID and emergency contact info. We'll call Marie Montgomery now. You were in a car accident, Miranda. We're going to give you something more for the pain, but it might knock you out."

Miranda closed her eyes.

Let it come. The pain was too much. She wasn't fully awake though. She couldn't give up, but sleep sounded so much better.

So. Much. Better.

DECKER SLAMMED THROUGH THE HOSPITAL DOORS, aware he looked like he was bat-shit crazy, but he didn't give a fuck. He'd missed a damn call because he'd been on the phone dealing with something for the job site and had lost it when he'd called back.

Fuck.

Griffin had called him immediately after, letting him

know what hospital to go to and the fact that they knew *nothing* about Miranda's condition.

She'd been hit by a fucking car.

In her own parking lot.

He stormed to the receptionist desk and planted his hands on the wood. "I need to see Miranda Montgomery."

The nurse behind the desk sighed but didn't look overly frightened at seeing a man his size yell and shout.

"Are you family?"

He opened his mouth to say yes, but stopped himself. Before he'd have thought so in a heartbeat, now he wasn't so sure. She was *his*, but damn it, it was different now.

"He's with us," Griffin said as he walked up to the desk. "Thanks, Jaycee."

The woman nodded then went back to her paperwork.

Decker swallowed hard then followed Griffin back to the waiting area. He didn't say anything—he couldn't. If he'd spoken just then, he might break down, and he couldn't do that. All he knew when his friend had called before was that he needed to come to the hospital because Miranda was hurt. She'd been rushed off to surgery before anyone had a chance to see her.

He had no idea what was broken and what had been cut or bruised. All he knew was she was lying on a table somewhere with doctors trying to fix her, and he was outside, helpless and useless.

He never thought he'd care about someone enough to feel this broken, this shattered. She had sneaked into his heart, and he was afraid if he lost her, he'd lose himself.

No, he knew that already.

She was his everything, the reason he had to be happy about his future, and now he had no idea what would happen next. God, he just wanted to find a way to make everything better, but he didn't have a magic wand. His hands broke things, molded them into something else, but they weren't meant to heal.

He was useless to her.

The waiting room was filled with Montgomerys.

When one of their own was in pain, they rallied. No matter what was going on in the rest of their lives, they put their worries to the side and cared for one another. He'd always envied that as a kid, and right now, he was so fucking grateful she had this, and had them.

Austin stood off in the corner, his gaze out the small window that served as another light source in the cramped room. A pale Sierra stood to his side, her head resting on his shoulder. She faced the room though, her eyes wet, her face drawn.

Leif sat in the chair next to Austin with Sasha on his lap. The boy read to the little girl, his words soft and low amongst the people in the room who worried about what they didn't know. Cliff sat next to Leif, his head on the other boy's shoulder. Decker wasn't sure if any of the three kids knew what was going on, but they'd all been through some hell of their own, so the sadness couldn't have been lost on them.

Meghan sat next to Cliff, her hands on her lap. She looked like she hadn't slept in weeks, and knowing her own personal torment, that could have been the case. Decker was surprised to see Luc there, sitting next to Meghan, but neither of them spoke. Luc had been part of the Montgomery clan years ago, and now that he was back, he seemed to have slipped right back into his old role.

Right now, Decker didn't care about anyone or anything, not when he didn't know what was going on with the woman he loved.

Loved, yet never told.

He was surprised to see Alex there, standing with a cup he hoped was filled with coffee in his hand. He shouldn't have been surprised though. While Alex might have seemed selfish lately, he loved his little sister something fierce.

Maya paced one side of the room, her hands clenched in fists. Each time she came back to the corner, her friend Jake would hug her then push her back so she could pace again. The other man looked ready to commit murder, and Decker felt that kindred spirit within him.

Wes and Storm stood next to the coffee area, their heads close together while they talked to one another. They spoke in hushed whispers, but again, Decker didn't care. All he wanted was Miranda, the one person he couldn't see.

"Decker," Marie said before she launched herself at him.

He caught her with ease, and he crushed her to his chest. She sobbed into his shoulder, and he had to blink back tears of his own as his throat grew suspiciously tight. The woman, who was more a mother to him than his own mother had ever been, always jumped in his arms like she was a young girl. It had started when Decker had shot up five inches seemingly overnight and he could no longer hug her the way he did when he was younger. He hadn't been used to hugs and came to need hers more than he'd realized. There was something about the way Marie hugged him that conveyed all the love and acceptance that came with the Montgomery family bond. Since he couldn't throw his arms around her anymore, she'd taken over and done the same.

He loved her so fucking much, and now her daughter, his Miranda, was hurt, and there was nothing they could do.

"I'm so glad you're here, honey," she whispered then patted his cheek. "You need a shave, but all my boys do."

He gave a watery chuckle then shook his head. "You're the only woman I'd shave for."

She raised a brow. "Am I?"

He sighed. "No. I'd do anything for her, Marie." He sucked in a breath. "Anything."

"I know, baby." Her lip wobbled, and Harry came up

behind her. She turned and hugged him. She didn't cry, but she did take deep breaths.

"What's the word?" Decker asked.

Harry sighed. "A car hit her, and then, according to witnesses, the man got out of the car and beat her."

Decker cursed and turned his back so they wouldn't see the murder on his face.

"Jack," he gritted out.

"Jack," Griffin growled. "The police are looking for him."

Decker snorted. "Yeah, because they did such a fucking good job before."

"They have witnesses and evidence now," Harry said, his voice low but smooth. He wasn't going to ignite the masses, but damn, Decker didn't know how the man did it. "I know the justice system fucked up, and believe me, we will be working on what we can do to achieve our own justice, but right now, we need to focus on Miranda. Jack will get what's coming to him, but our baby girl in there needs our support."

Decker swallowed hard then turned back around. Harry, despite the fact that he looked so much older because of his disease, held his head high.

"I'm not giving up," Decker answered back. "But fuck. I hate not knowing."

"We just need to wait," Austin said. "Have faith in the doctors here."

Decker nodded then went to one of the chairs to sit

down. If he stood, he'd pace, and then he'd make the others jumpy. Maya was already doing that.

Hours passed, and Meghan took all three children home. Luc stayed for a bit then left a couple hours later. Everyone took turns going on coffee runs and to get food. They made sure Sierra and Harry were taking care of themselves while the rest of them pretended to eat.

Decker wouldn't be able to focus until he could see Miranda safe and whole. But he wasn't entirely sure that would happen.

The doors to the surgical suite opened, and a man in scrubs walked out. Decker's stomach clenched, and he stood up. The other Montgomerys stood around him. Marie put her hand in his, and he squeezed back.

"Are you Miranda Montgomery's family?" the doctor asked.

"We all are," Harry said. "How's our baby girl?

The doctor nodded then ran a hand over his capped head. "She made it through surgery, but I'll be honest and say it was touch and go for a bit there. She had lacerations to her liver and spleen. We had to remove the latter, but she will live a normal life without it as long as we take a few precautions. She has a broken wrist and a dislocated shoulder. Both legs were broken, and we were able to set them without surgery. She will be in casts for a while. There wasn't any damage to her spine, thankfully, but she has sustained head trauma. We won't know the extent of brain injury, if any, until she comes out of the anesthesia."

The doctor went on and on about things that Decker knew he'd ask about later, but all he cared about was that she was *alive*.

Holy fuck, it had been bad, worse than he'd ever imagined, but she was *alive*.

"When can I see her?" Decker asked, his voice gruff. He'd apparently interrupted the doctor, but whatever.

Harry cleared his throat. "Yes, when can we see her?"

The doctor sighed, but nodded. "Tomorrow at the earliest. You all can go home now and get some rest. You can come back tomorrow and take turns seeing her."

Decker went back to the chair, knowing he wouldn't be leaving. The Montgomerys took their turns thanking the doctor before talking amongst themselves about who would be staying. He didn't care as long as they didn't try to make him leave. He'd be there until he saw her. There would be no moving him.

Eventually, Storm came and sat next to him, his forearms resting on his legs. "Everyone is going home to sleep. I'm staying since I'm the least likely to piss you off and cause you to yell or punch someone."

Decker lifted a brow. "You're doing a hell of a good job so far."

Storm shrugged then leaned back. "The others will take turns. We're not leaving her alone. Especially with Jack out on the loose."

Decker nodded. "I'll kill him if I see him."

"Another reason I'm here. You're no good to her behind bars."

The barb dug at him, though he knew Storm was right. His dad wasn't behind bars right now, as it was. But fuck, he'd gone over the edge once already. Now they had people drawing straws to see who could piss him off the least? How close was he to turning into his father? He already had the man's hands, the man's temper. What would break him? What would be the last straw?

The fact that he could easily see himself killing Jack without any remorse didn't worry him like it should have. Instead, it just showed him the man he truly was.

The man his father had made.

More hours passed, and when morning came, a shift change came with it. A new nurse walked into the waiting room and told them that one person could see Miranda now, and then they could take turns.

"Go ahead and see her," Storm said, taking out his phone. "You're not going to be functional until you do. I know the family is on their way, but I'll let them know what's going on."

Decker nodded then woodenly followed the nurse to Miranda's room. She was still in the ICU, but would be moved to a regular floor later if she remained stable. He wiped his hands with antibacterial crap at the door then took two steps into the room and froze.

Holy Mother of God.

Miranda's face was black and blue. She had casts on three of her limbs and a sling on the other. What skin that wasn't covered by bandages or the bedding was bruised or red. Her eyes were closed, and because she was sleeping, he knew that her pain level was manageable. When she woke up though, fuck, it wasn't going to be good.

He walked to her side and reached out for her uncasted hand, only to stop and pull himself back. There wasn't a place he could touch her and not hurt her. He let the tears fall into his beard, and he sucked in a breath.

The only thing he could think of was the redness on her ass, the bruises on her hips when he'd taken her hard against the wall, in his bed, and on his floor. He'd been so fucking rough with her, and yet look how fragile she was.

How was he any better than Jack?

Just because his marks on her had been hidden under her clothes didn't make them any less painful.

He sank down into the chair next to her, knowing that he had to end this. What would happen when he snapped? What would happen when he finally turned into his father? He couldn't be the person who hurt Miranda like this. He couldn't be the one who gave her more pain.

It felt as if someone was ripping his soul from his body, but he knew it was for the best. If he didn't leave now, he'd only hurt her in the future.

He stood up on shaky legs and leaned over, gently brushing a clear patch of skin with his lips.

"I love you so fucking much, Miranda. That's why I have to do this. I hope you understand. I know you're going to hate me, but it's for the best."

He knew she couldn't hear him and wouldn't understand when she woke up and he wasn't there.

But he couldn't be the person that she needed him to be.

He'd write her a note, tell her the reasons she was better off without him, and then find a way to live again.

With that, he walked out of the room, past the waiting room without stopping to talk to Storm. He and the family would figure it out eventually. They were better off without him. They all were.

Decker was meant to be alone. Though the Montgomerys had been a safe haven, they weren't for him.

It was time they realized that.

Decker finally had.

Chapter Twenty One

Miranda lifted her arm then cursed. Austin was right there, holding out her juice cup and putting the straw to her lips. She tentatively wrapped her lips around the straw and sucked, ignoring the pain in her head when she did so. She didn't have a concussion, but she had one hell of a headache.

Everyone kept saying she was lucky to be alive, yet a week later, she wasn't so sure. No, she couldn't be that melancholy, that depressed, but it sure hurt a hell of a lot to heal. Every inch of her body hurt to move. Well, that was when she was allowed to move at all anyway. Some things were strapped down or in a cast, so she could do no more than wiggle her toes in some instances. As long as she didn't move too fast, or move at all, she was fine.

Living again without being able to move was going to suck.

Yes, it was only temporary, but she didn't know for how long. The doctors were being very cagey when it came to timetables at this point because they didn't want her to overdo it. They only said it would take more time than she probably thought and to work on resting her body before she got to the next step. Her parents probably knew more details, but they were keeping them from her. They at least had the ability to research recovery times and methods, but she was locked in bed. That wouldn't last long, though, since she would be demanding answers soon. No one wanted her to worry and had been very vague, but positive. Too bad she liked numbers. Numbers kept her sane. She needed an end goal, and the doctors being vague because they probably didn't know themselves wouldn't help her recover.

After she was finally able to stay awake for more than an hour or two at a time, she might be able to find out when physical therapy would start and when she would be herself again.

She swallowed hard, struggling to keep the tears back.

She wasn't sure she'd ever truly be herself again.

God, she was so fucking scared. She honestly thought that had been the end of it.

She barely remembered the car hitting her, thankfully. She remembered only the confusion, then the fear when she was flying. She didn't remember the pain. Well, she remembered *some* of it, but that came only in spurts. Even then, the flaring agony that came in dreams was from after the crash...with Jack. She only remembered his shoes so she wouldn't have ever known it was him for sure without the witnesses who had screamed and run toward the two of them.

She didn't remember the witnesses. The first thing she remembered was waking up to find her mom and dad in the room, each holding a finger on her hand. They had been afraid to touch anything else, and from the look of her, she hadn't blamed them. She wasn't a pretty sight.

Her skin was now a lovely shade of black and blue, with little splashes of purple and green thrown in. Her stomach hurt, and she couldn't bend since she had a surgical wound from stem to stern. She had no spleen, and her liver was still healing. It could have been so much worse, though, and she knew it. Her heart, lungs, and kidneys were all okay.

Thank God.

"Miranda? Are you in pain? Should I call the doctor?"

She shook her head then winced. "I'm okay. Well, as long as I don't shake my head so hard."

Austin sighed then sat down in the chair next to the bed. "They said you're lucky that you didn't end up with a concussion, but with all the healing you're doing, you're bound to feel like shit. Here, sip some more juice. You're probably still dehydrated, which isn't helping your head."

She sipped then closed her eyes. "I wish I knew when we could break out of this joint."

Austin grunted. "Even if you break out, you're not

going home. You're coming to one of our houses. Probably mine since we have the space, and we don't want to tire Mom and Dad out."

"Ugh. I hate this. But yeah, I don't really want to step foot in that apartment again. You know?" Let alone the parking lot. Too many bad memories. She might have stayed at Decker's place...but he wasn't there.

She swallowed hard and put that thought from her head. Nope. Not going to go there.

"So you're okay with our place until you're healed and find another place of your own?"

She sighed. "Sierra's pregnant, Austin. Maybe I should stay with Griffin."

"Griffin is too angry to be nice to live with right now."

She winced then curled her lip. "Well, he has a right to be angry. I'm not too happy either."

Austin sighed. "I'm sorry, honey. I didn't mean to bring that up."

"Bring what up? The giant elephant in the room? Like the fact that the man I love took one look at me and ran away with his tail between his legs? Or the fact that he didn't have the common courtesy to tell me to my face? No, he ran out in the dark of night—okay, it was the morning, but whatever—and didn't bother to tell me he was leaving me."

Tears pricked her eyes, and she bit her lip, refusing to cry over him.

"He left a note," Austin said softly.

Yes. The note.

"A goddamn note, Austin. He said he wasn't good enough for me. He said he was afraid he'd turn into his father or Jack because he wasn't a good man. Well, fuck that, Austin. His words in that note were the most honest and open things he'd ever said to me, and yet they're all a crock of shit. He ran away because he was scared, and he left me alone." The tears came this time, and she sniffed. Crying hurt her head, and she honestly didn't want to cry over him. It hurt her heart too much...hurt everything.

"I'd beat him up for you, but Mom said you'd yell at me for that."

She let out a soft laugh then moaned when her stomach ached in protest. "Don't make me laugh. It pulls my incision."

Austin's eyes widened, and he shut his mouth.

She laughed again at his expression then winced.

"It's okay, Austin. I'm going to hurt for a while, and there's nothing we can do about it other than wait for my body to heal. As for you beating him up, yeah, I'd yell at you. First, I still love him, and it pisses me off that I do. Second, don't you think we've had enough violence in this family?"

Austin had the grace to look ashamed then leaned back in his chair. "He might come around, Miranda. He got scared. Hell, we all did."

"But none of you ran away."

Austin sighed. "None of us have the history he does. I

know his dad is out of jail again, and he's bothering Decker. His mom is still staying at the house, and Decker can't do anything to get her out. He's being pulled in a thousand directions, and he made a mistake."

She swallowed hard then leveled a look at her big brother. "That's all true, but it doesn't take away the fact that he hurt me. He *hurt* me while I was already down. He left without a word. I always knew that what we had might be temporary, but I didn't know he'd be so cruel about it. God, I *hate* his parents. Hate them. Yet he's *not* them. And until he realizes that, he's never going to be with me. Not fully."

Austin studied her face. "You're not a little girl anymore."

"No. No, I'm not. I'm a grown woman who got the crap beat out of her and then got kicked again. I'm done being a victim, Austin. I'm done being left behind."

Her brother ran a hand over his face and cursed. "Jesus, I want to kill that bastard."

"Which one?" she asked dryly.

Austin glared. "Both. One broke your body, the other your heart, and no one gets to do that to my little sister. Decker is lucky he was once considered family. That's the only reason I'm not knocking on his door right now kicking his ass. That and you don't want me to. As for Jack? He's behind bars and hard to get to."

She closed her eyes and swallowed hard. She didn't want to think about either man, but the fact that Jack was in jail made it easier to sleep at night. The police had caught him the next morning. He'd been in a cabin he owned three hours outside of Denver. The idiot honestly didn't think anyone would check to see what his investments were. Though considering how the original team on her case had fucked up royally, Jack probably thought he could get away with anything.

It turned out he got away with a lot in his life.

Apparently he'd hit his previous girlfriend. A lot. To the point that he'd left town and found a new job and a new life so he could run from getting caught. When Miranda's story had come forward, the other girl came out of the woodwork as well. Miranda was sure there would be other women that the blond man with bright blue eyes had hurt in his past. Now the man was getting justice, but at the cost of Miranda's health. He was being charged with attempted murder along with a few other things that Miranda didn't want to think about just then.

He wouldn't be hurting her again.

He wouldn't be hurting anyone.

The school had called, along with Mrs. Perkins of all people. The older English teacher seemed like she wanted to see Miranda fail, yet had wanted to help in any way she could. Everyone had rallied around her and told her that when she was ready, her job would be there. Her students apparently missed her, and while they were getting along with the sub, the woman wasn't her. When Miranda could hold her head up while not getting a headache, she'd warm at the thought.

She had a future to look forward to. She'd heal, and she'd be as whole as she could be with a shattered heart. Her job was there, and she'd find a way to walk through the halls without thinking of the man who'd put her in the hospital.

One day she might even be able to go on without thinking of the man who'd left her broken in a hospital bed.

She knew Decker had his own things to deal with, just like she knew that he'd left, not because she wasn't worthy, but because *he* thought he wasn't worthy.

While she might have been able to forgive him for leaving her when she wasn't in pain, wasn't almost dying, she didn't know if she could now.

Everything she thought she wanted with him had gone out the window, and now she had to pick up the pieces and move on.

If only it were that easy.

If only she still didn't love him.

But love wasn't enough. Decker had proven that.

FOR THE SECOND TIME THAT MONTH, DECKER FOUND himself in the hospital. His head ached from lack of sleep, not booze. He hadn't had a drink since the last time he'd walked through these doors and seen the woman he loved broken and bleeding.

He'd left her because he hadn't wanted to turn into his old man, and drinking his pain away would have only set him on the long path of darkness.

It was a step, but he'd already fucked up any chance of happiness. Now he just had to learn to live with what he had. He'd been doing that for years anyway; he would do it again. That taste of perfection with Miranda was over, and it was his fault.

But it was for her own good.

He'd only hurt her more, and she'd been hurt enough as it was.

Now he found himself once again in the hospital, but not for Miranda. No, now he was walking through the halls toward the other woman in his life, although, if he thought about it, she hadn't been a part of his life in far too long.

Though she should have been, goddamn it.

He'd gotten the call from the emergency room telling him that his mother was in the hospital. Apparently, Frank had beaten her so badly that there was no way to hide the bruises. Decker wasn't sure how his mom had even ended up in the place to begin with since she was usually so good at ignoring the pains. It hurt him to no end that she couldn't or wouldn't fight for herself. Decker was old enough to fight for her, yet she wouldn't ask for help, wouldn't take the help he offered. He just prayed that one day she'd realize that she didn't have to be with Frank... and that day wouldn't be too late.

He walked up to the reception desk and asked for Francine Kendrick. This time, he *was* family, though only through blood.

While last time he'd been frantic, his body stiff, his voice a low growl, this time he approached with more resignation. He didn't want to see what his mother would look like. He hated the fact he felt so helpless. There was nothing he could do short of kidnapping his mother to keep her away from his father. Even then, he thought that wouldn't be enough. Frank had done a number on Francine's mind, and Decker didn't know the answer. She came from a family where a woman stood by her husband no matter what. Vows were vows and were meant to be kept.

It didn't matter that those vows might one day kill her.

The nurse walked him back to her room. Apparently, whatever had happened wasn't as bad as Miranda's attack.

Jesus.

He could still picture Miranda's pale face under dark bruises. He'd heard at the job site that Miranda had been allowed to go to Griffin's house to live while she recovered. According to Luc, she had planned on staying at Austin's, but with the baby coming and Sierra having problems with the pregnancy already, she'd felt better at Griffin's.

The fact that he still worked for Wes and Storm made things awkward as hell, but with Tabby back from her forced vacation, she'd turned into the mediator. Wes wouldn't speak with him but passed notes through Tabby. Storm talked with him only about work then left him alone. Luc, alone, spoke to him like he wasn't the asshole he was, but Decker wasn't sure how long that would last.

He knew it would be best for him to pack up and find another job. Leaving Denver might even be better so he didn't hurt the Montgomerys more than he already had. He was a fucking Kendrick, and he knew things got worse before they, if ever, got better.

"Decker. You're here."

His mother's small voice hit him in the solar plexus, and he took a deep breath, steadying himself. He walked the rest of the way into the room and did his best to keep his face neutral.

Frank had done a number on her face and had broken her arm. Decker wasn't sure what else was wrong, but those were the things visible. That was too much as it was.

"Mom. Jesus. Are you in pain?"

She shook her head then winced. "I'll be fine. They have me on the good stuff that takes care of things. Decker. I need your help."

Hope burned through his chest, and he took three large steps to his mother's side. He picked up her free hand and let out a breath.

"Thank God. Okay, you can stay with me. I'll keep you safe while we file charges against Frank. Then we'll figure out the next steps. I'm here for you, Mom. Okay?"

She looked confused then pulled her hand away. "No, Decker. I fell."

His face shut down, and he slowly stood up, unbelieving. "You fell," he said softly, his voice emotionless. "That's a lie, and you know it."

She blinked back tears and shied away from him. He cursed and took another step back. She was so fucking afraid of Frank but wouldn't do anything about it. Now she looked at him like he was the same monster.

Maybe he was, but damn it, he couldn't let his mother continue on like this.

"I...I got the wrong kind of beer. It was right next to the one on sale, and I got confused. It's okay, honey, it won't happen again. But I need your help."

He'd heard this story before, heard it countless times when he'd been a kid. Why couldn't she see what the old man was doing? Why wasn't Decker enough to help her?

"Mom. Let me help you."

"You can, honey. You can. The police are looking for your dad. They want to charge him for this, and he's going to be real mad about it. I need your help with bail. You know I hate to ask for money, but I need help with your dad."

Whatever hope he had in his heart that came from that scared little boy broke inside him. She'd picked her husband over her son. No matter how many times Frank put her in the hospital, she would always choose him.

Decker had no idea how to break the cycle. He only knew his place.

He'd be the haven that she'd never reach for.

He'd make sure she knew he'd be there and try to find a way for her to get out, but unless she tried...

Everything would be lost.

"Mom. I'm not going to do that."

Her face fell, and he felt like he'd been punched. The look in her eyes...damn it. He was *not* his father.

He blinked.

He wasn't his dad.

Holy shit.

What had he done?

What had he done to Miranda?

"Decker, honey, I need you."

Shaken, he swallowed hard and took another step back. "I can't, Mom. If you want out, if you need a place to be safe, then I'm here. But I'm not going to help the man who put you here. I'm not going to help you get hurt again."

With that, he left his mother weeping in her bed. Maybe this time she'd ask for help that meant help for her and not the man who they both hated. Maybe this time it would be different.

Decker might not have hope, but he had the ability to not give up.

At least that's what he thought.

He'd given up on Miranda. No, that wasn't right. He'd

given up on himself, and he'd ruined it all. He'd walked away when she needed him the most, and there was no coming back from that. Even if she still wanted him, she'd never trust him again, and he didn't blame her.

He'd ruined it because he was scared.

He blamed it on his old man and his scars, but that was a cop-out. He'd ruined it all because he'd been afraid, and now he'd never forgive himself.

By the time he made it home, he was sick to his stomach and his hands shook. He didn't know what was coming, didn't know what he'd do next, but he knew it couldn't go on like this. If he spent the rest of his days hiding and scared, he'd become the one man who'd always frightened him, and then he wouldn't be a man at all.

He had no idea what to do next.

He'd thought he wasn't worthy of Miranda before, but now he knew that was even more the case.

He'd *left* her.

Yes, he wasn't his father, but the fact that he'd left her made whatever he did that much harder to come back from.

There was no coming back from that.

With a sigh, he got out of his truck and headed inside. Gunner came in through the doggie door and barked while dancing around Decker's legs. Decker leaned down and gave his dog a full-body rub. It was nice to see at least one person—dog or no—that was happy to see him. Actually, Gunner had been a bit depressed in the couple weeks

Miranda had been away. It seemed that she had charmed more than one male in this house.

And then Decker had gone and ruined it.

Something knocked into the door, and Decker frowned. Gunner growled by his side, and he shushed him.

"Go to the pantry," he ordered, pointing at the doorway. Gunner didn't look pleased, but followed directions.

Something was wrong, and Decker didn't want his dog hurt by whatever it was. Years of trying to protect those in his circle had taught him that.

Something smashed into the door that sounded like glass, and Decker sighed. Instead of going out there and facing whatever the fuck was going on, he called the cops. They told him they were on his way and to stay inside.

His front window shattered.

The glass sprayed into his living room, and he ducked behind his kitchen island as glass showered the floor.

"Boy! Get your fucking ass out here. I need your fucking help."

The man was a fucking idiot. A Class A idiot who was on the run from the police and decided to scream his presence at the top of his lungs. Decker stood, grabbing a rolling pin on his way. He wasn't about to grab a knife. With the way the drunk son of a bitch stumbled into his house, Decker would be the one more likely to get cut than the intruder.

"What the hell, Frank."

"Boy, don't you backtalk me. I need you to hide me. The cops are on my tail."

How the man had eluded them thus far, Decker didn't know. What he would do, though, was make sure the old man stayed put. The cops would be there soon, and hopefully, breaking and entering would extend any sentence the old man was likely to get.

"You can't just break into my house. You're not welcome here. You never were. And when the cops catch you, I won't help you. You deserve to be behind bars. You deserve to go to fucking hell."

Frank wavered on his feet. "I helped raise you, boy. You have to help me."

"No. I really don't. I'm done with you. I'm done thinking that you can control my life, my actions. Even when I thought I was through with you, you were still there in the back of my mind fucking up my life."

"You can't blame me for all your problems. You lost that little piece of Montgomery ass on your own."

"Can't deny that, but you're done haunting my thoughts, my actions. I'm not you. I've never been the man you are, and I'll never be."

The sirens in the distance grew louder, and Frank's eyes widened. "You son of a bitch." The man lunged, and Decker moved out of the way, letting him fall to the ground. Frank got back up again, swayed, and then tried to punch Decker.

Decker ducked out of the way then took Frank by the arm, pinning him to the wall.

"We're done," he growled. "Done."

Frank slammed his head back, knocking Decker in the chin. Decker staggered back and threw up his hands as Frank tried to hit him again.

The cops broke the door down, shouting for everyone to get to the floor. Frank lunged one more time, but the biggest cop took him down before Decker got hit.

It was over.

It had to be.

By the time the cops took his statement and hauled Frank off in handcuffs, Decker was ready to sleep for a few days. Instead, he boarded his window up and explained what had happened to the neighbors. They offered condolences and didn't look at him like he was scum. In fact, their derision was reserved for his father, not for him.

Maybe if he'd figured that out sooner, he wouldn't have lost the only person who'd ever mattered to him.

No, that wasn't quite true. Other people mattered a whole hell of a lot, but he'd only fallen in love with one of them.

Before he thought better of it, he found himself in front of the Montgomerys'. He needed...he needed a *mom*. He knocked once then blinked out of whatever haze he was in. What the fuck was he thinking? He'd burned those bridges. He'd left Miranda, and now he didn't have the support system he'd never thought he'd truly needed.

He turned away and walked toward his car, his soul broken.

"Decker?"

Marie's voice hit him, and he froze.

"Decker, honey, what's wrong?"

He turned, his hands shaking. "I...I..."

"Come inside, honey. We'll fix it."

She sounded so sure, but he knew that wasn't the case. "Frank's in jail again, and Mom wants me to bail him out," he blurted. "I can't stay here, Marie. You know that. I fucked up. I fucked up bad. I'm never going to have Miranda again. I lost her because I pushed her away."

Marie raised her chin. "Get in here, baby. We'll fix it. We're family, honey."

He shook his head, and she stomped her way up to him. She was so tiny compared to him. In fact, she couldn't have been that much bigger than Miranda.

"You are my son, Decker. I know we never had the chance to make it formal, but I raised you along with my other children. Yes, you fucked up with my baby girl, but the man I raised will fix that. You need to grovel, get on your knees, and show that girl you're the man she needs. You need to be there for her no matter what. No more running away."

"She shouldn't forgive me."

Marie shook her head. "She just might. She won't forget, but then again, neither will you. Now get your ass in the house, and we'll make your night better. You need food and company. That man..." She shook her head. "That man who called himself your father is *nothing*. He's out of your life, and we're going to make sure it stays that way. As for Francine, well, if she needs a way out, we're here. I'm never going to be able to forgive what happened to you as a boy, but I will *never* blame the woman for what Frank did. Now get in the house, Decker. We love you, honey. We'll fix this."

He swallowed hard then nodded, wrapping his arm around Marie's shoulder. She did the same to his waist, and he sighed.

Harry and Marie were the parents that had raised him. They were the ones he would strive to emulate, not the mess he'd come from.

If only he'd seen that earlier, maybe he wouldn't have lost Miranda. Maybe Marie was right and he could grovel his way back. He'd do anything to have her back.

He just hoped she'd take him.

Chapter Twenty Two

M iranda covered her face with her hands.

"I told you it was bad," Griffin said softly. "But now Frank is out of the picture, and Decker had Francine moved to her sister's place. That part is over."

She nodded then sucked in a breath. Her legs and one of her arms were still in casts, but the rest of her was on the mend. She couldn't walk or do anything on her own, but she wasn't crying every time she moved.

She and Griffin had just become *really* close.

Thank God she could bathe herself if he wrapped her casts because, yeah, no thanks.

"I can't believe his dad broke into his house like that. He really went off the rails." She laid her head back on the couch and tried to get comfortable. That was easier said than done these days.

Griffin sat down on the coffee table in front of her. "Mom said Decker was starting to actually move on."

She frowned. "From what?" Her pulse picked up, and she bit her lip.

Her brother shook his head and cursed. "Damn it, that's not what I mean. I'm sorry. I meant that he's moving on from his *father*. Not from you." He closed his eyes. "Fuck. I'm so sorry. This is just weird. I'm not used to having to shield myself from you or him. Not that it matters because you're the one in pain, in more ways than one. I'm going to just shut up now. You'd think I'd be better with words considering what I do for a living."

A tear rolled down her cheek, and she shook her head, grateful it didn't hurt when she did that anymore. It wasn't Griffin's fault that things were awkward. That blame landed on her and Decker's shoulders. She didn't want to be the person that split Decker off from the group. She knew she'd have to deal with the fact that Decker *needed* to be part of her family, even if he wasn't with her. He might not have the last name, but her parents had adopted him long before she'd fallen in love with him.

Now she had to deal with the consequences.

She didn't want people to take sides, although they already had. Her mom and dad, though, hadn't. They'd been supportive of the both of them, even if they did it for different reasons. That was just one of the many reasons she loved her parents.

But now she was healing and alone, and Decker was finding out who he really was...and alone.

God, this sucked.

"You want me to make you something to eat?" Griffin asked, clearly trying to change the subject.

"I'm not hungry, but if you are, go ahead." She raised a brow when he didn't move. "Go work or something, Grif. You don't need to sit and watch me. It's not like your presence actually knits the bones together." She'd tried to joke, but when he winced, she knew she'd made the wrong move. "I'm sorry. I'm okay, Grif. I promise. Go work on the next great American novel, and if I need anything, I'll ring this little bell." In demonstration, she picked it up off the couch and gave it a few rings.

Griffin squinted then rubbed his jaw. "I swear that thing has the perfect resonance to make my fillings hurt. What the hell was Austin thinking?"

Miranda laughed. "I'm thinking he just wanted to make sure I could get you if I needed you."

Griffin stood, grumbling under his breath. "Leif is getting a fucking drum set for Christmas."

"I'm pretty sure Maya was planning on getting him that."

He cursed and ran a hand over his head. "Fine, an electric guitar. The kid can be his own one-man band and annoy the hell out of Austin."

"I think with the new baby on the way, they'll have enough noise going on."

Her brother gave her a small smile then waved as he went back to his office. The man needed to work, and since she'd been staying there, she knew he wasn't doing as much as he should have.

In addition to that, with her incapacitated and him being a slob, the house was starting to get a bit cramped. Thankfully Meghan had hired—with help from Wes and Storm—a maid to help. Meghan had wanted to come over and help, but Miranda had told her no. Her sister had enough crap going on in her life right now, and she needed to focus on her kids and her future. Miranda would be here healing when Meghan needed a break, but right then, other priorities needed to be in focus.

Being alone in the living room left her with her thoughts, and sometimes that wasn't a good thing. She couldn't help but think of Decker and his so-called healing.

Maybe he was finally finding a way to live with the man he was, not the man he thought he was, but she didn't know.

She missed her friend, missed the man she'd fallen in love with, but she couldn't heal her body and help him heal his soul if he didn't want it. It wasn't as if she wanted to be the one to make things better for him, but it would have been nice if he'd figured things out *before* ripping her heart from her chest.

God, she hated how weak she sounded. She'd have to push him from her heart and her thoughts if she wanted to move on. She had to remember she had her job when she got back, a family that loved her, and based on the way things were crumbling down around them, *needed* her, and a future she could figure out...on her own.

She could do that, but it didn't mean she wanted to.

She wasn't sure where she could fit Decker in her life now. He didn't want to risk whatever they had, so he'd thrown it away, but now, according to her parents, he was in *their* lives, which meant, eventually, he'd be in *her* life again. She didn't find it selfish of her parents to have taken him in. Far from it. He'd always been there, and she'd been the one to change the rules. Plus, Decker needed them.

She just wished he needed her.

The doorbell rang, and she sighed. She wished she could answer it on her own, but there was no way with these casts on.

She waited for Griffin to come out of his office and answer, but no one came.

The doorbell rang again, and Miranda closed her eyes. Her brother must have started writing. Sometimes he got so caught up, he missed things like doorbells...and proper hygiene.

No wonder Austin got her the bell that hurt Griffin's teeth. He couldn't ignore that. She picked it up and rang it a few times until her brother staggered out of the hallway.

"Dear God, stop it. For the love of God, please stop it."

She pointed to the door with the bell, and Griffin rolled his eyes, a faint blush marring his cheeks.

"Sorry, got caught up."

The doorbell rang again.

"I'm coming, I'm coming." He opened the door, and Miranda watched his body freeze. "What the fuck are you doing here?"

She tried to look past her brother to see who it was, but she couldn't move the right way. It didn't help that she had a feeling she knew who it was from Griffin's reaction. She didn't know if she wanted to be right or not.

"Can I please talk with Miranda?"

Decker's deep voice slid over her, and she trembled. She didn't know if it was from need, ache, or tension, and she didn't know if she was ready. God, she hated being weak. No, this wasn't weakness. This was just too much all at once. She hadn't seen him since before the accident. The others said he'd stayed all night in the waiting room and then had been the first to see her. The fact that he'd left right after that made her want to scream, but he'd written that he'd done it to protect her.

Stupid man.

She didn't need *protecting*.

She looked down at her casts. Those were extenuating circumstances.

"She doesn't want to see you, man," Griffin said back. "In fact, I'm not sure I want to see you either. You're a fucking asshole for what you did to her."

"I know I am, Grif. God, I'm a fucking idiot on top of

all that. I'm so fucking sorry I broke your trust, but I need to see Miranda."

Tears pricked the back of her eyes, but she forced them back. She'd done enough crying over what she'd lost. She didn't want to do it again.

"She doesn't want to see you," Griffin repeated. "You need to go." Her brother let out a sigh that seared her soul. "Maybe...maybe one day I'll want to see you again too, but right now, all I see is the man who hurt my baby sister, and I don't think I can deal with that."

A lone tear slid down her cheek, and she cursed herself. Damn it. She did *not* want to cry again, and yet the fact that her brother was also hurting just made it too much to bear.

"Griffin," she called out, her voice hoarse. "Let him in. I'll talk with him."

Griffin looked over his shoulder and frowned. "You don't have to. He can leave, and we can move on. I don't want you to overwork yourself while you're healing."

She held up her casted arm. "I'm healing right now, and I can heal while I talk to him. Let him in. It will only prolong the inevitable if we kick him out right now. Okay?"

Griffin sighed then looked back at Decker. "I'd say if you hurt her, I'd kill you, but you already did that."

She winced at his words.

"Just...just don't do something that we're all going to regret," Griffin said softly then moved out of the way before looking at her. "I'm going to be in my office. Ring that damn bell if you need me." He kissed her on the head before stomping back to his office.

With her brother out of the room, she finally turned back to Decker.

Her heart thudded.

Stupid heart.

He stood in the doorway, the sunlight behind him framing his body so he looked like a wicked angel. Apparently, her meds were making her loopy.

She refused to meet his eyes just then, afraid of what she'd say once she did. Instead, she looked down to see Gunner at his master's feet. The dog's long tongue was hanging out of his mouth, but his eyes looked solemn.

"Hey, boy," she said, her voice a little higher than usual. "I've missed you." It was safer to talk to the dog than the man.

Gunner looked up at Decker then came at her. Decker whistled, and Gunner stopped.

"It's okay. As long as he doesn't jump on me, I'll be fine." She still didn't look at Decker when she said the words.

"Be careful, Gunner," Decker cautioned.

The dog slowly made his way to her, sniffing along her casts, before putting his wet nose in her hand. She let out a giggle, surprised that she'd missed Gunner as much as she did.

"Oh, honey, you are a sight for sore eyes," she said softly.

Gunner panted, and she rubbed his head. She couldn't reach much else, but he looked happy. She knew that she was delaying the inevitable, but she wasn't sure she could take looking up.

"Miranda."

She closed her eyes and kept petting Gunner. God, it hurt so freaking much. "You left me," she said softly. "You fucking left me alone and bleeding in a hospital room. You left a fucking *note*. Do you realize how that made me feel? Like I was *nothing*. Like I wasn't worth your words or your time."

She swallowed hard then opened her eyes. Decker was on his knees in front of her, squished between Gunner and the footstool.

"I'm so fucking sorry, Mir." His eyes darkened, and she saw the pain in them. She just wasn't sure it was all worth it.

She loved his man, loved him with everything she had, yet he'd thrown it all away.

"I loved you, Decker."

"Loved? Past tense?" His voice cracked, but she ignored it. If she didn't, she might change her mind—though she wasn't sure what she was going to do to begin with.

She licked her lips and petted Gunner's head again.

Decker didn't touch her, but she could feel the heat of his gaze.

"I don't know, Decker. No, I do know. I still love you." It occurred to her she'd never said it to him before this. "Damn it. It wasn't supposed to be like this. It wasn't supposed to hurt this much. Love wasn't supposed to make me feel like I'm dying inside, Decker. Don't you get that? I gave you everything I had, and you threw it all away. I know I didn't tell you I loved you before the accident, but it showed in all my actions. I didn't want to scare you away like I did that day in the kitchen, and then you got scared anyway. I don't know what to do, Deck. I don't know what to think."

He reached out to cup her face then must have thought better of it. Good, because if he touched her, she wasn't sure what she'd do.

"I knew, Miranda. Deep down, I knew. I told myself you didn't though. Told myself that you couldn't love a man like me, a man with a family like mine. I was wrong, so fucking wrong. I put my fear of who I could be over what we actually had in front of us. I should have told you the same, Miranda. I should have told you that I loved you."

She gasped, blinking. "No. You don't get to do this. You don't get to throw my love back in my face and also say it back. That's not how things work." She couldn't move, and she hated feeling trapped. Yet she didn't ring the bell for Griffin to come save her.

She'd save herself.

"I'm not doing that, Miranda. Please. Please, just listen. Okay? I know I have no right to ask that of you, but I'm asking anyway. After I'm done, if you don't want to hear from me, I'll go away. I'll leave you alone, leave Denver, leave everything. I'll do whatever you need me to do so you're happy."

She shook her head. "I'm not happy, Decker, and nothing about you leaving could make me happy. I'm not going to hurt you because I'm hurt. But I'll listen to what you want to say." She met his gaze and saw the love mixed with hope there, and this time, she didn't turn away. She didn't know what she was going to do next, but she knew she had to listen. If she didn't, she'd make the same mistake he made in the hospital. If she ran away because she was scared, she'd regret it. Decker clearly had, but that didn't make everything okay.

"I'm not the man my father is. It took me too fucking long to realize that. He is a drunk, a cheat, a liar, and an abuser. He took my mother's life in every way possible while not killing her. I know that if he'd been around longer, he'd have eventually gone too far and killed her. I was so fucking afraid that one day I'd snap and be like him."

She shook her head. "You know that's not the case, Decker."

"I do know that. Now. Actions make the man. Not fear. I've never once done the things he has. I'm not a drunk. I'm not an abuser. What scared me more than I thought possible was thinking of the bruises and red marks I'd left on your skin the night before your accident."

Her eyes widened, finally understanding. "Decker, no. Those...those were something between the two of us. I *wanted* you to spank me. I wanted you to grip my hips that hard. It was something between two people who loved each other. That is *nothing* like what your dad did to your mom." She licked her lips. "If you think that, then it cheapens everything we did. Do you get that?"

She winced, remembering the fact that Griffin could probably hear everything she was saying, but she didn't care. Not really. They all had their secrets and their own needs. Griffin would just have to deal with it.

"I get it, Mir. I so fucking get it. I used what we had as an excuse. I was scared. I'm man enough to admit that. In doing so, though, I hurt the one person who means more than anything to me." He reached out and touched her fingers. It was the only part of her arm he could get to since she still wore the cast.

"I love you, Miranda Montgomery. I love what we had, what we could have. I was a fool to walk away thinking I was protecting you. I never should have made that choice for you. For that, I'm doubly sorry. You are not the type of woman who would ever let a man make her choices for her, and that's what I did. I don't know how to ever make that up to you. But I'm going to spend the rest of my life trying, if you let me."

He squeezed her fingers, and she squeezed back without thinking. The hope in his eyes flared, and she swallowed hard.

"I don't know if I can trust you, Decker."

There. She'd said it.

He nodded and the hope didn't leave his eyes. "I know. I'm so fucking sorry for that. I can make all the promises in the world and know in my heart I'll keep them, but unless you can take a chance on me, then I don't know what to do."

He lifted her hand and kissed her fingertips.

She let him.

"I'll do everything I can to prove that I'm worthy of you, Mir."

She shook her head, and his face fell. "Decker, you were always worthy of me. That wasn't the issue. It was you thinking you weren't good enough in the first place."

He nodded. "I'm not going to turn into my dad," he said, his voice stronger this time. "I'm going to love you until the day I die, Miranda. Let me love you. Be with me. You don't have to forgive me because what I did was unforgivable, but love me anyway."

She bit her lip. "I do forgive you, Decker. You did it because you were stupid and not thinking. Or maybe you were thinking too much."

He swallowed hard, and she watched his throat work. "Will you still love me? Will you let me try to make it up to you?"

She took a deep breath and nodded, taking the plunge. She'd loved Decker Kendrick for what seemed like forever. Twists and turns along the path were things she'd known would come, though she hadn't known they would hurt as much as they had. If she ran away because she was scared of being hurt, then she didn't love him enough.

And she did.

Love him enough.

She reached out with her free hand and cupped his face. He turned and kissed her palm. "I love you, Decker. I love you enough to move on from what happened."

He smiled then, his eyes bright. "I'm going to show you everything, Mir. Show you exactly how much I love you. I don't want you to ever feel like you can't trust me, can't lean on me. I'll be the man you need, the man you want."

She smiled then. "Oh, Decker. You already are."

He leaned in then and brushed his lips against hers. She sank into him, craving him. She'd missed this, missed *him* so much she could barely breathe.

He pulled back and leaned his forehead against hers. "I won't do more than that until you're healed. I don't want to hurt you."

She saw the truth in his eyes and smiled. "I can live with that."

"I hope so. And while you're doing that, why don't you come to my place?" He cleared his throat. "*Our* place. I can help you recover there."

She met his gaze and warmed. "I like the sound of that."

He kissed her again, and she fell in love with him once more. Things were never going to be easy, but that's what love was. It wasn't a fairy tale dreamed up by a little girl who liked the boy across the way. Love was something that flared between two people who were right for each other, even if they didn't see it right away.

She'd loved Decker Kendrick since she was a little girl. Now she was all grown up and living a life of her own, with the man she'd never thought she'd have.

Not a bad way to heal.

Or to live.

———

THREE MONTHS LATER.

DECKER GRINNED AS MIRANDA ARCHED AGAINST HIM. "That's it baby, take me. Take all of me."

She wrapped her legs around his waist and pulled him deeper. "Start moving, Decker. I swear I'm going to reach down and make myself come if you don't start doing your job."

Decker swooped in for a deep kiss, fucking her mouth with his tongue as he pumped his hips in the same rhythm. She gasped beneath him, writhing and moaning.

He pulled back and moved down to suck one nipple into his mouth. He bit down on the bud, loving the way she shook under him. Her fingers tangled in his hair, pressing him closer. He flicked her nipple with his tongue then pulled back, giving the same attention to her other breast.

"Decker, I'm going to..." She trailed off as she came, her pussy clenching around his cock.

It was too much, and he followed her, filling her up even as he kept thrusting.

"Jesus Christ, I love you."

She smiled up at him, her eyes dreamy, her motions lazy as she ran her hands up and down his back.

"I love you too." She touched a sore part on his back, and he winced. "Shit. I'm sorry. I forgot your new ink is back there."

He smiled and kissed her. "It's why I was on top."

She snorted and rolled her eyes. "I love the fact that you have the Montgomery brand on your back. You're officially one of us."

His chest grew tight at the words, and he nodded. Austin and Maya had each had a hand at his ink, and he'd never felt like he'd belonged more.

He had the ink on his back, the connection to a family he never thought he'd have, and the love of a woman that made him reach for more.

He'd crossed the boundaries of temptation to gain it all, yet he'd do it again in a heartbeat.

Decker couldn't have asked for more.

He had his Montgomery. He was one lucky man.

The End

Up next, Meghan and her former best friend Luc find their romance in Harder than Words!

A Note from Carrie Ann

Thank you so much for reading **TEMPTING BOUNDARIES!**

This is one of my favorite tropes and Decker and Miranda were not easy on me!

Up next, Meghan and her former best friend Luc find their romance in Harder than Words!

Montgomery Ink Denver:

Book 4.5: Hidden Ink
Book 5: Ink Enduring
Book 6: Ink Exposed
Book 6.5: Adoring Ink
Book 6.6: Love, Honor, & Ink
Book 7: Inked Expressions
Book 7.3: Dropout
Book 7.5: Executive Ink
Book 8: Inked Memories
Book 8.5: Inked Nights
Book 8.7: Second Chance Ink
Book 8.5: Montgomery Midnight Kisses
Bonus: Inked Kingdom

If you want to make sure you know what's coming next from me, you can sign up for my newsletter at www. CarrieAnnRyan.com; follow me on twitter at @CarrieAnnRyan, or like my Facebook page. I also have a Facebook Fan Club where we have trivia, chats, and other goodies. You guys are the reason I get to do what I do and I thank you.

Make sure you're signed up for my MAILING LIST so you can know when the next releases are available as well as find giveaways and FREE READS.

Happy Reading!

Also from Carrie Ann Ryan

The Montgomery Ink Legacy Series:
Book 1: Bittersweet Promises

The Wilder Brothers Series:
Book 1: One Way Back to Me
Book 2: Always the One for Me

The Aspen Pack Series:
Book 1: Etched in Honor

The Montgomery Ink: Fort Collins Series:
Book 1: Inked Persuasion
Book 2: Inked Obsession
Book 3: Inked Devotion
Book 3.5: Nothing But Ink
Book 4: Inked Craving

Book 5: Inked Temptation

The Montgomery Ink: Boulder Series:
Book 1: Wrapped in Ink
Book 2: Sated in Ink
Book 3: Embraced in Ink
Book 3: Moments in Ink
Book 4: Seduced in Ink
Book 4.5: Captured in Ink
Book 4.7: Inked Fantasy
Book 4.8: A Very Montgomery Christmas

Montgomery Ink: Colorado Springs
Book 1: Fallen Ink
Book 2: Restless Ink
Book 2.5: Ashes to Ink
Book 3: Jagged Ink
Book 3.5: Ink by Numbers

Montgomery Ink Denver:
Book 0.5: Ink Inspired
Book 0.6: Ink Reunited
Book 1: Delicate Ink
Book 1.5: Forever Ink
Book 2: Tempting Boundaries
Book 3: Harder than Words
Book 3.5: Finally Found You
Book 4: Written in Ink

Book 4.5: Hidden Ink
Book 5: Ink Enduring
Book 6: Ink Exposed
Book 6.5: Adoring Ink
Book 6.6: Love, Honor, & Ink
Book 7: Inked Expressions
Book 7.3: Dropout
Book 7.5: Executive Ink
Book 8: Inked Memories
Book 8.5: Inked Nights
Book 8.7: Second Chance Ink
Book 8.5: Montgomery Midnight Kisses
Bonus: Inked Kingdom

The On My Own Series:
Book 0.5: My First Glance
Book 1: My One Night
Book 2: My Rebound
Book 3: My Next Play
Book 4: My Bad Decisions

The Promise Me Series:
Book 1: Forever Only Once
Book 2: From That Moment
Book 3: Far From Destined
Book 4: From Our First

The Less Than Series:

Book 3: Mated in Mist
Book 4: Wolf Betrayed
Book 5: Fractured Silence
Book 6: Destiny Disgraced
Book 7: Eternal Mourning
Book 8: Strength Enduring
Book 9: Forever Broken
Book 10: Mated in Darkness
Book 11: Fated in Winter

Redwood Pack Series:

Book 1: An Alpha's Path
Book 2: A Taste for a Mate
Book 3: Trinity Bound
Book 3.5: A Night Away
Book 4: Enforcer's Redemption
Book 4.5: Blurred Expectations
Book 4.7: Forgiveness
Book 5: Shattered Emotions
Book 6: Hidden Destiny
Book 6.5: A Beta's Haven
Book 7: Fighting Fate
Book 7.5: Loving the Omega
Book 7.7: The Hunted Heart
Book 8: Wicked Wolf

The Elements of Five Series:

Book 1: From Breath and Ruin

Book 2: From Flame and Ash

Book 3: From Spirit and Binding

Book 4: From Shadow and Silence

Dante's Circle Series:

Book 1: Dust of My Wings

Book 2: Her Warriors' Three Wishes

Book 3: An Unlucky Moon

Book 3.5: His Choice

Book 4: Tangled Innocence

Book 5: Fierce Enchantment

Book 6: An Immortal's Song

Book 7: Prowled Darkness

Book 8: Dante's Circle Reborn

Holiday, Montana Series:

Book 1: Charmed Spirits

Book 2: Santa's Executive

Book 3: Finding Abigail

Book 4: Her Lucky Love

Book 5: Dreams of Ivory

The Branded Pack Series:
(Written with Alexandra Ivy)

Book 1: Stolen and Forgiven

Book 2: Abandoned and Unseen

Book 3: Buried and Shadowed

About the Author

Carrie Ann Ryan is the New York Times and USA Today bestselling author of contemporary, paranormal, and young adult romance. Her works include the Montgomery Ink, Redwood Pack, Fractured Connections, and Elements of Five series, which have sold over 3.0 million books worldwide. She started writing while in graduate school for her advanced degree in chemistry and hasn't stopped since. Carrie Ann has written over seventy-five novels and novellas with more in the works. When she's not losing herself in her emotional and action-packed worlds, she's reading as much as she can while wrangling her clowder of cats who have more followers than she does.

www.CarrieAnnRyan.com

Made in the USA
Middletown, DE
01 April 2022

63475234R00210